POMONA AFTON
Can Totally Catch a Killer

Also by Bellamy Rose

Pomona Afton Can So Solve a Murder

Praise for *Pomona Afton Can So Solve a Murder*

"Enormously fun, witty, and warm, Pomona Afton is the heiress-turned-underdog that you'll definitely be rooting for."

—Kristen Perrin, nationally bestselling author of *How to Solve Your Own Murder*

"Pomona Afton is the heroine you don't want to like and end up loving! Other characters might make lemonade out of their lemons, but Pom crafts a single-batch, artisanal lemon drop martini. She's smart, resourceful, and unstoppable—and she's going to be one of the most unforgettable heroines of 2025."

—Deanna Raybourn, *New York Times* bestselling author of *Killers of a Certain Age*

"Spoiled hotel heiress Pomona Afton joins the ranks of Katharine Hepburn in *The Philadelphia Story*, Blair Waldorf in *Gossip Girl*, and Paris Hilton in real life in this droll and sophisticated mystery. . . . Pomona Afton can definitely, absolutely, and confidently solve her grandmother's murder. It's a pleasure to watch her do it."

—Oprah Daily

"Readers who love a great transformation story, ridiculously charming characters, and the chance to have a little chuckle while they're rooting for all the right things to happen will find satisfaction on every page. . . . Rose (aka Amanda Elliot) has written a romp that will appeal to fans of Elle Cosimano, Sophie Kinsella, and Meg Cabot."

—*Booklist* (starred review)

"A super fun spin on the amateur sleuth story with a great dash of romance, Pomona Afton joins the list of spoiled yet lovable heiresses like Cher Horowitz and London Tipton. I couldn't put it down!"

—Mia P. Manansala, author of the bestselling Tita Rosie's Kitchen Mystery series

"This charming and hilarious case of whodunit is perfect for fans of *Only Murders in the Building* looking for an added romance bonus! I read the whole book in one sitting."

—Jo Segura, *USA Today* bestselling author of *Raiders of the Lost Heart*

"*Clueless* meets *Clue* . . . the funniest whodunit I've read this year."

—L. M. Chilton, author of *Swiped*

"Pomona Afton is the perfect antihero you love to hate (but mainly love), and this book is the ultimate chic accessory to murder. A glam and glorious mystery."

—Kat Ailes, critically acclaimed author of *The Expectant Detectives*

"Fans of *Only Murders in the Building* will enjoy this fun mystery rom-com by Rose (aka Amanda Elliot)."

—*Library Journal* (starred review)

"Bellamy Rose pens a frolicking riches-to-rags romcozy. Can this spoiled hotel heiress find redemption and a murderer without mussing her manicure? From socialite to sleuth, Pomona Afton will stop at nothing (even if her investigation takes her all the way to the outer boroughs of NYC) to find her grandmother's killer, salvage her trust fund, and discover that she's more than meets the eye."

—Olivia Blacke, author of *A New Lease on Death*

POMONA AFTON
Can Totally Catch a Killer

A Novel

Bellamy Rose

EMILY BESTLER BOOKS

ATRIA

New York Amsterdam/Antwerp London
Toronto Sydney/Melbourne New Delhi

ATRIA
An Imprint of Simon & Schuster, LLC
1230 Avenue of the Americas
New York, NY 10020

For more than 100 years, Simon & Schuster has championed authors and the stories they create. By respecting the copyright of an author's intellectual property, you enable Simon & Schuster and the author to continue publishing exceptional books for years to come. We thank you for supporting the author's copyright by purchasing an authorized edition of this book.

No amount of this book may be reproduced or stored in any format, nor may it be uploaded to any website, database, language-learning model, or other repository, retrieval, or artificial intelligence system without express permission. All rights reserved. Inquiries may be directed to Simon & Schuster, 1230 Avenue of the Americas, New York, NY 10020 or permissions@simonandschuster.com.

This book is a work of fiction. Any references to historical events, real people, or real places are used fictitiously. Other names, characters, places, and events are products of the author's imagination, and any resemblance to actual events or places or persons, living or dead, is entirely coincidental.

Copyright © 2026 by Amanda Panitch

All rights reserved, including the right to reproduce this book or portions thereof in any form whatsoever. For information, address Atria Books Subsidiary Rights Department, 1230 Avenue of the Americas, New York, NY 10020.

First Emily Bestler Books/Atria Paperback edition April 2026

EMILY BESTLER BOOKS/ATRIA PAPERBACK
and colophon are registered trademarks of Simon & Schuster, LLC

Simon & Schuster strongly believes in freedom of expression and stands against censorship in all its forms. For more information, visit BooksBelong.com.

For information about special discounts for bulk purchases, please contact Simon & Schuster Special Sales at 1-866-506-1949 or business@simonandschuster.com.

The Simon & Schuster Speakers Bureau can bring authors to your live event. For more information or to book an event, contact the Simon & Schuster Speakers Bureau at 1-866-248-3049 or visit our website at www.simonspeakers.com.

Interior design by Davina Mock-Maniscalco

Manufactured in the United States of America

1 3 5 7 9 10 8 6 4 2

Library of Congress Control Number: 2025948616

ISBN 978-1-6680-7568-5 (pbk)
ISBN 978-1-6680-7570-8 (ebook)

Let's stay in touch! Scan here to get book recommendations, exclusive offers, and more delivered to your inbox.

This book is for Betsy, Nat, and Madeline,
who are totally the best in-laws ever.

CHAPTER One

Throwing a party really isn't that complicated. All you need are decent food and drinks. A venue large enough to hold your guests without crowding them. Decorations to wow them—maybe some fresh seasonal flowers, a dinosaur skeleton or two, a few principals from the New York Philharmonic or the Metropolitan Opera to fiddle away in the background. Enough space on the roof for a helipad. And then, of course, the little extra touches that make a party truly special.

"Are you absolutely, positively *sure* we can't do the themed peacocks?" I asked my former and also current best friend (my life is complicated) Vienna across the shiny chrome table covered with pans of sweet roll dough. It was warm back here in the bakery kitchen, great for rising dough and less great for my hair, which was currently sticking sweatily to the back of my neck.

"I've held multiple galas there," Vienna said. She was sitting perfectly straight on a stool even though it didn't have a back to lean against, her legs crossed elegantly at the ankle. Her signature sleek French twist kept her black hair off her elegant swan neck, upon which glistened not a single drop of sweat. "So I can tell you with confidence and for the third time that, yes, non-service animals are barred from the main building of the New York Public Library."

Could I sneak them in? The last time I went to a gala there, my friend Millicent had smuggled in her emotional support Pekingese, and the staff hadn't even noticed. To be fair, fluffy purses were in style that year and they might have mistaken it for one. Though peacocks were probably less likely to get kicked out for eating a chunk of a 1600s atlas on display.

"The peacocks come trained," I said. "And they're an essential part of my vision. Imagine the guests mingling while peacocks in my theme colors of violet and white are strutting around, introducing a bit of wild excitement into an otherwise ordinary party."

This party wasn't just any party—it was the first gala for my very own nonprofit focused on helping disadvantaged students with scholarships and whatever else they needed to stay in school, on which I'd spent a lot of blood and sweat and tears and money and also a lot of other people's blood and sweat and tears and money over the course of the past year building. Over that year, I'd gotten to know these kids, learned all about the help they required, and understood that it fell to me to be the heroine they needed. In order to get that help, I had to impress a bunch of important people, which meant the gala had to be perfect, and perfect meant themed peacocks. Obviously.

Vienna raised one perfectly shaped eyebrow. "A beautiful vision. But I assume they've already told you no."

I sighed. My assistant, Lina, had indeed forwarded me her emails where she'd basically begged the venue to change their policy for a night. They hadn't budged. Then she'd forwarded me the emails she'd sent to a bunch of service dog agencies asking if it was possible to get a flock of peacocks certified as service animals, to which people had only responded to ask if this was a prank. "I suppose it would be bad form to get kicked out of the venue the night of my first gala for breaking the rules."

"Good publicity, though," Vienna said.

I sighed. "Only if you're one of those people who thinks all publicity is good publicity." No shade to those people—I used to be one of them, after all. Before the murder of my grandmother last year, I'd been a tabloid darling, reveling in the buzz of influencers discussing whether my post-club nip slip had been deliberate or if I realized that the fast-food chain I'd been starring in commercials for was under federal investigation for heavy metals in their meat (respectively, yes and no, though I did use the opportunity of the latter to ask a reporter, in my best baby voice, if that meant people were finding gold bars in their burgers, which made me into a meme).

But now? Now that I'd not only solved the murder of my grandmother but had survived months living in an apartment without a doorman or even a chef, I was a new woman. Honestly, getting herself murdered and basically forcing me to be the one to solve it was the nicest thing my grandmother had ever done for me. Old Pom would've strutted at the head of her peacock parade, grinning at the flashing cameras and already salivating to see what the *New York Post* was going to say.

New Pom wanted to be taken seriously. Which, as it turned out, was kind of hard when the entire world was used to laughing at you like everything you said and did was a joke.

"You know, one of my artists went through a bird period," Vienna said. I bit my tongue, still fighting the Old Pom urge to play stupid even after a year, and ask if it was really possible for someone to transform into a bird. "We can see if he'll let us include some of his works at the venue instead of live peacocks? I'm sure he'd be thrilled to get so many eyes on his art, and it would capture the spirit of what you want."

"That's a great idea," I mused, and not just because it helped mine come to life. It would help both me and Vienna with our missions at once: she headed a nonprofit that worked with young artists of color. "Is he already on the guest list? Text Lina his name and she'll put him on." I thought for another moment. "You know what else is a great idea? Peanut butter and jelly rolls."

"I assume that's for the bakery and not the gala."

"Right." I surveyed the rolls rising under cloth before me. I'd come to the bakery—*my* bakery, I reminded myself with a shot of pride—to test out new fillings for the bakery's—*my* bakery's; I was still getting used to achieving things—famous sweet rolls. In about a half hour we'd put them in the oven, then do a taste test. The winners would become rotating specials. (Which I'd hired people to bake, obviously. Having my trust fund back meant that I got to do the fun parts of owning a bakery, like formulating and taste-testing new flavors of sweet rolls, and leave the less-fun parts, like waking up at three o'clock every morning to bake full batches of them, to people I paid.) "Do you think your artist might be able to make a special piece for the event? One with a peacock in my colors?"

"I'll ask him." She pulled out her phone. I watched her type, still feeling lucky that she was here in the first place. We'd gone through a very painful and very public friend breakup a couple of years ago, when she'd grown out of the party girl phase and I hadn't. We'd reconnected once I'd grown out of it, too, and decided I wanted to do more with my life. "I can't imagine he wouldn't pull an all-nighter for an opportunity like this."

"Fantastic."

My phone buzzed. My assistant, Lina. "Hello?"

"Hello!" she said brightly into my ear. Lina was the . . . stepniece of one of the board members of the family company, I think? Or something like that. She'd graduated from college recently and wanted some nonprofit experience before going on to grad school or hunting down an MBA to marry. "I have an update for you on the Chelsea project."

"Great. Tell me everything."

She started talking about permits and land use and blah, blah, blah. I nodded along and focused on how great it would feel when the project was done and I was smiling for the cameras on the building's front steps as I cut the shiny pink ribbon crossing the doorway, surrounded by the delighted faces of the kids I was helping. My nonprofit had started out focusing on giving scholarships to students at New York City colleges and universities, but I'd learned over the past year that sometimes a scholarship wasn't enough to help many students stay in school: a number were housing or food insecure, or they didn't have a quiet or safe place to study, or they had to work odd hours that made it difficult to go to class or get assignments done on time.

So, the project: a building that could help my students with all those things, centrally located between many of the city's campuses. It would have a fully stocked kitchen, places to nap or sleep for a bit until they got back on their feet, a library where they could focus and study. A brilliant idea, if I could say so myself. (I could.)

". . . so we're right on track with all that," Lina finished.

"Great," I said, then paused. "And . . . everything is okay with Mr. Phlume?"

My idea may have been brilliant, but, as it turned out, even my gorgeously reestablished trust fund had limits. Renting and maintaining a big enough building in central Manhattan would've eaten up too much of it for my comfort. So when real estate tycoon Conrad Phlume had approached me, offering us the use of one of his currently vacant buildings at an absurdly low cost in exchange for tax write-offs and grunt work on the inside, how could I say no?

"I mean, he's a giant asshole, but yes, everything's okay with Mr. Phlume," Lina said.

A few months ago, everybody who was everybody collectively decided they'd had enough of Conrad Phlume. Enough of his leers and wandering hands. Enough of his nasty jokes at other people's expense and blustering speeches about how women didn't belong in the boardroom. He'd been knocked off the entire city's guest list.

And the price of readmission? Giving me a building. Did I love the idea? No. But I'd be able to do so much good with it, and all I had to do was grit my teeth and let him stare at my ass for a night. "Great. Keep me updated."

"Will do."

As I hung up, my phone went off. First with my timer—I swept the cheesecloth covering all my pans of rising sweet rolls off so that I could pop them into the preheated ovens—and then with a flurry of texts. I grimaced at them while putting down my pot holders. Ugh. The first couple were from Millicent and Coriander, my old friends who'd helped me perfect the art of dancing on tables and getting in and out of cars without flashing anyone. I didn't hate them or anything. It wasn't like they'd killed my grandmother and then tried to kill me when I figured it out, like our other friend, Opal.

But not trying to kill you was a pretty low bar for friendship.

Hey Pom!!! I feel like I haven't seen you in forever!!!

I know, right??? It's like you've been avoiding us or something lol

The mature thing to do would probably be to talk to them like an adult and tell them kindly that I wasn't avoiding them, I was just really busy. That was a lie, but it would mean I wouldn't have to tell them I was actually avoiding them because they were bad for my image and also kind of annoying. It was bad enough I'd been forced to invite them to my gala, but the choice was between that or dealing with a flurry of posts and articles speculating about our friend breakup that would overshadow all the good I was trying to do.

Sigh. Ignore.

The next was from my brother, Nicholas. Hey, traitor. Can you offer to take Jessica shopping for your gala? She's second-guessing everything in her closet and might show up naked.

I rolled my eyes. Well, since you put it so kindly. I didn't think it was that terrible to want to distance myself from the family company, Afton Hotels, after everything that happened last year. Both the "family" part and the "company" part had proven themselves pretty toxic. But Nicholas did not quite agree, nor did he approve of my decision to host my gala somewhere other than the flagship hotel.

But I shrugged it off. He'd just have to deal with it. I still loved my brother. And I probably owed Jessica, his fiancée, more than a shopping trip, considering how I'd wrongly accused her of murder and all. I continued, I'll see if she wants to go this weekend.

He didn't thank me, which was to be expected from Nicholas. Okay. Also, did you realize you're hosting your first gala while Mom and Dad are abroad? Mom is upset about it.

Aw, that's too bad ☹ I had no idea.

I did have an idea. It had been entirely my idea, actually, to have Lina sneakily check with my mom's assistant for her schedule. My parents could enjoy their seventh honeymoon in Tuscany, and I could enjoy having a gala without them in attendance.

You should call her.

I will. I definitely would not.

Messages dealt with, I tucked my phone back into my Poquette belt bag, its bubble-gum-pink stripes matching the pot holders I'd specifically commissioned for everyone who worked at the bakery. "What do you think about my guest list?"

"Can I see it?"

I grabbed my tablet from the nearby counter, blowing a puff of flour off the screen, and handed it over to Vienna. We were already almost at capacity from RSVPs—we'd barely need to contact anyone on the backup list I'd generated to keep the place from looking embarrassingly empty in case no one wanted to come. Much of the guest list was made up of people who'd donated large amounts of money to the nonprofit; others were people I wanted to impress with my transformation and show I was ready to be taken seriously; more had been chosen by me and Vienna to keep things interesting. Nobody wanted to go to a gala if the only people there were other boring, normal rich people. "The artists from your list are all coming, and the girl from that new Broadway show too."

Vienna scrolled, the shiny screen reflecting in her dark eyes. "Wow. I can't believe they're all yeses."

I sucked in a deep breath, trying to quell the nerves that sentence had unleashed in my stomach. She didn't have to clarify who "they all" were: they were the top tier, the upper crust, the other nonprofit owners and museum board sitters and city award winners. In short, all of the people who would have previously never been seen with Pomona Afton.

Probably they were only coming to my gala because they thought it would go down in flames and they'd get to cluck their tongues at me again. But I'd show them. They'd see. They'd have to stop looking down their noses at me once they saw how serious I was about wanting to help people. They'd have to start looking . . . up their noses at me? Did that make sense?

Vienna continued, "What about the journalist who wrote that viral 'eat the rich' piece?"

I grimaced. "You don't think he'd start a fight?"

Vienna shrugged, cracking a smile. "The one thing I've learned about throwing galas is that you want them to be a little spicy, as long as you personally or your organization aren't involved in the drama. Just a little. Otherwise they blend in with all the other galas and nobody remembers you well enough to donate."

She was probably right. Most of the galas I'd attended blurred together, but I did still remember a gala my grandmother threw back when I was a teenager, when she invited both my mom and the ex-boyfriend my mom cheated on with my dad. I still remembered that the gala had been to benefit something about preserving ancient rock formations in parks because my mom had taken a miniature replica of one of those ancient rock formations and thrown it at my grandma's head.

Note: make sure our centerpieces weren't easily throwable.

"Makes sense," I said, texting Lina to dig up his contact info. Make sure to drop how many billionaires and almost-billionaires will be there and tipsy, I added, making a mental note to seat them apart so that the reporter could only approach the billionaires while everyone was mingling, giving the billionaires an escape hatch. Spicy was good, but not hot enough to make my donors cry. "What else should I remember?"

"Figure out who your fattest targets are," Vienna said promptly, as if she'd been waiting for me to ask. "Not literally. You want to make sure you're spending a lot of time chatting up and flattering a few people who both have a ton of money and might be especially inclined toward your cause for some personal reason."

I thought for a moment, scanning the list again. "Ooh, probably Kevin Miller."

"The TED Talk guy?"

"Yeah," I said, tapping his name. I didn't know him super well, since he was closer to my parents' age than mine, but he was a regular on the gala circuit. "The one who built himself up from nothing and never shuts up about it, so I'm thinking he'll probably want to help other people build themselves up from nothing, right?"

"Hopefully."

"Oh, and Denise Ryan."

"The divorcée?"

"She hates being called that," I said. No matter how accurate it was, considering she'd inherited her massive fortune when her ex-husband, a tech mogul, divorced her for, surprisingly, an older woman. Dude subverting expectations over here. "She made that public vow to give away all her money. If she's giving it away, I'll take it."

Vienna smirked. "Sounds like a good bet."

"And there's Jack Wohl." He'd founded the hedge fund my parents and the family business invested in. He had an interest in keeping them invested in his company, and hopefully he'd assume one way of keeping them happy was investing in their daughter.

"Though he has those connections to Greystone, right?" I grimaced. Greystone Inc. was the most malevolent entity in the corporate finance world, which was full of malevolent entities—over the years they'd been called out for burning enormous stretches of rainforest, using child slave labor in its cobalt mines, causing the extinction of multiple species of panda, and more.

Vienna stared down at the tablet. "He's not part of them, though, right? Just associated with them?"

"No, but I'm not sure how much that matters." Vienna's crowd would never accept me if they found out I was taking money from a place like Greystone. They'd probably love it if I was—they could continue staring down their noses and shaking their heads at me. And the amount of good I'd be doing for the kids would be offset by the amount of harm I'd be doing elsewhere. "I'll have to verify that—"

The door to the kitchen swung open, cutting me off as I swiveled to see who was there. Maybe Ellie or Sage, two of my workers who knew I delighted in being called in when jerks asked to see the manager so that I could dramatically puff myself up like one of those really fluffy pigeons and tell them to go stuff themselves because *I* was the manager.

But no, it was Gabe. My lips broke automatically into a smile upon seeing that familiar swoop of black hair, the defined cheekbones dusted with stubble, the smoldering dark glare. Though his eyes weren't smoldering now. Or glaring, the way they'd been when I first turned up on his doorstep (to be fair, I started out as a terrible roommate). They'd brightened as soon as they'd seen me, even though I wasn't wearing any makeup and my hair was up in a quick actually-messy-not-artfully-messy bun and there was flour all over my yoga pants.

"Hey," he said, and it was truly amazing how one measly word had the power to make me feel so warm inside. "I was told something about sweet rolls that needed taste testing?"

"They've still got about fifteen minutes in the oven," I said.

Gabe turned as if to go. "Okay, see you then."

I rolled my eyes affectionately as he turned back around, then swooped in to give me a kiss. "How was your day?" I asked.

"It was fine," he said, and apparently "fine" meant that not one but two teenagers had told him that he made history sound interesting, which was about the highest compliment you could get from a teenager. Having just graduated with his master's degree in education, he was spending the spring and summer tutoring until his official job as a history teacher at a high school in East Harlem started this fall. "I have no idea how they know about me and you, but it seems that dating Pomona Afton makes me extremely cool."

"Hell yes, it does," said Vienna from her stool, and Gabe jumped a little bit as if he hadn't noticed her, even though she was right there. Because the man only had eyes for me. Yes, I loved it.

"Oh, hey, Vienna," he said. "How's everything?"

"Good, good," she said. "We're figuring out some of the final pieces for the big night."

Which seemed to have been far more difficult than his day spent with teenagers who adored him. "The seating chart for the gala is simply *impossible*," I said with a gusty sigh that I hoped conveyed the difficulty but also that I was world-weary enough that it wouldn't conquer me. "Coriander's slept with so many people's husbands that the only place I can put her without insulting anyone is in the corner behind a bookshelf, which is apparently against fire code. And I didn't think the Race CEO would RSVP yes, but he did, which is a problem because I've invited a couple of former employees he fired for embezzling, and I can't uninvite them because I want them to give some of the money they embezzled to the kids."

"The stakes are high," Gabe said, and not even sarcastically. It felt good to hear someone say that nonsarcastically, because it was true. My seating chart woes might sound silly and frivolous, but the goal of this gala was to make people donate money to help kids, and they wouldn't do that if they were in a foul mood from sitting beside someone who'd stolen their money or their husband.

"They are high," Vienna said, her voice tight. I hoped she didn't think he was being sarcastic. Gabe always spoke in a kind of measured way, so it could be hard for people who didn't know him well to tell. "But if anyone can do it, it's our girl."

"One hundred percent," Gabe said.

Tears prickled the backs of my eyes. I cleared my throat. Something that I still wasn't quite used to: people believing in me. "You guys."

The timer dinged. "Quick," Gabe said. "While she's distracted by the happy tears, we eat all the sweet rolls."

"You *guys*." With them at my side, I could do anything.

CHAPTER *Two*

Except fix the seating chart, as it turned out. No matter how hard I worked at it, there was always someone in the wrong spot. In the end I made the executive and somewhat cowardly decision to put Coriander's table setting under her middle name, Lynn, and convince her that fake thick-framed glasses were not only the height of fashion at the moment but that she'd be perfectly on theme if she wore them. Hopefully none of the wronged wives would recognize her. Also, hopefully Coriander wouldn't pitch a fit when she noticed I wasn't wearing said fake thick-framed glasses myself, as I may have hinted I would be.

The day of the gala dawned cloudy and a little chilly for spring, which was actually perfect, because clouds made for better photo lighting, and the cold meant I'd get to wear my faux-fur wrap and silk gloves without looking like I was trying too hard. I blinked into the hazy sun filtering through my bedroom window at a low angle, appreciating both the view of Central Park and the way the light illuminated the vintage porcelain planters I'd installed on the mantel. I'd never been able to do that in my apartment at the Afton—my grandma would always send an employee in to throw them out so that I wouldn't get dirt or water leakage on hotel property. Here, in my own space, I could do whatever I wanted. Hopefully not leak water into my floor, but if I wanted to, I could.

Wait a second. The sun should not be filtering in through my bedroom window at all, considering I'd closed the blackout curtains last night and Gabe knew better than to wake me up before eight.

There could only be one culprit. I rolled over with a theatrical groan to glare at Vienna, who stood next to Gabe's empty side of the bed, calmly examining her nails. It took her a moment to raise her eyes to meet mine. "Well, it's about time."

"You could have called," I grumbled.

"I did. You didn't pick up. Come on, sleeping beauty."

I'd been all ready to keep glaring, but apparently all it took for me to get up without complaint was to make me feel pretty even though I had bed head and remnants of eye cream giving my face a ghostly pallor. I pushed myself up. Squeaky Meatball, who'd been curled up at the foot of the bed, gave a rusty meow of protest. I didn't know what he was complaining about—*he* could continue doing his best croissant cosplay as long as he wanted. Cats didn't have to plan galas. Or attend them. Or do anything, really. Old Pom had kind of been like a cat. "You're killing me. I was so nervous about today that I couldn't fall asleep. I barely got, like, eight and a half hours."

"You're doing better than me," she said, and it was only then that I registered that the bags under her eyes were bigger than Poquette's new totes, the ones that could fit both a laptop and a Stanley Cup. "Come on. Have you checked in with everyone? There's always some vendor that doesn't come through or something that goes wrong."

"Lina's got that under control, I'm sure," I said. I reached for my phone. Gabe had already left for work, but he'd texted me encouragement and even an emoji heart, which for him was nearly the equivalent of tearing open his chest to show me his actual heart. "What's wrong?"

"Nothing's wrong," she said, but she didn't look me in the eye as she said it. "And yes, I'm sure your assistant is doing a fine job, but this is *your* night. You're the one who cares most about everything. It's your name and reputation on the line, and your cause that you feel the most strongly about."

I took a deep, slightly shaky breath. Yes. It was my name and reputation there on the line. After tonight, that name would have a very different reputation. No longer would people hear the name "Pomona Afton" and think, *girl with an admittedly glamorous mug shot who has never had a thought deeper than a kiddie pool.*

And it was my cause too. The press could claim that I was only starting a nonprofit for social cachet all they wanted, but I knew the truth. I'd seen firsthand last year the struggles that people like Gabe went through in order to get an education, and had learned since all about people who had it even worse. It wasn't fair. The world wasn't fair—I'd been given so much, and they'd been given so little. It was on me to help even the score, so that fewer Gabes would have to struggle.

"And you're going to kill it," Vienna said with a tiny smile, holding out my belt bag. "Now come on. Get dressed."

Thoroughly energized and more than a little anxious, I brushed my teeth in the green marble bathroom I'd designed (the idea: if my makeup looked good reflected against green marble, it would look good literally anywhere), threw my hair into a bun, and changed into a cute casual denim zip-up dress. Finally, I looked presentable—wait: I slipped on a pair of big sunglasses; *now* I looked presentable. "Okay. Let's start with the guest list."

And thus I was thrown into a whirlwind of activity—the best kind of whirlwind, because it didn't mess up my hair. I scanned the final RSVPs and sent Lina in the direction of a few second-tier socialites who wouldn't be insulted by a last-minute invite, then checked to make sure the bakery was doing okay with tonight's dessert order (somehow Sage had written down rhubarb only, when the tarts were supposed to include strawberry too). And I plucked a few photos of French heiresses wearing thick-framed glasses off my feed to send Coriander in case she was wavering.

"Ugh." I grimaced at my phone an hour later. Vienna and I had progressed to the breakfast nook of the eat-in kitchen, where she was pouring herself an ice water with cucumber and I was hunched at the table squinting at my tablet. "I guess I can't really be annoyed at someone who's, like, giving us a building, but could Conrad Phlume just stop for a second? He won't stop texting me. He just asked for a gluten-free meal with a side of garlic bread. Like, why?"

"Because he's a giant asshole?" Vienna turned with the heavy crystal glass at her lips. "Don't listen to anything he says."

I sighed. "I have to listen to everything he says. He's giving us a *building.*"

She winced. Just for a split second, and it was half blocked by a cucumber slice, but I know what I saw. "Vienna, are you sure nothing's wrong?"

"I told you, I'm fine." She took another sip. The ice in her glass clinked against the sides—her hand was shaking.

"You're definitely not fine," I said. "What's going on?"

She stared at me for a second. Set the glass down on the gleaming granite countertop. Awfully close to the edge—it wouldn't even be a challenge for Squeaky to knock off. "You know I love you, Pom, right?"

"Yes," I said cautiously.

"And I would never do anything to hurt you."

I mean, she'd hurt me pretty badly when she friend-dumped me a couple of years ago, but I wouldn't bring that up. "Okay?"

She stared at me again. Her lips parted.

Then she shook her head. "It doesn't matter," she said. "After tonight, it'll be over anyway." She cleared her throat. "Have you heard back from the venue?"

Later on, I'd be furious at myself for not pressing her. But at the moment, in my defense, my phone was pinging nonstop and my mind was running a mile a minute with all I had to accomplish before the event of a lifetime that very night. So I let it go. Told myself I'd press her tomorrow. "Apparently they don't have any violet tablecloths. Just purple. It's a disaster."

You'd think I'd be exhausted by the time it came to get dressed for the gala, but somehow it was the opposite: I felt a little like I'd downed eight espresso martinis (really do not recommend; emergency room lighting looks good on nobody). "I'm definitely going to need your help zipping me up," I told Vienna. "Alexa Vinchy dresses are great and all, but it's like she has a competition with herself about making the smallest, sharpest zipper covered in the most snaggable material she can possibly fit on one dress."

It was worth it, though, I knew as I admired myself in the mirror, smoothing the jagged ruffles that kept the poofy skirt from getting cutesy. The dress had a lot going on besides the ruffles—a jewel-colored mosaic pattern on the bodice; an asymmetric hem; gauze puffing up to my collarbone—but it all worked together. The moment I tried it on, I'd looked my reflection up and down and thought, *Yes. Yes, this is it. This is the dress that will make me the center of attention.*

And then, of course, there were the shoes. After my best friend had murdered my grandmother with my mother's famous stiletto heel and pictures of those heels had been splashed across every newspaper and social media account in the world, I had two options: give in to the salacious mob who would whisper furiously if I dared wear heels again and start wearing flats, or teeter tall and proud back into society.

Not going to lie, I did the first one for a little while. But now I surveyed the nude lace heels I'd be wearing later, flexing my toes in anticipation. It was about being tall and proud and all that, true. But also? I couldn't help but feel a little dark thrill every time someone clocked who I was and what I was wearing.

"You look incredible," said Vienna as we admired ourselves side by side in the mirror.

"You do too," I said, and it was true: she stunned in a simple black sheath dressed up by a dazzling diamond lariat necklace and matching earrings, each one a big square-cut diamond swinging on the bottom of a thin gold chain. I touched one briefly, watched it swing. "Where did you get these?"

She turned her head so that they sparkled. "My mom got them back in the eighties, so they're vintage. She finally let me borrow them."

"They're beautiful," I said, spinning back to the mirror to regard myself once more. The last thing I hadn't been able to figure out was my jewelry situation—I was wearing a thin gold chain around my neck, but I knew it wasn't quite right. "You know, they've inspired me. Do you mind if I wear a similar pair?" One I'd inherited from my dead grandmother once the will had finally been sorted out. "Or is that twinning too hard?"

"You know I love to twin with you," Vienna said, which was enough to send me hustling toward the jewelry safe hidden in my second walk-in closet. "Besides, nobody's going to be looking at me tonight. All eyes will be on you!"

Exactly what I wanted to hear. The more people were focused on me, the more they'd be focused on what I had to say about my nonprofit. I removed my necklace and put in my earrings, which were the same design but on a slightly shorter chain. Lowered my hands. Admired myself. "Perfect."

"Beyond perfect," Vienna said. "They make your eyes sparkle too. That's what my mom said about the earrings on me: that they sparkle like my eyes. Even though my eyes are dark, so it doesn't really make sense."

"Nice," I said, and by that I meant, *It must be nice to have a mother who gives you compliments instead of telling you that the diamonds make you look dull in comparison.* I could practically hear what she'd say about me now. *Knee-length skirts make your legs look stumpy, Pom. And don't you think you could use more blush so that your cheeks don't look so sallow against—*

"Pardon?" Vienna said, and wait, that wasn't my inner self-critic that sounded suspiciously like my mother, but *my actual mother*. In my apartment. Where I'd specifically banned her from entering by stealing back the spare key she'd stolen from me.

I spun around, a headache already pulsing at my temples, but my fake smile was fixed on before I finished the revolution. "Hi. I thought you were still going to be in Italy for another two weeks? Also, how did you get in here?"

My mother swooped in to kiss me on both cheeks, her lily perfume so sweet it made me a little nauseous. (Fun fact: lilies are extraordinarily toxic to many animals, including house cats.) "Oh, darling, you couldn't possibly lock your parents out of your apartment. What if there was an emergency?" She dabbed at the corners of her eyes, which were stone dry. I'd heard rumors from the staff that she'd gotten her tear ducts removed during her eyelid lift so that she'd never have to worry about looking weak or smudging her mascara. Probably they were false, but when it came to my mother, you never knew. "Right, honey?"

It was right then I realized my father was there too. He had a tendency to blend into the background, with his graying hair and black tux and—

Oh no. Black tux. And my mom . . . was wearing a shimmery silver gown so tight you could see the divots of her hips.

Gala attire.

"Oh, Vienna, hello," Mom was saying, pursing her lips at my best friend. "Pom, are you going through a lesbian phase again?"

One, Vienna was bisexual, not a lesbian. Two, my mother knew perfectly well I was in a committed relationship with "the nanny's son." Three, I'd never gone through a lesbian phase; my mother was just terrified of female friendship. And finally, most important, my parents were here, when they should have been in Italy, and they were dressed in gala attire, which meant—

"You're coming to the gala, aren't you?" I said faintly, and if Gabe were around, I totally would have taken this opportunity to swoon into his arms.

"Of course we're coming to the gala," Mom said. "We could never miss our baby's very first gala, right, dear?"

My dad cleared his throat. I got the very distinct impression that he'd much rather be in Tuscany right now, drinking glasses of wine that had been aged in crumbling castle cellars alongside mummified skeletons and hidden Nazi gold. "You're always right, dear."

"Of course I am," Mom said. "Now, Pom, is that really what you're wearing? Is it too late to—"

"Pom, is that your phone?" Vienna interrupted.

I blinked at her. No, it hadn't been my phone. I hadn't heard any—oh. *Oh.* "Oh, wow, yes," I said, pulling out my phone and clapping it to my ear. "Hello? Oh my God, are you serious? Alligators? In the moat?" I lowered the phone, wincing at my parents. "I really have to deal with this. Sorry."

My mom was glaring at me. "What moat?" But my dad had already wrapped his arm around her shoulders and was steering her toward the door, giving me an apologetic glance over his shoulder.

"Dear, we can't keep distracting Pom. We'll see her soon."

She called after me, "You really need to work on your . . ." but the door closed in her face and that was that.

I heaved a heavy sigh, tossing my phone on the bed, and followed it with my body, landing face down in the blankets. (It was okay. Kai hadn't come to do my hair and makeup yet.) "Ughhhh."

"I thought they were supposed to be in Italy," Vienna said, her voice muffled by the feathers around my ears.

"They were," I groaned, as weary as if I hadn't slept in four days (something I thought I'd done once during a bender in Ibiza, until Millicent told me I'd passed out on her shoulder each night at the club while dancing. Apparently a member of the minor

Austro-Hungarian nobility had tried to grind with me and I'd snored in his face).

"They didn't RSVP, did they?"

"They didn't." But these were my parents. They wouldn't have bothered with something so pedestrian as RSVPing to their daughter's first gala. My mom's plan was definitely to show up at the door and make a stink until they were let in. "I don't even know where to put them."

"So don't put them anywhere," Vienna said. I lifted my head from the bed so I could see her face. It was dead serious.

"What are you talking about?" It wasn't like they could sit on the floor. Judging by the fit of my mom's dress, she might not even be able to bend her knees.

"I'm saying don't let them in," she said. "They didn't RSVP. They aren't supposed to be there. They're not particularly nice to you. Just . . . tell them the venue's at capacity and there isn't enough space."

I sighed. I couldn't even let myself imagine it—it would be too tempting. "I can't."

"Why not?"

"They're my parents," I said weakly. It had already caused enough family drama that I wasn't holding my first gala at the Afton. If I didn't let them come . . . well, I didn't know exactly what would happen, but I knew it would be nuclear.

"Just because they're—"

"There will definitely be a few no-shows," I thought aloud, not at all because Vienna was totally right and I couldn't handle hearing it, no way, absolutely not. "I'll be able to slot them in somewhere. I'll figure it out."

She bit her lip. "If you're sure."

"I'm positive," I said firmly. By the time we got to the gala, I'd have the perfect solution ready. It would come to me, and everything would be great.

It *had* to be.

CHAPTER Three

In my previous life, I didn't spend a lot of time in libraries. Public libraries, at least—the amount of gold shining in a place like the Morgan Library had made it a great place for photos that brought out the flecks of gold in my brown eyes, especially when it was after hours and I could dim the lighting as much as I wanted. But public libraries, full of free books and clunky desktop computers and . . . the public? No. If I wanted a book or a computer, I just bought it. If I wanted to become conversational in ASL or access a career network, I'd hire a tutor or DM one of my millions of followers who could help.

So when Vienna had first suggested the New York Public Library as a location for the gala, I'd been exceedingly skeptical. "I toured the local branch after my parents made a big donation on my behalf," I said, deciding not to mention that it had been after I'd broken in at night on a party dare to steal the porniest book I could find (who knew the library would have security when the books were all free anyway?). "The carpet was brown and looked like it smelled like mushrooms, and the ceiling was drop and paneled, and the books were just regular books, not even pretty gold-foiled special editions that would look good with gala attire."

"I was thinking the main branch," Vienna said, and . . . oh, that made more sense. I hadn't been to a gala there in ages, probably since prepuberty, which was why it hadn't been top of mind—the kind of organizations that held galas in spaces like libraries didn't tend to want Pomona Afton on the invite list. "Not only is it a beautiful space, but I think holding it there would be good publicity for you. All payments to use the space go toward the library itself, and pretty much all of your scholarship recipients use the library, so it's almost like you're making a double donation."

Pomona Afton, doubly generous. I liked the sound of that.

And I loved the way the New York Public Library looked right now, its tall white pillars aglow in the dusk. The famous pair of lions, Patience and Fortitude, guarded the entrance. People raised phones and cameras in the air as I posed against the backdrop emblazoned with THE POMONA AFTON FOUNDATION. The people taking pictures shouted intelligent questions about my organization's mission and what advice I would give to students looking to apply for one of my scholarships and what fillings I'd selected for my signature pink donuts this evening.

JUST KIDDING. "Pom, now that you and Vienna are friends again, can you tell us about your fight?" "Pom, now that Opal's been sentenced to life in prison, do you think any of your other friends might be murderers too?" "Pom, there's a rumor going around that you're pregnant, can you confirm?"

Why were the rumors always that I was pregnant and not that I was, say, perfectly happy being a cat parent for now? But I couldn't yell or even calmly contradict them without them starting rumors that I was on that new drug that made your skin incredibly dewy and your eyelashes long and lush in exchange for wild mood swings. So I just smiled and posed and stuck to my canned lines about how delighted I was to be kicking off my very first nonprofit with all of my nonmurderer family and friends, and then I was whisked inside to the main hall.

My heels clacked on gray-veined marble, which also shone up the walls and alllll the way above me in the cavernous domed ceiling. Elegant staircases soared upward to a veranda overlooking the main space, which was scattered with round white tables and glittering with candles refracted through the light of champagne flutes.

"It looks incredible," I said, turning to Vienna, but she was already striding in the other direction. To do what? The gala hadn't even officially started yet. Barely anyone was even here.

I turned back when someone clapped me on the shoulder so hard that a less adept heel-wearer might have toppled. "Pomona Afton," someone roared in my ear, someone who—I wrinkled my nose—had already consumed enough whiskey to the point where I was glad there weren't any open flames at mouth level. "You look absolutely gorgeous in that dress."

I managed to plaster on a smile by the time we made eye contact, but only because I had the extra few seconds it took him to raise his eyes up from my boobs. "Good evening, Mr. Phlume," I said. "It's wonderful to see you."

He puffed up his chest, which I had on good authority was already puffed up via inserts to make his slim frame a little more imposing. Other than the slimness it seemed no personal trainer or customized diet could conquer, he was average-looking in every way: dishwater-brown hair; ordinary features; a scruffy beard he probably thought made him look a little more interesting but that just looked unkempt. "How could I miss a gala honoring yours truly?"

I couldn't help but bristle a little bit at that. Excuse me, but this gala was honoring *me* truly.

And the kids.

I forced that smile to go brighter, brighter, brighter than the sun. For the kids. Because helping those kids meant making him happy. "You are absolutely the guest of honor," I said. "I hope you've got your grand speech ready."

I had mic-cutting power and would use it if he started talking about how he'd grown up working hard and earning everything he had and that was all my scholarship kids had to do too. Conrad Phlume had made all his money the old-fashioned way: by inheriting it. His father was descended from some oil baron or something and bought up a bunch of real estate in the city back when it was cheap, then started letting his son manage his holdings before passing them down altogether. Getting lectured to work hard by someone who'd never worked hard in their life was extremely annoying. Or so Gabe has told me.

That family wealth had been enough to keep the invitations coming, despite his increasingly boorish personality. Apparently he'd always been annoying, but had taken a hard turn into intolerable a few years ago after falling down some conspiratorial Facebook rabbit hole. Giving me a building at a big, splashy, widely publicized event was his way of buying his ticket back in, because everybody else would start hoping he'd give them a building too.

I wondered how many buildings Opal would have to buy someone to be invited to their gala. Probably one, because, being real, my crowd had short memories and really loved money, even if they liked to pretend that they were above it. In a way, even though we never talked about money, all we talked about was money.

Pardon me. Sometimes, since rising like a resplendent phoenix from the ashes of my before-life, I liked to wax philosophic. Probably something about growing more mature. Anyway, I'd kept Conrad Phlume's involvement on the down-low in preparation for the grand announcement tonight, and also because I didn't want people to no-show so that they wouldn't have to hang out with him. Maybe I shouldn't have kept it secret, though—my parents had been ahead of the curve and had never invited him to any of their galas, despite his wealth. Same with my grandmother, which was maybe the one thing she and my mother had ever agreed on. If they knew he was coming, maybe they wouldn't show.

Honestly, it served them right. Maybe I should even seat

them near Conrad. He'd think it was an absolute honor to be seated with the parents of the gala-thrower. *That* would teach them to RSVP.

Quite cheered, I gave Conrad what was now a genuine smile. I'd totally missed what he'd been blathering on about, so hopefully I wasn't smiling about something horrible, like the time I'd pretended I knew French at a party with the Belgian ambassador's son so that he'd think I was cool and cultured and later found out I'd been nodding and smiling along to his story about his family's collection of artifacts they'd stolen from various colonized countries in an assortment of horrible, blood-soaked ways. Though, as it turned out, an undercover Interpol officer had been at the party in hopes of finding some of those artifacts, and the son's attempt to impress me had ended with several of those artifacts getting returned. Really, that whole saga should have ended with INTERPOL giving me an award and maybe a really cool piece of art (not stolen).

"Lovely," I told Conrad. Mental note: tell that story to more people tonight to demonstrate how cultured and altruistic and clever I am. (Mental footnote: leave out the part where I had no idea what I was hearing.) "Please, have a drink. The champagne is very good, but they're slinging a signature cocktail in my honor too." The Pomona Afton: a little sweet, a little spicy, and deceptively strong. Also, pink. "And let me know if there's anything else that you need." I stepped away before he could actually tell me anything else that he needed.

I kind of wanted a The Pomona Afton, but had to keep my mind sharp tonight. Also, I had to greet the people who were filtering in. I shook hands, smiled wide, gave plummy, practiced laughs to old, tired jokes, and said "no comment" to every nosy person who asked about Opal. I also dodged waiters, who were starting to circle the room with trays of tuna tartare on sesame crackers and tiny avocado toasts topped with roe. Old Pom wouldn't have acknowledged them except to shoot annoyed glances their way if they stepped into her path; New Pom made sure to smile if they caught her eye.

The one person I didn't see while circulating through the steadily more crowded room? Vienna. I kept one eye out for her, wanting to make sure she was having a good time after whatever was going on earlier.

"Pom!" As soon as I registered that the voice belonged to Jessica, her arms were around me. She smelled like she'd just finished baking something with apples and vanilla. "A million congratulations! I'm so proud of you!"

I gave her a genuine smile as she released me. She was beaming so hard in my direction that it almost made up for the lack of smile coming from Nicholas. If I were to commission a custom cocktail for my brother tonight, it would consist mostly of lemon juice. With the seeds. "Pomona," he said flatly, his arms crossed. "Congratulations. The room looks nice. Though—"

"Though not as nice as if I'd held it at the Afton, I know," I finished for him. He looked a little stunned by my daring. "I appreciate you coming anyway."

He sniffed. "I wouldn't miss my sister's first gala. Even if she's—"

"Even if she's a traitor to the family. I know." I leaned in and gave him a hug. It was like hugging a mannequin. "Jessica, you look stunning."

"Thank you!" I'd taken her shopping after all and helped her find a gauzy blue-violet crepe dress that had been, to her great and inexplicable pleasure, on clearance. Hopefully she'd just stick to telling everybody who complimented her on it that it had pockets. "Pom, you'll come wedding dress shopping with me, won't you? I mean, I haven't even started the wedding planning process, but—"

"Say no more." I linked arms with my future sister-in-law. "I'll start working on a spreadsheet."

"A spreadsheet?" She blinked at me. "I was thinking we just

go to the *Say Yes to the Dress* store and try stuff on until I find something I like."

I heaved a sigh. "We'll loop back on this soon." Jessica really didn't know anything.

"Okaaaaay." She sounded like I'd told her we'd be wedding dress shopping inside a bear cage. "By the way, is your friend okay? I just saw her over there looking like she was about to cry."

"My friend? You mean Vienna?" I followed Jessica's pointer finger to the far corner of the room, where . . . Was that the tip of Vienna's sleek black chignon peeking up over that bookshelf? "Excuse me."

I nodded goodbye to my brother, who grabbed a The Pomona Afton off a circulating tray, and Jessica, then hustled toward the side corner, nodding hello and giving my busy smile to several small donors and the girl from Broadway, who I really wanted to talk to later (namely to ask an important question: If the part of Elle Woods in the *Legally Blonde* revival vibed with somebody's very soul but they could neither sing, act, nor dance, could they still hypothetically be stunt-cast on Broadway?).

I reached the bookcase Vienna was hiding (???) behind just in time to hear her speak and realize that she wasn't alone. She was saying, in a low, tense voice, "You've got to give me more time. I don't have it yet."

"Tonight was your deadline." I blinked in surprise, because the voice belonged to my guest of honor. Conrad Phlume. "If you can't—"

"Please," Vienna said. "Give me one more day."

"Perhaps there's another way—"

"Oh my God, Pom, why are you hiding away here in the corner?"

Before I could turn myself, I was physically grabbed by the shoulder and turned by two tiny, bony, illogically strong hands. My cheek was bumped by a hollow jawbone and the corner of a thick glasses frame. The smells of freesia and lavender drifted past me.

"Millicent, Coriander," I said, trying to turn back and failing. How was Coriander so strong when she refused to do any exercise that made her sweat? "So good to see you, but—"

"Oh my God, Pom, you look amazing," Coriander said, pushing me away at arm's length—I almost hit a pillar—so that she could look me up and down. "*Love* that dress. It's so . . . bohemian."

Was that a compliment or an insult? Did she know what "bohemian" meant? It didn't matter. I just smiled and nodded. "You look amazing too. Both of you. Especially you, Coriander. Those glasses are so wow."

I tried to turn back toward the corner where Vienna and Conrad were seemingly conspiring, but now the pillar was in my way. I was trapped staring at Millicent and Coriander as their hands moved to their hips and they ducked their chins, posing. Coriander's mermaid dress was so tight it was a mystery how she could walk in it, but at least it didn't swamp her tiny frame the way the paper bag dress she wore to the last gala had, and her blond hair (expertly dyed) really popped against the iridescent navy. Her glasses looked terrible, but that was on me. Meanwhile, Millicent had gone for grandeur in a long, flowing ball gown in bloodred. She'd also chosen red eye shadow around her enormous deep, dark eyes, which on most people would have made them look sick, but which gave her a look just on the attractive side of dangerous.

I stepped forward and spun around before either one could accost me again. There! The corner! Where . . . Vienna's bun no longer protruded, and I could no longer hear her or Conrad's voices. Either they'd ducked down to hide or they'd finished their conversation and moved on.

Plastering on a wide fake smile to hide my disappointment,

I looked back over at Millicent and Coriander. They didn't let their poses fall until I gave them a nod of approval. "Well, it's so great to see you. Thank you so much for coming," I said, then looked past them as if seeing another friend I wanted to talk to, the universal signal of moving on.

My friends were very good at ignoring what other people wanted, though. "Wait, Pom," Coriander said breathlessly. "I wanted to ask your advice . . ."

Just then, I actually did see someone past them I wanted to talk to. Someone I very much wanted to talk to, in fact, even after more than a year together, which, according to my mom, was about when couples started to hate each other. "Gabe!" I said, and my smile morphed into something genuine.

That faltered a little bit when I realized how uncomfortable he looked—he was scratching the back of his neck and shifting a little in his tux. "Are you okay?" I asked him. He certainly looked it, in the slim-fitting black tux I'd insisted on having made for him after the debacle of our first gala together. I never wanted to speak of it again.

Coriander, however, would. "You look nice *tonight*," she said.

Gabe forced a smile. He was not nearly as practiced at it as I was, so he kind of resembled one of those corpses that had been dead for a long time, when its lips started peeling back from its teeth. A really healthy-looking corpse, with warm, golden skin and dark eyes fringed by thick eyelashes I knew at least three women personally who would pay to harvest. "Thank you."

"Yeah," Millicent added. "*Tonight*, you look really good." They tittered, as if I were too dumb to parse what they were actually saying.

(To be fair, when Gabe told me he had it all under control for our first gala together, who would think that would mean he'd show up in a *rental tux*? And not even from a designer rental tux company, but the one our building super recommended because he'd rented a tux there for his father-in-law's funeral?)

I linked my elbow through that of my corpse-boyfriend. A gold cuff link, a "gift from my father" that I'd purchased and wrapped and discreetly handed to my father to hand back to us, glinted at his wrist beside my diamond tennis bracelet. "Gabe, come with me. There's someone I want you to meet."

With that, I was able to excuse us from Millicent and Coriander and pull Gabe to the corner where Vienna and Conrad had been talking. Maybe they were hiding back here. I rounded the corner and—

Nothing. Just a waiter on her phone; she glanced up at me with wide eyes and stuttered an apology before darting off too fast for me to assure her that I didn't mind her being on her phone. I had, after all, spent my grandfather's funeral riveted not to whatever boring eulogies they were saying about him but to the ugly breakup between Coriander's boyfriend and his not-so-secret affair partner playing out in the group chat, so who was I to judge?

"Who am I meeting?" Gabe asked, raising an eyebrow at the empty nook.

Well. I could still spin this to my advantage. I spun around, backing into the bookshelf, nudging a few books out of the way as I pulled Gabe into me. "Me."

I closed my eyes as his lips found mine. Some of the fireworks might have stopped popping a year into our relationship, but fireworks were loud and annoying anyway. I was happy with his warmth, the feeling of safety I felt wrapped in his arms, the way each kiss still sent heat flooding through my belly. One of his hands cupped my cheek, fingers delicately brushing the edge of my hairline but not actually stroking my hair (which I appreciated, considering that hitting the wrong bobby pin might make the whole thing explode). As we pulled apart I sighed, a little bit of the day's tension draining out of me. "Okay. I really needed that."

"I'm always at your service," Gabe said, cracking a smile. I rested my head on his shoulder. "Is everything going okay so far? I'm sorry I couldn't come earlier. I would've rescheduled, but my student takes his SATs tomorrow, so—"

"Don't worry. I understand." I didn't, not really—I'd never been involved in anything I couldn't change at my whim. But his life was different, and even if I didn't quite get it, I tried my best. "Everything's going well, I think. The caterers and bartenders were all here on time, and everyone seems happy. Conrad hasn't mortally offended anyone yet." I inhaled deeply through my nose, out through my mouth. "Though the night is still young." I pulled back and linked my arm through his. "We should mingle."

He gestured gallantly with his free arm. "After you."

We spent some time circulating, making small talk about the news and complimenting people's outfits (the begging for donations would come later, once everybody had consumed a The Pomona Afton or two or five). After a bit, I spotted that familiar sleek black chignon. "Oh, there's Vienna."

I wanted to ask her what she'd been doing with Conrad Phlume, but, as I approached, I realized she was holding court with a group of people who looked around our age, maybe a little younger, all dressed in ways that impressed me but that were drawing stares from many of the older people in attendance: one who presented as female but wore a tartan tux; another presenting as male with a long, fuzzy beard who had on a flowing bright orange gown. Vienna lifted a hand in a pageant princess wave. "Speak of the devil herself," she said. "Everyone, I'm so glad for you to meet Pomona Afton, our hostess tonight."

It always tickled me when people introduced me. Like everybody doesn't already know who I am. I inclined my head, preening like one of the themed peacocks that were devastatingly not in attendance. "Thank you so much for attending tonight and supporting such an important cause," I said. Though, from their age and the fact that I didn't recognize them, I suspected that they wouldn't be donating. They had to be Vienna's gaggle of artists. "If any of you have—"

Orange Gown waved a hand impatiently to shut me up. I shut up, mostly out of shock that someone would dare do that to me. "Yes, the scholarships are great and all. But I *must* hear about how you solved a *murder*. *That's* the most exciting thing I've ever heard."

I was immediately a little queasy. Shifting from foot to foot to recenter myself didn't help, because my heels were so high it was a little like I was on the deck of a yacht in stormy seas. Maybe I should flash the heel at them like a threat. "Oh, I wouldn't say that," I told them. "I mean, yes, it's true, I did solve a murder. And . . ."

Yes, it was exciting—that'd been what I was about to say, because technically it was true. But . . . I don't know, saying it like that to this crowd of people looking at me like I was onstage performing for them? It felt a little icky. I went on, "It was my grandmother who died, and my close friend who killed her. So yes, I solved it, but it wasn't like I was happy about it in the end."

None of them seemed abashed. "Oh, we didn't meant it like that," said one of the others, a squat Black man in a violently purple tux. "It's like my birds. The goal isn't for you to feel peace and serenity looking at them, but to feel the adrenaline pumping through your system, for you to reflect on the mortality of your human body and the earth we live on. That's excitement, is it not?"

The one part that stood out to me in that jumble of buzzwords was "birds." That, combined with the purplest purple tux I'd ever seen . . . "You must be Isaiah Franklin," I said, appreciating that I'd been gifted this glorious change of subject. "It's such a delight to meet you. I love your work and I so appreciate the peacock you made for the event." I realized that, while Vienna had told me he'd agreed to make one and transport it to the gala, I hadn't seen it yet. "Where did they put it? I'm dying to see it."

"I hope you don't mean literally," said Tartan Tux, and the group burst into laughter, Gabe included. Not his real laughter, his fake social laughter, which sounded a bit like he'd gagged on a gazpacho shooter.

Isaiah pointed somewhere behind me. "They were able to hang it from the railing there."

I turned, then gasped, then choked on all the air I'd gasped.

Isaiah had made us a peacock as requested, yes. I couldn't fault him for that. I could fault myself for not specifying that the peacock should be, I don't know, *not horrible*. It was spun of white and purple feathers, as I'd asked, but the feathers had been spattered with something dark red—hopefully not real blood—and where its eyes should have been gaped empty sockets. And the tail, where I'd envisioned a splendid fanlike display to match the centerpieces, was made up of knives. Rusty ones, jagged ones, small ones, large ones, sleek ones, bulky ones. No wonder they'd had to hang it up; it was probably a liability issue sitting on the floor in case somebody tripped nearby.

"It's quite something, isn't it?" Vienna said, her voice strained.

Back to my fake smile, which by now was threatening to split my face in two. "It's very . . . meaningful."

"It's a commentary on murder," Isaiah said, raising his eyebrows, as if it should be obvious. "I wanted to nod to what you've been through, while delving even further into human and bird psychology. Peacocks will eat almost anything, gulping down a mouse or lizard even as it screams." Vivid. "It made me connect murder to the peacock to the human experience. Perhaps the ultimate form of art is murder."

Gabe laughed, his real laugh this time, which was as bright as a new floral spring collection and warm as a new line of faux-fur muffs. But the artists, who were all nodding approvingly, looked at him as if he'd dared to mix mustard and cyan. He sobered immediately with a quick glance at me that felt like an apology. "Oh. Sorry. I thought you were joking."

"Joking?" Isaiah echoed, eyes wide. "*Joking?* Murder opens up the innermost chambers of the body that are meant to remain closed and chaste and unbroken, and spills all of its secrets to the world, who says it doesn't want to look but in reality cannot turn away. How is that anything but art?"

I don't know, maybe a monstrous crime that destroyed entire families and shattered hearts? I mean, my grandmother's murder had nearly destroyed my entire life. Not emotionally, of course, just logistically. I managed not to say that—for Vienna's sake, considering she was looking even more pained now—but couldn't resist asking, "Does that make the murderer an artist?"

Isaiah wrinkled his nose, offended that I'd even asked. "The ultimate artist, some might say."

Only somebody who'd never been around murder for real would say that. "Well, it was great to meet you all, and Isaiah, I appreciate you lending us your work for the night."

All the artists cooed in response, with Isaiah's coming last. "Pomona, it's not on loan, it's a gift. For your good work." He smiled toothily at me, and, for once, I couldn't force my fake smile in response. A shiver ran down my spine as I nodded quickly and beat it. Did he mean my good work with the non-profit, or my good work with murder?

Either way, it felt like a bad omen.

CHAPTER *Four*

The next hour passed in a dizzying blur of faces and names and compliments, mostly for me. I parked Gabe with Nicholas and Jessica for a bit to give him a break from all the schmoozing. Though the worried look he gave me when I did it told me he knew the real reason. "I'm not embarrassing you, am I?"

"Of course not," I said vehemently, which was only a little bit of a lie. The rental tux situation had been largely forgotten by everyone who wasn't a petty little bitch, but Gabe hadn't helped himself this evening by blurting out to Denise Ryan, the billionaire divorcée, that he was a huge fan of the ex-husband who'd cheated on her. "I'm just looking out for you."

Without Gabe sweating through his tux beside me, I talked to a bunch of people I knew. Millicent's parents. Some of my parents' friends. Fred, the Afton CFO, who I'd thought might retire and move to Florida after he blew up at me last year (to be fair, it was after I'd accused him of murder), but who'd come trotting back after everything was solved and resumed his job like nothing had ever happened. A couple of people I swore I knew but couldn't pinpoint.

"Did we meet at Vienna's last show? Vienna Soo, Artists in the World? It was at the Whitney?" I asked one, a woman maybe ten years older than me who I definitely knew somehow. I squinted at her heart-shaped face, dark hair, catlike green eyes, though not hard enough to look creepy (hopefully). She looked *so* familiar. "Or the Met Gala? I finally got the invite last year. I was the one in the birdcage? It might have been hard to see my face under all the feathers."

The woman—her older husband had introduced her as Cora Jean-Pierre—shook her head, wincing a little bit. "Um, I saw pictures of it? But no, you wouldn't have met me there. Sorry. Uh, I'm going to get one of those delicious-looking waffles." And she fled. Maybe I'd squinted too hard? Or maybe she'd just been really into the waffles. Understandably, since I personally had told Ellie and Sage to make sure that they used a little barley flour to add an earthy depth that would contrast really well with the rich mascarpone topping.

Before I could think too much about it, I spotted a group I hadn't expected to see here, not even with the elegantly scrawled RSVPs (they only employed assistants with calligraphy on their résumés, I assumed). The blue bloods. I sucked in a deep breath. I hated to admit it to myself, but tonight wasn't entirely about the kids I was trying to help.

I mean, it was mostly about them. But it was also for me: an audition, almost, for the new life I wanted. And this new life involved impressing this particular group of people who I very much wanted to be my new friends. Some of them had partied with me back in the day before embarking on their new, grown-up life paths of looking down on everybody else. Sure enough, they were standing in a tight circle, glancing around them, little smirks on their faces. What was it? Was my string quartet playing too loud? My caviar pulled from the wrong sea?

I fixed a bright but hopefully demure smile on my face (I was not used to demure) as I sashayed in their direction. "Libby, hi! Kitty, so glad you could come. John, delightful to see you." I moved around the rest of the circle, air-kissing cheeks and ignoring the eye flicks of judgment my dress was getting. I didn't get it—it covered up all the important bits and it wasn't *that* loud. Right? Now I was second-guessing myself. Libby's and Kitty's dresses were both muted in color and conservative in cut, though the diamonds on their earlobes and fingers were big and sparkly enough to make up for it. My voice climbed a half octave. "I think everything has been going very well so far!"

I regretted it immediately. Desperate. Sure enough, Libby's and Kitty's eyes met with a judgmental eyebrow raise. "Very well."

If I was remembering correctly, Libby's full name was Elizabeth Katherine Montserrat-Rand, and she was the descendant of a nineteenth-century railroad baron. Kitty's was Katherine Elizabeth Hart, and her ancestors had owned half the city back in the day (and a whole bunch of people, but they kind of glossed over that). Their friend John's great-great-great-grandfather had competed with Libby's on the rails, but they'd gotten over that sometime in the past hundred and fifty or so years. Their parents would never have flicked an eyelash in the direction of my parents—*new* money—but times were changing. I mean, they were friends with Vienna, and her mom had been a pop star, for heaven's sake.

I let that bolster me, lifted my chin. "I'm so glad I had Vienna's help." Couldn't hurt to remind them that they were tight with my very best friend. "I hope my debut goes as well as hers did."

"It would be hard for it to go better," Libby murmured. What did that even mean? I bristled but didn't let it show. Only smiled brighter.

Besides, it was kind of true. Back when Vienna had decided to transform from party girl into serious person, she'd started her foundation practically overnight, making a splash immediately with family money. She didn't even have to suck up to any assholes like Conrad Phlume. The *New York Times* did a massive, glowing write-up on her, everywhere else followed, and suddenly everyone was taking her seriously. It had been incredible.

"Anyway," Kitty said, taking a sip of her drink. She wasn't holding a The Pomona Afton, I was a bit aggrieved to see. None of them were, actually. They were all drinking wine. I was suddenly seized with doubt. Was it tacky to have a drink themed after yourself at your gala? I smoothed down my skirt, hopefully not leaving streaks of sweat on the fabric. "So good seeing you, Pomona." Ugh, my full name. She raised one elegantly shaped eyebrow. She'd probably never had someone accidentally wax an entire one off, then panic about what to do with the other one (did they have to match?). "Looking forward to seeing how this all turns out."

The others nodded, and I went to say—oh, wait. They were dismissing me. I was *not* used to being dismissed. But I wasn't going to bulldoze past their disdain. I just nodded and scuttled off and tried not to worry too much about how this would all turn out.

When the time came to usher everyone to their seats for dinner and speeches, it was a relief to get to sit down for a moment, even though, with the exception of Kitty and Libby and them, the feedback had all been glowing. Sometimes being universally beloved and admired could be exhausting. I sank down into my seat at the head table to guzzle a glass or five of ice-cold spring water, only to be immediately accosted by Conrad Phlume.

"Pomona, I have some edits to my speech," he said, chest puffed out again. His wife, Bibi, trailed behind him, elegant in a simple but well-cut black gown and confident in her undyed silver hair. I went to acknowledge her with at least a nod, but she was intently focused on the ceiling. I glanced up just in case I'd missed another horrible murder-knife bird hanging from it, but thank God, there was nothing up there but marble arches. Honestly, I couldn't blame her for not wanting to catch my eye. Imagine going to an event where everybody knew you were married to Conrad Phlume. How embarrassing.

"Edits to your speech?" I formed my fake smile into a

fake-regretful frown. "I'm sorry, Mr. Phlume. Library policy forbids changes to any public speeches once they've been approved by its representatives." That was a lie, but it was always easier to blame someone other than yourself. "What you already have is so great, though."

"Hmph," he grumbled. "Fine." He narrowed his eyes at me. "You know, your guests aren't being all that nice to me."

What was I supposed to say to that? *Well, maybe if you were nicer to people, they'd be nicer to you*? "I'm sorry to hear that."

His glare turned for a moment toward his wife. "Maybe they'd want to spend more time with me if she made more of an effort. Just look at that pooch. She's never even had children, you know. Only women who've ruined their bodies with childbirth should look like that." And he actually—actually—reached over and pinched the bulge of her hip.

My mouth dropped open. It was rare that I had no idea what to say, but . . . I had no idea what to say. *You're such an asshole? How even dare you? She's not even close to having a pooch*? (Not that what he said would be acceptable if she were.) *Childbirth doesn't "ruin" people's bodies, and, by the way, I'd like to see you go through pregnancy and childbirth and see how you feel about* your *body?*

Bibi didn't seem especially bothered—she just rolled her eyes toward the ceiling, then back down—which somehow made the whole thing worse. Like she was used to it. I wanted to give her a giant hug, during which I would whisper in her ear, *Why are you married to this man? Do you need help? Squeeze once if yes, but not too hard, because this dress is already so tight that squeezing any tighter might cut off my circulation.*

I honestly knew very little about her that could answer that question. All my years in society had made it very clear who Conrad Phlume was—a boor, a jerk, an extremely rich and sometimes generous asshole—but the wife by his side was more of an enigma. Honestly, I was surprised she was age-appropriate. Conrad struck me as the kind of guy who'd want a twenty-two-year-old with giant fake boobs on his arm.

He was talking again. I blinked hard and shut my mouth before he could comment on how blobby my molars were. ". . . eat their sneers and stares once they hear what I have to say."

"Great," I said. "Just don't forget, the library won't allow any additions to the speech."

He snorted, tipping his head back. Tufts of graying hair poked from each of his nostrils. "They won't get that upset with someone who can pay for a new branch. Trust me."

Before I could argue with him, he drifted back toward his table, wife in tow. I fought the urge to touch her apologetically on the shoulder as she went. *I'm sorry I didn't speak up for you. I'm sorry I care about this building he's giving me more than I care about you.*

Back at his table, my parents were glaring at me, each other, and the room in general. Everywhere but at Conrad, which meant he was what they *really* wanted to be glaring at. That cheered me considerably. Served them right for not RSVPing.

Hopefully the people I'd put on Conrad's other side were less miserable—they were two of my golden geese, and I hoped Conrad would brag enough and be obnoxious enough that he'd goad them into wanting to outdo him. Kevin Miller, because he'd grown up like my scholarship recipients and would hopefully sympathize with other kids trying to climb the ladder, and Jack Wohl, because he'd grown up in Greenwich and had taken a helicopter to his boarding school in New Hampshire and would want to donate a lot to make society think he cared about poor people (he probably didn't, but his money worked the same either way).

As Conrad and Bibi settled back into their seats, though, the two men seemed more into having their own conversation than bringing in the guest of honor. Jack was gesturing so hard, he almost knocked Bibi's water glass into her lap.

They looked up as I stood and tapped my spoon on my champagne flute with a delicate *ting* that somehow reverberated around the room. Gabe and Vienna smiled at me from my right and left sides (I probably should have seated my donors next to me, but I'd known I'd spend so much time with them during the rest of the party and really wanted a break to talk to the people who mattered). "Welcome to the inaugural gala for the Pomona Afton Foundation," I said. The room was so quiet you could've heard a tiny dog taking one delicate bite from an old book. (Which, thankfully, I was not hearing, though Denise Ryan had somehow snuck her Pomeranian in and was giving it bits of her bread to nibble on.) "I can't express how excited I am to be helping students get an education. With your help, of course."

I went on for a bit, sharing some stories about my scholarship recipients and what they were doing with the money—one budding software engineer, another aspiring social worker, a few teachers (I had a soft spot for teachers, clearly). I shouted out several of the people who'd made generous donations. And, of course, I talked about my inspirations for the pastries served tonight.

And then it was time to pass the mic. "My guest of honor tonight is Conrad Phlume. Mr. Phlume needs no introduction, but I'll give one anyway." This one got a snicker around the room. "New York City's most famous real estate developer, he holds buildings all over the city, and he was kind and generous enough to loan us a building to use as our center. I appreciate him very much. Mr. Phlume, take it away."

I sat to scattered applause that, excuse me, should have been a lot stronger. From the amount of times I'd practiced that speech in my bedroom mirror and to various captive audiences (mostly Gabe and Squeaky Meatball), I knew I'd been excellent.

Gabe leaned in as Conrad began to speak—so far, fortunately, keeping to the words I'd approved (a bland and somewhat nonsensical story about how growing up wealthy had actually inflicted more hardships upon him than growing up poor would have). "Your parents are glaring so hard at Conrad Phlume that he might catch fire," he whispered. "I'd say you should have them frisked for weapons if I didn't already know your mom's shoe could be one."

I'd already snuck a glance at her feet before to check; when her famous stilettos had been taken by the police in evidence bags from Opal's closet and splashed across the front page of every tabloid, she'd been both scarred and tarred. She was wearing gladiator sandals tonight, which she'd always told me made her legs look stumpy. "I suppose she could use the laces to strangle him," I mused. "But yeah, I know. He's been persona non grata for, what, a year or two now? But my parents were ahead of the curve. He was never invited to any of our family galas."

I peered at them again, wondering if Conrad had made a pass at my mom or something in the past. They'd be pretty well suited as a couple, honestly. Assuming they didn't kill each other.

Some unfamiliar words in Conrad's speech clashed against my ear. Words that I had decidedly *not* approved. ". . . the business of secrets," he said, and then he was staring at me. I blinked, hoping that somehow he was just about to surprise me with an extra few compliments or something. "When you know someone's secret, it gives you power. Power that can give you the world."

A clatter of glass from beside me. Vienna had jumped so hard she'd jarred her tableware. "Vee, are you okay?" I whispered.

She didn't respond. She was staring at Conrad, her face a murky gray. "I'm fine."

Conrad Phlume had gone back to his prepared speech, talking about the building in Chelsea he was lending to us and some of its history as a grand residence before falling into disrepair and dilapidation, but the drama wasn't over. He stopped short as his wife stood beside him, her jaw clenched hard enough to break teeth.

"Dear," he began, but she leaned in and whispered. She might not have meant anyone to hear it, but it went right into his mic.

"I'm done. Have fun with that skank."

She reared back, looking momentarily startled at how loud she'd been, then gave a tiny shrug and tossed her hair before storming off toward the restrooms. I was dying to follow, but as the host, I couldn't move.

Like she'd read my mind, Vienna stood and also strode off toward the restrooms. What a good best friend.

The rest of Conrad Phlume's speech passed without great incident, and so did our dinner, which was resoundingly mediocre—the salad a little wilted, the chicken breast dry. Gabe devoured his entire plate in a matter of moments, though. A little too fast. Libby, seated on his other side, was giving him side-eye. I should speak to him about his speed of consumption.

Vienna returned in time to pick at her food. "I'm dying to ask you what Bibi said," I whispered in her ear. "But I guess I'll have to wait until later. Don't want to risk anyone overhearing."

She picked up a forkful of salmon, grimaced at it, and let it drop back to her plate. "Don't bother. Nothing interesting happened. All we said to each other was 'excuse me' as I was going into the bathroom."

Well, that was disappointing. I turned my attention to Vienna's plate, from which she'd eaten almost nothing. Understandable, considering it wasn't very good, but also, Vienna had a history of not eating enough during times of stress. She went practically skeletal while we were waiting for college acceptances back in the day. "Are you okay?"

"Fine," she said. As if anticipating my next point, she stuck a big forkful of roasted carrot into her mouth and chewed hard. Okay, so she still didn't want to talk about it. Sure enough, she changed the subject. "How are you feeling about your inaugural gala? I think it's gone quite well so far."

"I'm feeling pretty good," I said, glancing over at the side entrance again. Bibi had emerged, gliding past the crowd with her sharp chin held high as if she didn't feel all the stares on her. She sat down beside her husband to pick at her salad.

Soon enough, it was time for the after-dinner mingling to commence. A string quartet played light but delicate tunes in the corner as our hopefully full and sated and slightly tipsy guests were given the opportunity to donate big checks before the champagne buzz or urge to compete with one another wore off.

I, for one, beelined for the three white whales. Denise Ryan first. As I approached her, I ran through the notes my assistant, Lina, had made me in my head, careful not to mouth anything out loud. "Denise! So glad you could make it!"

"Pom," she said, smiling wide and white. "So glad you invited me."

I had no idea how true that was. Since her widely publicized divorce and the even more widely publicized vow she'd taken to give her entire half of her ex's tech fortune away, she'd been invited to every single gala in every single city in every single state. If anything, I was honored that she'd shown up here when she could've been off helping struggling farm workers in SoCal or investing in small theaters downtown. "How is dual-coast life?" I asked. I'd read she was now splitting her time between her old home in Seattle and here in the city, closer to her parents and siblings in the Philly area where she'd grown up. "I've been considering starting a West Coast branch of Pomona's Treats."

"Oh, please start one in Seattle," she said. "Whenever I'm there I so miss your chai spice buns."

I doubted that she'd ever stepped foot in my bakery or let one of my buns pass her lips (or any buns, considering the way she was encased in a size-zero bandage dress at age fifty-four), but I appreciated whatever assistant had told her about them. "You know, I haven't spent a lot of time in Seattle. Whenever I've been out west, it's mostly been LA."

"Oh, Seattle is wonderful," she said. "You must come visit. You're welcome to stay with me, of course."

There would certainly be plenty of room; she'd supposedly gotten the house in the divorce, all eleven bedrooms and fourteen bathrooms of it. "Oh, thank you. That would be delightful."

"Of course," she said, teeth gleaming with her smile. The cello thrummed in the background. "Though of course it's far more fun here. The lights. The sound. The energy. God, it's incredible. If my younger self could see me now . . ."

Denise's past was no secret: it had been plastered over every newspaper that wrote an article about her divorce, which was every single newspaper. She'd met her ex-husband when they were students together at Penn. He'd gotten his degree in engineering; she'd studied English. After school, she'd done unpaid publishing internships during the day and bartended at night. All the articles called her a former bartender, which seemed unfair, considering the main reason she was bartending was to make enough money to support the two of them while he was working full-time on the fledgling company that eventually blew up.

"I bet your younger self would be so proud of you," I told her. "It's incredible what you're doing. Deciding to give all your money away to worthy causes . . ."

She didn't take the heavy hint. "Honestly, I think younger me would be more excited about the fashion and the food and the celebrities." Her laugh was open-mouthed, genuine. "I got invited to the Met Gala, and my ex didn't. That alone would've floored her."

I didn't remember seeing her there, but, to be fair, it had been hard to see much of anything through the birdcage bars. (Or go to the bathroom. Though photos at the Met Gala were forbidden, someone had snuck one that had gone viral of last year's Oscar winners for best actress *and* best supporting actress helping me lift the birdcage over my head so I could fit into a stall.) "Amazing," I gushed. "But anyway, I bet what would really floor her is how much she could help some scholarship students afford school and living expenses while working their way up. We could even name one after you."

"Oh, that would be so lovely," she said, clasping one of my hands and giving it a squeeze. "You can, of course, expect a contribution to your very worthy organization." She dropped my hand. "I'll have to get it to you later, though—somehow I left my checkbook at home."

"Oh, we take—" I started, but she was already patting me on the shoulder and bumping her cheek against mine in a goodbye. Which was totally fine. With these people, a commitment to contribute was basically just as good as the contribution itself. They wouldn't want to be embarrassed if it leaked out that they were promising money they didn't give. They'd never get invited to a gala again.

On to the next shiny golden goose. I swanned over to Kevin Miller, who was lurking by the chocolate fountain. "Kevin, such a joy to see you," I said, leaning in for a handshake. His nearly crushed my fingers, but I held my own by not crying. "Your new book was amazing. So inspiring. I'm thinking about getting a copy for each of my students."

I hadn't read his book. I'd read the back, if it counted. It sounded the same as all his other books, TED Talks, and talk show appearances: basically a recounting of his childhood as a street urchin with ashes on his cheeks and no shoes, then a sermon on how he'd risen from those cheek ashes to become one of the richest men in the US. But the compliment worked—he beamed, his ruddy face going ruddier. He ran a hand through his head of thick dark hair. Threads of silver winked at me. "Aw, shucks. Thank you. Ping me if you want me to sign them," he said, his old-school New Yawk accent still strong after years of being surrounded by Waspy mid-Atlantic diction. "I'm happy to. I always like paying it forward."

Ugh, now I'd actually have to buy his stupid book. A while ago, one of my students had broached the idea of bringing him in to speak. But for all of Kevin's blabbering about how he'd started out poor and eventually become part of high society with penthouses and mansions galore, he kind of skated over the details of how exactly he got all that money. My bet? He was involved in something sketchy he couldn't elaborate on without the IRS training its beady eyes on him. "Wow, that's so generous of you," I said. "Speaking of paying it forward, I—"

"You know, I grew up in Chelsea," he said, head tilting, eyes shimmering nostalgically in the direction of the ceiling. Great. What I really wanted was another recap of his street urchin years. "Chelsea was a very different place then, rich and poor all mixed together. I would pass those grand brownstones, like the one Conrad is lending you, and wish I lived somewhere like that."

"Mmm," I said. Vienna lived in a Chelsea brownstone. It was indeed beautiful, but it also had a lot of stairs. So many stairs. Navigating those stairs drunk and on heels when we'd stumble home in the middle of the night was a medal-worthy Olympic feat.

"It's a shame the one Conrad's lending you fell into such disrepair in the eighties and nineties, but that's also an opportunity," Kevin said. "You could really get into the place's bones. Renovate it however you want."

"That's a fun idea," I said brightly. "But I think it's a little too much for what we want to use the building for. Our plan is just to do the basics—fix the flooring, take down the torn-up wallpaper, clear out the broken furniture, and dump all the moldy boxes in the basement. It'll work perfectly well for our purposes."

"Yes, but the opportunity." His eyes gleamed. "I offered to buy it off Conrad, but he told me he couldn't sell because he'd already promised it to you. You could tell him it's okay, and then how about you have your pick from the buildings in my portfolio? I've got a great little duplex in Queens."

Queens. I suppressed a shudder. I'd had quite enough of Queens after nearly being murdered there, thank you very much.

"That's very kind of you, but location is everything. We really need something centrally located."

"I also have some vacant apartments up in Inwood—"

How stupid did this guy think I was? Just because I hadn't climbed the ladder like him didn't mean I couldn't see the view from the top. That house in Chelsea was worth way more than anything in his outer-borough portfolio.

Maybe this was how he'd climbed the ladder. Stepping on other people's fingers as they clung to the rungs.

"Thank you, I'll consider it," I said as sweetly as I could. "But tonight I'm here to focus on—"

"I hear your family is closing the Afton Scottsdale." He talked over me, eyes keen. "Is that true?"

I hadn't been to the Afton Scottsdale in years—all the light reflecting off the dyed blond hair, giant veneers, and garish jewelry in the area hurt my eyes. "I have no idea," I said. "That's probably a question for my dad. He's the one in charge."

That keen glint in his eyes again. "Is he?"

What even kind of question was that? "Yes. He's over there." I turned to point at my parents' table, but they were no longer at their seats. Maybe they'd decided they'd shown their faces enough not to lose them and fled. "Well. You probably have his number; you can text him. Anyway! You received a number of scholarships to help you through college and business school, right?" He didn't interrupt me this time, which was encouraging. "I imagine you're very grateful to the people who gave you access to those opportunities you wouldn't have been able to get ahead without. Imagine how good it would feel to pay that forward."

"I'm sure. I'll consider it and get back to you," he said, a little sourly. His eyes landed on someone over my shoulder. Maybe my dad. "Ah, there you are. Come—"

I beat it before I could get sucked into some boring conversation about the family business. Two of my golden geese hadn't laid any eggs so far, but there was still number three, my parents' hedge fund manager, Jack Wohl . . . who, I had to admit after three full circles of the room, was nowhere to be found. I could only hope that he'd suffered some kind of bathroom emergency or wardrobe malfunction, that he was somewhere in the wings and would reemerge later. Because the alternative was to admit that the gala might be a bust.

That *I* was a bust. Because what would it say if my very first gala was a bust? If this organization and goal that I'd spent all year working on fell flat? If I failed the kids I'd been promising to help? God, I couldn't even think of their faces. What if I'd spent all year doing my best to become a better person and my best wasn't good enough? I could practically see Libby and Kitty and John snickering behind a pillar. Silently and with solemn faces, because they were too well-bred to actually snicker in public.

No. That couldn't be what happened. It couldn't. Because even the thought of abandoning the kids and heading out to party with Millicent and Coriander—who, I thought with an unpleasant lurch in my stomach, were also nowhere to be seen right now—didn't feel good at all. Which meant I'd progressed as a person, right? That I was better?

What did better mean, anyway?

"Pomona!" someone cried, clapped me on the shoulder, pulled me into their circle. "Tell me about your . . ."

My worries faded as I circled the room again, made conversation, solicited smaller donations that would add up to multiple scholarships. Things were going fine. My first gala would be a success. Nothing bad would—

A scream echoed through the room, silencing all the chatter with the force of a slap. My head whipped in its direction.

Just in time to see the body tumbling from the second-floor railing and landing, with the most horrific squelch I'd ever heard, atop the hanging murder peacock.

CHAPTER *Five*

So it was safe to say that I'd been wrong. Something bad, something terrible, had happened. But that wasn't the thought whirling around my head as I waited, with the rest of my guests, to talk to the police, Gabe's arm wrapped around me like a blanket.

It was, *This again?*

Knowing one murder victim had been enough for one lifetime. Being involved in one murder investigation had been *quite* enough for one lifetime, thank you very much. I still had nightmares about it. They'd lessened with time, but I wasn't sure they'd ever completely go away.

At least they'd mostly replaced the stress dreams I used to have about finally getting that invite to the Met Gala only to discover I'd shown up without my clothes and that the theme was *not* Naked Glory.

Gabe pressed a kiss to the top of my head. "It's going to be okay," he said into my hair. A chilly breeze followed it, making me burrow deeper into his warmth. Everybody from the gala who hadn't disobeyed the police and made a run for it or who wasn't dead was currently gathered outside on the steps of the New York Public Library, drawing stares from tourists walking by.

"You don't know that," I said into his neck. It was easier to argue with him when I wasn't looking him in the eye. "Who was it? I can't find Vienna. I can't find—"

"It was definitely a man," he said. "I definitely saw that before everybody started screaming and running out and the police told us to leave. An older man. With gray hair."

I pulled back from Gabe's shoulder, scanning the crowd. "I don't see my dad," I said, panic swelling in my chest, threatening to push my heart out my throat. What if this was my last interaction with my dad? Me sitting him next to someone he hated? And he—

Oh. There he was. Off in the corner talking to my mom, Nicholas, and Jessica. A shiver of relief ran down my spine. Not enough to go talk to them, but it was there all the same.

"See?" Gabe's voice was a rumble all through me; his arms were strong and warm around me against the chill of the air. "It's not your dad. Take a deep breath through your nose."

I took a deep breath through my nose. It didn't help. It just made me want a hot dog, because there was a hot dog cart stationed on the sidewalk nearby and I'd barely managed to choke down any of my mediocre chicken. Maybe for my next gala I should have the hot dog cart guys cater.

If I had a next gala. "I can't believe someone was murdered at my first gala." I clenched my fists, wanting so badly to scream but knowing that I couldn't. People were probably taking photos of me now, waiting for me to do something crazy. "I just . . . I can't even. My life is ruined. My nonprofit is ruined. Nobody's going to donate to my cause now." I glanced frantically around, seeking out Libby, Kitty, and John. They were nowhere to be seen. Probably they'd left their names with the police and gone home, because you could do that when you had more money than God and a family tree that included multiple presidents, governors, and senators (the piddly House representatives didn't even merit a mention).

"First of all, we don't know that the victim was murdered," Gabe said. "It's unlikely he was murdered, statistically. He probably drank too much champagne, leaned too far over that too-low second-floor railing, and had the bad luck to land on that monstrosity."

"I don't know," I said, because statistics hadn't always been on my side before. How many people could say that they'd been yachtjacked not once but twice? "And that railing wasn't high, but it also wasn't that low."

"And second of all," he said, ignoring my extremely sound point. "Even if he was murdered, your life is not ruined. It wasn't your fault. Nobody will blame you."

My laugh was short and sharp and tired. "Of course they'll blame me." The resignation was already setting in. "I've spent this past year working so hard to change the way people think of me. I haven't been clubbing once. I haven't gotten drunk. I've spent evenings at the theater, going to art openings, attending gala after gala. I've been keeping my head down, trying to repel the kinds of stories people always run about me."

"And this doesn't change that," Gabe said, but I barely heard him.

"They'll spin it as me somehow engineering it for attention. Nobody will say I committed the murder, but they'll talk about how my grandma's murder made me even more famous than I already was, and—"

"Ms. Afton?"

My hand fluttered to my chest. Two detectives were standing behind me, faces grave. "Yes?"

"Could we speak with you inside for a moment?"

I could feel every single eye crawling on me as I passed them.

Inside, the detectives ushered me to what seemed to be someone's office, a cluttered space of papers and books. They stopped before the desk, not sitting. I didn't sit either. "Who was it?" I asked, the dread heavy in my stomach.

The first detective fiddled with his glasses. "It seems that the victim was a Mr. Conrad Phlume."

I gasped, hand flying to my mouth. Tears sprang to my eyes. "Oh God. Oh no."

The detective frowned sympathetically. "I'm so sorry. Did you know him well?"

It seemed rude to say, *No, I loathed him, but he was supposed to give me a house*, so I just nodded and hoped the detective wouldn't ask any more questions. Which was probably not a wish that was going to come true, considering he was a detective.

"I'm sorry for your loss," he said. "What was your relationship with the deceased?"

I cleared my throat, which was suddenly very dry. "He was a major donor to my nonprofit, the Pomona Afton Foundation." And then, because, well, it wasn't like the detective was in mourning and he probably knew something about laws: "If he'd promised us a major contribution but hadn't actually signed it over to us yet, does it still belong to us?"

"I believe that's a question for his next of kin," the detective said.

As far as I knew, Conrad didn't have any kids, which made his next of kin his wife, Bibi . . . who'd stormed out during his toast. There was a sinking feeling in my stomach that maybe she wouldn't exactly want to see his wishes through. "I see." A pause. "Was he . . . do you know if he was . . ."

"Murdered?" the second detective finished. "We can't say anything for sure, obviously. We'll need to wait for the full autopsy results. But . . ." She frowned. "The victim has marks on his face and hands that indicate he may have been in a physical altercation before falling over the railing. And the force with which he hit the peacock sculpture . . . well. Again, we can't be 100 percent sure at this point . . ."

I wasn't stupid. I could read between the lines. Someone had beaten him up and pushed him over the railing. I let out a long, low exhale. Fantastic. Somehow I didn't think the murder of the guest of honor at my first gala would make people excited about being the guest of honor at the next one.

"We'll likely want to call you in for a longer chat once we've learned more," said the first detective. "But, in the meantime, I understand that the victim wasn't all that popular." That was a delicate understatement. "Can you think of anyone tonight at the gala who might have had a reason to confront Mr. Phlume?"

A reason to beat him up and shove him over a railing to his death, they meant. I sighed. "Like you said, he wasn't very popular. I don't think anybody there really liked him. But I don't know who would *kill* him."

"I understand. Thank you," said the first detective. "We'll talk to you again soon, but please be in touch if you think of anything. And I assume that you or the venue can provide a full guest list?"

I nodded. "Of course."

"Thank you," said the first detective. "I have one more question for you before you go. This was found in the victim's hand. I'm assuming it wasn't his—do you know who it might have belonged to?"

He held up a small clear evidence bag. Inside, something winked at me. A large diamond. Attached to a thin gold chain. Which was attached to, I realized as cold spread through my chest, an earring back.

I reached automatically for my earlobes, but both of my earrings were firmly in place. I fiddled with a chain, which was slightly shorter than the chain of the earring in the evidence bag.

Which meant it had to be Vienna's.

I opened my mouth, then closed it. Opened it, closed it.

"Do you recognize it?" the detective pressed.

I had a split second to decide what to do. They'd figure out it was Vienna's eventually, right? She was wearing it in all the pictures from tonight. And then they'd be suspicious of me for lying about it. I loved Vienna, but I also loved myself. And it didn't matter anyway—it wasn't like Vienna had killed Conrad Phlume. There was no way.

So I told him. And, as I scurried back to Gabe and burrowed into his chest to avoid the dark stares from the rest of my guests, I hoped I'd done the right thing.

CHAPTER
Six

They say that all publicity is good publicity. Who "they" are, I don't know. I was decidedly not part of "them," after I woke in the morning and grabbed my phone off the nightstand to see news reports about the murder at the gala all over social media set to the soundtrack of the poorly received title track from the only album of my short-lived singing career. (How was young Pom to know that the lyric "Pink is dead and I'm the killer" would age so poorly?)

"Shouldn't they all know that I didn't write my own music?" I said aloud. Gabe stirred awake. I waited for him to ask what was wrong, but he only settled onto his pillow like he was going back to sleep, so I let out an enormous gust of a sigh.

That got him up. He propped himself on an elbow, wincing at the sunlight filtering around the edges of our blackout curtains and rubbing his eyes. "What's wrong?"

"Everything," I said, as dramatically as possible. "I'm ruined."

He sat up all the way, running a hand through his hair that made it, if possible, even more mussed. Sometimes I just wanted to lean in and take a bite of him. Was that weird? It was probably weird. "You're not ruined. It's going to be okay."

"It's not going to be okay. A man is dead."

"Yes, a man you didn't like even a little bit," Gabe said. "I mean, yes, it's sad, but it's not going to ruin your life. And even if his widow won't sign the building over to you, you'll find another building. It's going to be okay."

At least he didn't try to tell me that all publicity is good publicity. Just in case he was thinking it, I held out my phone so that he could scroll through some of the top results from this morning's Google Alert. His eyes widened as he flicked his finger. "Oh, wow. Okay. Um."

"Yeah." I knew what he was seeing: headlines claiming that I was delighted about the murder because solving the last one (excuse me, "stumbling upon the answer," according to one particularly infuriating subheading) had given me so much good publicity; influencers who'd met me once claiming that they knew me and I'd probably killed Conrad myself to stay relevant; one self-proclaimed witch claiming that I was cursed (which, might there be something to that? Mental note to give her a call). "My reputation was finally improving. Libby and Kitty and them actually showed at my gala. And now . . ."

"At least it's not just you," Gabe said grimly, handing my phone back. Because, of course, Vienna was in the public's eye too. She might have faded from view over her past few years of doing good and keeping her underwear on in public, but everybody knew her from being my best friend. We'd done a short-lived reality show together right after we graduated from college where we traveled around the globe together trying the weirdest foods producers could find. (A GIF of her vomiting into the Nile after trying a sheep's eyeball still showed up in my comments sections all the time.) "I guess the thing about her earring leaked. Everybody thinks the two of you did it together."

"Of course they do," I said. Because the two drunken college grads who couldn't even stomach haggis could definitely go in on a murder together.

As absurd as the idea was, though, it was gaining steam. I

texted her, Hey, how are you doing? Hesitated before sending. Added an emoji heart. Sent. I was *such* a good friend.

The three typing bubbles popped up immediately. I sat there staring at them, waiting for the response. She was typing, typing, typing for ages . . .

And then they disappeared. Leaving me staring at my question, which was sitting there all alone and awkward, like me when the Oscar winners left the bathroom at the Met Gala before they could help me get my birdcage back on. Which, of course, led to the second viral photo featuring strategically placed feathers from that night.

But enough about that. I tossed my phone aside, smarting a little. "Can we call your brother?"

Gabe, who in the meantime had gone out to the kitchen, called back, "We just saw him last week."

I followed the sound of Gabe's voice, Squeaky winding his way around my ankles the whole way, either in such delight to see me that he couldn't sit still or because he thought it would be funny to trip me and watch me face-plant in his water bowl. You could never really tell with cats. They were kind of like my old model frenemies that way.

Gabe stopped short in front of his coffeemaker as he saw me holding out his phone. I leaned down to scratch Squeaky's ears without breaking eye contact with my boyfriend, who said, "Oh no. No way."

"There's no harm in it," I wheedled. Squeaky purred louder than a coffee grinder, his black fur shining almost reddish in the light that poured through our floor-to-ceiling windows. Central Park sprawled green outside the windows of the living room behind us in addition to our bedroom, and I usually made time to admire it every morning, but not today. Too much to do. "If there's something he can't tell us, he just won't. I'm not trying to get him in trouble."

Gabe's older brother, Caleb, was a detective with the NYPD. He probably wouldn't be on this case, just like he wasn't on the case of my grandmother, but it was useful having someone on the inside to catch all the gossip. Plus, he loved the fill-your-own donuts we served at the bakery with an enthusiasm that did nothing for the related stereotype.

Gabe sighed. "Fine." He dialed his brother and placed the phone flat on our kitchen table before putting it on speaker. I grabbed the Brita pitcher to fill Squeaky's Murano confetti glass bowl I'd brought back from Italy, then plopped some of his chicken, quinoa, and carrot mixture that the cat chef had left for him into his bowl (because Millicent had asked me this question in all seriousness: a chef for cats, not a cat who was a chef).

I sat down just as Caleb answered. "What do you want, farthead?"

I've had plenty of issues with Nicholas, but sometimes I was glad my own older brother was all about suits and poetry and propriety. Most of his insults for me had been Shakespearean, which had been great, because it was hard to be insulted by a nickname when you had no idea what it meant.

Before Gabe could respond with something equally juvenile, I butted in (hee). "Hey, Caleb. It's Pom."

"Oh, hey, Pom," he said. "You got strawberry filling in yet?"

"Soon," I promised. "I'll text you as soon as I do. I'm actually thinking about adding a touch of jalapeño, what do you think?"

"Sounds amazing," he said enthusiastically.

Of course it did. All my ideas (at least all of my pastry-related ideas) were amazing. I continued, encouraged, "Hey, we just wanted to pick your brain."

His voice immediately put up walls. "You know I can't tell you anything that's not already public information."

"Of course not. I wouldn't expect you to," I said. "We're more looking for vibes."

"Vibes?"

Vibes? Gabe mouthed at me, mystified.

How were they not familiar with vibes? Vibes were how I made most of my decisions. "Just, like, the general feeling around the department," I said breezily. "No concrete information. No secrets. I'm worried about my friend Vienna. Do they really think she did it?"

Caleb was silent for a moment. If they were just doing their due diligence in clearing her, he'd say so quickly. Which didn't bode well. After way too long, he said, "No comment."

Meaning, yes. Crap. It had to be the earring, though I couldn't help but flash back to that tense conversation between Vienna and Conrad I'd overheard at the very beginning of the night. Maybe somebody else had overheard it too. Still. "I mean, the earring could've gotten there in so many ways," I said. "Maybe it fell out and Conrad Phlume, a good upstanding citizen, picked it up so that he could return it later."

Caleb sighed. "Sure. Maybe." He was silent for a moment again. "Your friend, like the rest of your crowd, has the best lawyers and lots of money to donate to the campaign of whatever well-placed official will advocate on her behalf. You don't have to worry about her unless she did it."

"But she couldn't have done it," I said. "Vienna would never kill someone. What if it was some waiter? Conrad Phlume probably yelled at a bunch of waiters that night."

"The entire catering and venue staff were seen on the lower floor or in the basement cleaning up around the time of the murder," Caleb said.

"Then what about his wife? You know she hissed at him in the middle of his speech and stormed out, right?"

"Yes, I have heard that," Caleb said. "But you know, it's not the earring alone that points to your friend, it's all the . . ." He stopped himself short. I let out an exasperated breath.

"All the what?"

"You know I can't tell you that, Pom." He sounded as exasperated as I did.

"Come on, you can't hint like that and then *not* tell us."

"It wasn't a hint. I didn't even say anything."

"Sounded like a hint to me," I said. "Just give us one more tiny hint. Point us in the right direction."

"I have to go." Booooo. "Have a good day, Pom. Not you, farthead."

He hung up without even saying goodbye, like he was worried I'd wheedle the information out of him. I probably would. I was exceptionally good at wheedling. It was basically how I'd solved the last murder.

Speaking of which. "Oh no," Gabe said.

"What?" I said innocently. My eyes were as big and doe-like as those of the vintage cat clock on the kitchen wall, the one whose tail swung with every tick.

"I see that look on your face."

"What look on my face?"

"What was it?" Gabe asked. "Vienna being in trouble? The articles saying that you're stupid and that you blundered into solving your grandmother's murder? The risk of nobody coming to your next gala?"

I shrugged. "All of the above?"

"You do remember what happened last time we investigated a murder, right?" Gabe said. "You were almost stabbed to death with a shoe."

Honestly, that hadn't even been the most traumatic part. I'd thought Opal was my best friend, for goodness' sake. I'd also gone through most of my family members as suspects. There was nothing like making you question a relationship you'd always taken for granted like thinking—or ultimately finding out—that they were a murderer. It was hard to get close to anyone now, thinking what they might be hiding.

What if someone close to me was the killer again? I didn't know if I could take it.

"I'm not saying we should immediately go out and start interrogating people," I said.

My phone dinged. I picked it up. It was a text from Lina, my assistant. Pom, I'm so sorry, but I have to resign my position effective immediately. Thanks for understanding. I hope I can still use you as a reference in the future.

My lips tightened. Oh, I understood. Her step-uncle on the family board wanted her away from any hint of controversy or wrongdoing. Because that's what I was now. A flaming beacon of controversy and wrongdoing.

How could an entire year of do-gooding and look-smarting have plummeted over the railing with Conrad Phlume?

I put my phone aside without responding to Lina. Who needed her anyway? I could handle everything myself. "Maybe we should just try asking a few questions. Point the police in the right direction."

Gabe sighed. "If that's what you really want." He stood. "I guess I should go get the detective hats."

I assumed he meant that figuratively.

CHAPTER Seven

Gabe did not mean it figuratively. As it turned out, he had purchased us actual detective hats. Fedoras. Light brown fedoras, the kind a detective in an old black-and-white noir film would look sharp in.

I did not look sharp in it. For one, it clashed with my hair. For two, it clashed with the darling pink wallpaper in our living room that I'd sourced from the elite wallpaperers of Slovakia (if you know, you know). For three, I'd never had the face for a fedora. Too long.

Gabe did, though to be fair, he had the face for every kind of hat. Also for going without a hat. He just had a great face.

"I didn't buy them thinking we were going to be solving another murder," he said, when I gave him the questioning look that meant exactly that. "They were supposed to be a surprise for the one-year anniversary of when we solved the last one."

"What, so we could relive the highlights?"

"I mean, there were *some* highlights," Gabe said defensively. "We did fall in love."

"True." We were currently not reliving any highlights; we were reliving the most tedious part, aka when we sat on Gabe's couch and made lists of all possible suspects. At least this time we weren't confined to Gabe's terrible lumpy old three-seater he'd actually gotten used from a stranger without even thinking about how many people had probably had sex on it. Our new couch was the softest suede in ivory, a color I'd purchased without considering that we owned a black cat. Like I said, I made most of my decisions on vibes. "Okay, so Caleb confirmed that all the people working the event had alibis, which means that the murderer has to be someone who was attending the gala. Is there any way we can narrow it down?"

Gabe bit his lower lip as he thought. "Was anyone taking photos at the time?"

"I assume everyone. Let's check the feed." Within minutes, I had a time-stamped feed of photos from the gala. "Okay, these here are all from the five minutes before the murder. If we compile everyone we see in the background, we should be able to cross a bunch of people off our list."

I wished I still had an assistant who could do this for me. Plan B: I stood and smiled angelically at my beloved boyfriend. "Should I run to the bakery and pick up some fuel for the task?"

"Let me guess," Gabe said. "I might as well get started while you're gone and, ideally, will be done by the time you get back."

"I love you so much," I said.

"I love you too," he said. "But you're forgetting that I have no idea who most of these people are."

I moaned, flopping back down on the couch. The sunlight streaming over Central Park and into our windows suddenly seemed to mock me. I'd been so close to getting out of this. So close. I gazed longingly out the window, envying the tiny passersby below their freedom, their carefreeness, their social circles that were probably murderer-free.

Several hours later, I stared up at the ceiling, blinking hard, afterimages of guests permanently tattooed beneath my eyelids. "Okay. Is that all?"

"I think so," Gabe said, comparing the list we'd made with the zoomed-in images on my laptop. There had been several people who'd been too blurry or obscured to confidently identify, and of course there were people who'd been there out of anybody's frame, but we'd prepared a list that counted out a bunch of my guests. Which left a bunch more under suspicion, but it was a start. "Okay, so we've got our list to make now. Let's start with people who have motive and who aren't on the list."

"Murder Artist has to be on there," I said immediately. "Not only did he tell us explicitly that he was a murder fan, his peacock took part in the crime. I forget his name, but let me check with Li—oh." Couldn't do that. I turned to the guest list. "I'll probably recognize it when I—okay, Isaiah Franklin. Make him number one."

"Done," Gabe said. "And Conrad Phlume's wife has to be on there, too, right? After that outburst."

"Don't they say it's always the spouse?" I added her to the list. "Who else?"

We stared at the list for another few minutes. Gabe finally said hesitantly, "Do you think there's even a chance it might be—"

"No," I said immediately. "No way."

"But she seems to have—"

"It wasn't Vienna," I interrupted. "It's not possible." Before he could argue with me, I clicked back to the feed and refreshed. The hashtag reloaded. I cringed at the top photo: a very unflattering photo of me, one taken from the under-chin angle (why did that angle even exist?) with my mouth half open and nose pores on full display.

The cringe only lasted a second, though. It didn't faze me that much. The world had seen way worse of me. See: the paparazzi competition over who could get the "best" upskirt photo after I turned eighteen. There was nothing like the entire world getting to see the red, inflamed evidence of your very first bikini wax.

It took me another second to realize that I wasn't the only person in that photo: Vienna was there too. It was an old one, back from when we were doing the reality show; her arm was wrapped over my shoulder, clearly relying on me to hold her up. We were probably drunk or high (we were drunk or high a lot of the time those days). Unfairly, she looked way better than me—she'd had the foresight to tilt her chin down, and her hair was messy in a way that looked like it was on purpose even though it most likely wasn't.

Gabe, looking over my shoulder, sucked in a breath through his teeth. "The caption," he clarified, so that I wouldn't think he was wincing at my face.

I leaned in. The words seemed awfully small. Did I need glasses? Maybe I was being punished by the universe for convincing Coriander to wear those hideous frames, for which she'd already featured in, according to the group chat, at least two "Worst Dressed at the Murder Scene" compilations, which really should not be a thing.

> Pomona Afton's grand entrance into the do-gooder scene was supposed to be akin to a butterfly emerging from a cocoon: wasted party girl caterpillar to saintly butterfly. Saints don't get their biggest donors killed, though. Pom, maybe you should hop back up on a table, where you belong. Better to get attention by flashing your underwear at cameras than helping your fellow fake-do-gooder friend kill someone who only wanted to do good for real.

"Wow, okay," I said. Not going to lie, reading that made me feel a little nauseous, and the thought of all the people I wanted so badly to impress reading it made me feel like I might actually vomit. I was used to bad press—but not when I was actually trying to do something good. Part of me wanted to listen to whoever this anonymous asshole with no profile picture but a mastery of the hashtags was. Just admit defeat. Go back to doing what was easy.

No. I couldn't do that. My eyes flicked toward Gabe. For one, Gabe didn't love Old Pom. Right?

I thrust my shoulders back. I would be strong. I'd get through this.

My phone buzzed. The unflattering picture of me disappeared from the screen and was replaced with a picture of my mother. Suddenly I wanted the unflattering photo back.

Maybe I'd be lucky and she was accidentally butt-dialing me. I hit the green button. "Hello?" I said quietly, so that I wouldn't alert her head in the event I was indeed talking to her butt.

"Pom? You sound exhausted," she said. I was not lucky today. To be fair, she'd been extra cautious about butt-dialing people since her old habit had exposed the fact that her shoe had been my grandma's murder weapon.

"That's funny, because I'm the opposite of exhausted," I said. "There's nothing that makes you sleep soundly like someone getting murdered at your very first gala. It's so calming."

I could practically hear her rolling her eyes through the phone. She said, "I hope this call isn't being recorded, because you know everyone would have those words plastered all over the headlines without any regard to your supposed 'sarcasm.'"

If the paparazzi had managed to tap into my phone, they already would've plastered the headlines with quotes from my debate with Vienna about whether it was unethical to try out one of those spas where they use blood diamond dust in their massages. "Mom, why are you calling?"

She sniffed into the phone. "My goodness, Pom. Can a mother not call her daughter to see how she's doing the morning after a horrific event?"

"I'm here too," said my dad. She must have me on speakerphone. I could picture them in the living room of their Afton penthouse, my grandmother's old apartment, my mom in her tight black workout clothes all sweaty on my grandma's white couch (just because she could); my dad kind of hovering in the background, stubble on his cheeks, wearing khaki shorts that exposed knobby knees. "How are you doing, Pom? I've been worried about you."

I knew better than to let myself relax whenever my mom was involved, but I let my shoulders fall a fraction anyway. Gabe got up from the table with the crumb-covered dishes in hand to take to the sink. "Oh. Well, I can't say I'm doing great. It's so hard to know that someone wasn't only hurt at an event I'd hoped would be a good thing, but—"

"Richard, don't get blood on the couch," she snapped. "I heard your friend was arrested?"

"Why is Dad getting blood on the couch?" I asked. "Is he okay?" It would be so like my mom to call for a chat while my dad was bleeding out in the background.

"Another nosebleed. He always gets them," my mom said. "Anyway, Vienna was arrested? Is that true?"

I sighed. Of course she just wanted gossip. "Vienna was not arrested, at least last I heard." I would've heard, right? Even if she hadn't texted me back?

"Do you think she did it?"

"Yes, Mom. Of course I think my best friend did it. Are you telling me you don't think *your* best friend's murdered anyone? How pedestrian."

"Honestly, Pomona." My mom bristled. "You know with mine it's a gray area." But I'd shut her up, at least for a few seconds, and that was a victory. Those few seconds were enough time for my dad to get some words in.

Unfortunately, he seemed to have forgotten about his concern for me. He said, rather self-importantly, "It's not a gray area because she used a beach umbrella and was technically found not at fault because it was such a windy day."

"I've already had to testify to that enough," Mom said. "My skin looked terrible in that drab courtroom lighting. Thank goodness they didn't allow photos, though it's not like that sketch artist did me any favors. Did you see how that man depicted my neck? It was like I hadn't even gotten that surgery. Well, surgeries."

I sighed through my nose.

"Anyway, I was asking about your friend because apparently she was sleeping with Conrad Phlume."

I popped bolt upright. "What are you talking about?"

My mom's voice oozed with delight at getting to break the news. "My friend saw them out together at that stodgy old red sauce joint on Seventy-Fifth. All cuddled up together in a booth in the back. They both looked sick when my friend went over to say hello."

My mom might have been terrible in a lot of ways, but she wasn't a liar. At least not about things like this (her age was another story. She was the oldest-looking forty-year-old in the country, probably).

Which meant Vienna was the one who'd lied. Not explicitly—I wondered what she would say if I confronted her directly about it, though she'd have to text me back for that. But she hadn't said anything about cozying up to Conrad Phlume during our whole time preparing this gala that was partially in his honor (but mostly mine). "Hmm," I said noncommittally. Really, Vienna? *Conrad Phlume? That's* who you have an affair with?

No. No way. Vienna had integrity. There was no way she'd knowingly help a man cheat on his wife.

Especially not if that man was *Conrad Phlume.*

"That poor woman," Mom said smugly. "Getting cheated on like that again. Just like Denise Ryan."

"It's not her fault," I said. "Either of their faults. Denise at least seems way happier without her ex."

"She must be lacking something that would make him stay," she said. "Look at my marriage. Your father and I have been faithful to each other for thirty years. Meanwhile, in his first marriage, he cheated and left her behind, all sad and alone, because I was an objectively better person and partner."

"That's not fair," I told her.

"How dare you say I'm a bad wife?"

I sighed. "That's not what I said."

"I'm just saying it as I see it," said my mom. "She lost, and I won."

"Dear," Dad said. "Is being married to me for thirty years actually winning?"

I couldn't help but laugh. That was probably the funniest thing my father had ever said, at least intentionally. As far as I was concerned, my parents deserved each other. His first wife had won that marriage by getting out. Which probably sounded terrible, but it was true.

At least this time my parents weren't suspects! What a relief!

"Roberta thought so," my mom huffed. "Remember how hard she fought the divorce?"

"She wasn't exactly fighting the divorce," Dad said mildly. "She wanted the Nantucket house."

"*I* wanted the Nantucket house," Mom spat.

"To be fair," Dad said, "it had been in her family for generations."

Okay, I had to get this back on track. "Is there anything else you wanted to discuss?"

"Honestly, Pomona," Mom said. "Sometimes you can be so . . ."

Gabe squeezed my arm. I jumped a little. I'd almost forgotten he was there, but his presence reminded me that, hello, I did not have to take this. "I have to go," I said, and pulled the phone away from my ear before my mom could neg me about how I couldn't possibly have anything more interesting going on than talking to them.

It sounded cliché, but the moment my phone was down, it felt like a weight had been lifted from my shoulders. I rolled them, relishing the sound of the crack. "The funny thing is that Mom would trash Denise Ryan *before* the divorce too," I told Gabe, and also Squeaky, who was purring so hard at my feet I was a little worried he might drill his way down through the floor and into the vacant apartment below us (the owner was holding out to sell for a better market, which was fine with me, because I didn't have to feel guilty about doing a virtual solo tango class at ten p.m.). "Whenever she'd see her at a gala, Mom would talk smack about how she was new money and she'd had the nerve to marry into it, not inherit it or make it—actually, the term she used was a lot grosser—and how she'd never be anything more than a bartender from Pennsylvania."

I hoped she'd steered clear of that talk around Jessica, who was marrying into our money by marrying my brother. Probably she hadn't. God, I owed Jessica so many drinks.

Gabe said, "Not surprising coming from your mom."

She hadn't said much of anything about Gabe, at least around me—not because she hadn't tried, because I would literally stand up and leave the room whenever she did—but I could only imagine she'd think way worse about him, since he was a man. No matter that Gabe insisted on paying me rent and utilities so that he wouldn't feel like he was freeloading. No matter that, when we'd discussed the future, he said he was fine signing a prenup in regard to the family money.

I cleared my throat delicately. "By the way, did you see that spread in *Vogue Italia*? The one about fall weddings in Tuscany?"

He cocked his head at me, smirking a little. "It would've been hard to miss, considering you opened the magazine right to the spread and left it on the kitchen counter in front of my coffee machine."

If there was one thing you (and countless journalists) could say about me, it was not that I was subtle. "What did you think?"

"It looked beautiful," he said. "But I'm not sure a wedding in Tuscany is for me. Too picturesque. All those rolling hills make me queasy."

I rolled my eyes, shoving him gently, shoulder to shoulder. "Rolling hills make you queasy?"

"I'm just speaking my truth." But there was a sparkle in his eye. "Your cousin Freddy's wedding in Jackson Hole, though? That was something."

"I can work with that," I said. We might not have been engaged yet, but I knew it was coming. Nobody could date me for a year and not want to marry me. And you could never start planning the party of a lifetime too early. "Maybe during the early winter, when the snow is still sparkly. I'll have Jessica as a bridesmaid, obviously, and Vienna . . ." I trailed off. I was going to say Vienna would be my maid of honor, but what if . . . what if . . .

"Don't go down that road, Pom. You have no idea if Vienna—"

"But she was hiding things from me," I said. I swallowed hard, trying to keep down the tears threatening to choke me. My neck ached from the whiplash the turn in this conversation had given me. "Opal was my friend and she was a killer. Another person close to me can't be a killer!"

"Oh, Pom." Gabe wrapped me in his arms, pulling me close into his chest. I breathed in deep, his smell of lemon and soap and coffee endlessly comforting. "It's not your fault, you know."

"I know it's not my fault." I sniffled. "But what does it say about me if I keep welcoming killers into my friend circle? Nobody will want to be my friend."

I felt a little like I was in elementary school again, the other girls giving me the cold shoulder because my pony bit some of their ponies during dressage practice. I couldn't blame anybody or anyhorse for not wanting to dance with us after that.

"It's not a reflection on you," Gabe said into the top of my head. "The universe is full of random chance. You being born into a billionaire family is probably less likely than you befriending two killers. There are more killers in the world than billionaires, I bet." He let that discomfiting statistic sit for a moment. I wondered what would happen if all the killers ganged up against the billionaires. They'd totally win. Billionaires were soft. "And you don't know anything yet. One dinner does not an affair make, and even if she was having an affair with him, that doesn't mean she killed him."

I took a deep breath. "Right. You're right." It just cemented the need to look into other alternatives. So that I couldn't stew in the horrible maybe of it all. "That means we only have two main leads on this list, right? The scary bird artist and Bibi."

"It's going to be hard to get to Bibi, I bet."

That was true, though I'd need to reach out at some point to see what was going on with the building Conrad had promised me. I'd have to wait a respectful amount of time after the murder, of course. Poking her on it today would be callous. "The artist, then." He was the only one who'd explicitly admitted to wanting to murder someone that night. It would be irresponsible not to talk to him.

It turned out he was pretty easy to pin down—he had a show opening the next night. "It's in Brooklyn." I grimaced as I scrolled to the bottom of the online feature. "But at least it's in one of the cool parts."

"Don't forget your hat!" Gabe said enthusiastically.

CHAPTER Eight

I did forget my hat. If by "forget" you meant "stuffed so far in the back of my closet that it practically went into the next apartment, where Sandra Gelman's teacup Pomeranian would probably use it as a tiny, very unfashionable dog bed."

"So sad," I told Gabe, doing my absolute girlfriend best to sound regretful. He removed his, resting it in his lap.

"It doesn't work if it's only one of us," he said. "I just look like a douchebag."

As opposed to us both wearing them, in which case we would've looked like *two* douchebags. Much better. I gave him a sympathetic smile. "Sorry."

Neither of our outfits would've worked with a tan fedora (to be fair, the only real outfit that works with a tan fedora is a 1950s-style suit, but to make that work you really have to look like Humphrey Bogart). I'd styled us to hopefully blend in with the arty crowd tonight, which Humphrey Bogart would not. I was wearing a skirt from Rita Ngo, a fashion designer I'd discovered last year when she was graduating from FIT (I'd almost busted with pride when she invited me to sit in the front row of her very first Fashion Week show); its black-and-white plaid pattern was splashed over by bright red, yellow, and blue graffiti, which was actually very delicate embroidery. Gabe wore a well-fitted black

T-shirt and loose, ripped jeans with a lion medallion above the knee from Henri Maquet, a gift I'd bought for him that was really a gift to myself (of a fashionable boyfriend).

Gabe couldn't stop rubbing the lion medallion as we sat in the back of a black car, which was coasting down the west side of Manhattan toward Brooklyn. "You know, we could've just taken the subway. There's a stop a block over from the gallery."

We CoUlD'vE jUsT tAkEn ThE sUbWaY. Suuuure. When I got my trust fund back, I'd resolved never to take the subway again, except maybe for photo ops or ironic purposes or for the brochure of my nonprofit, where I wanted to look very Humble and Of The People.

"What?" Gabe asked. Whoops. I hadn't meant to snort in his face like that. "The subway really isn't that bad, you know. You survived taking it all last year."

"I also survived getting an emergency appendectomy, and I'd rather not repeat that experience," I said. "Remember the show-time dancer who almost kicked me in the head? And the time it was brutally hot in the station and the train was delayed, so I sweated through one of my only outfits when I couldn't afford dry cleaning and the washing machine was in your building's murder basement?" I paused, shuddering a little from the horror.

"As I recall, you bribed me with cookies into doing your laundry."

"Yeah, and you put one of my cashmere sweaters in the dryer."

Gabe rolled his eyes, shifting in his seat. What, was the buttery leather of the car seat too comfortable for him? Was the whirring of the air conditioner too calming in contrast to the subway's clamor of headphones-less people playing annoying videos on their phones and crying children and staticky announcements over the speakers that nobody could understand but that, by virtue of not understanding, might leave you unaware that the train was skipping your stop and send you sailing blissfully unaware into another borough? (Yes, I was speaking from experience.) "It didn't have a tag saying *not* to put it in the dryer."

"Custom-made couture typically doesn't have tags, Gabe."

"Right. Of course," he said. "Want to stop talking about laundry and start talking about our plan for the interrogation?"

I thought back to the gala, to the few short minutes I'd spent talking to Isaiah Franklin. "From what I remember, the guy was a smirky asshole. We're not going to get anywhere if we just start asking him questions."

"Okay," Gabe said. "So what do you think? Should we pretend we want to buy his art?"

"Artists will do anything to get people to buy their art, so that's a good bet," I said. "Follow my lead?"

"I always do."

The car coasted to a stop on a block of Bushwick that was hard to describe as anything but *filthy*. Discarded fancy coffee cups and print newspapers soggy with various unidentified liquids littered the bare, treeless sidewalk. The buildings, mostly long, low warehouses, were gray and featureless. The people passing by—mostly white, mostly young—looked grungy, some in an appropriative-dreadlocks kind of way, others in a wearing-clothes-that-obviously-hadn't-been-washed-in-weeks kind of way (honestly, I'd gained a new appreciation for that look after living in an apartment where the laundry machines were in a scary, cockroach-ridden basement).

I wrinkled my nose. "I understand that it's okay for me to be seen here because Bushwick is 'cool,' but I'll never understand why."

"I had cousins who lived here before they were priced out," Gabe said, stepping onto the sidewalk and turning to give me his hand. I took it, hoping he wouldn't let go, even though I was wearing platform sneakers that weren't that hard to walk in. "They didn't understand either. If they're lucky, nobody will decide their new neighborhood is cool."

"It's in Queens, so I doubt it." Now that I was out of the car, I could hear music pulsing from one of the buildings, heavy with bass. These structures used to be warehouses used for shipping; now that the industry had moved somewhere else, they'd been repurposed for everything from clubs to apartments to art galleries. We headed into one featureless door to the latter, which was thankfully not the place with thumping music.

The space was perfect for an art gallery, I had to admit: the bland featurelessness of the cavernous warehouse really allowed for all focus to be on the art hanging from the walls and rising from pedestals scattered around the bare concrete floor. Even though it was cool outside, the gallery was warm and a little muggy. I was glad I'd gone for a corset cami top to go with my skirt.

The crowd inside was more of an eclectic mix than the crowd outside. There were artists, who were identifiable by their either extremely colorful or stark monotone looks; some were probably friends of the exhibiting artist, while others had come to scope out the competition or tell themselves how much better their own artwork was. Some people had wandered in from outside or seen a post about the exhibit in some local rag, and wandered the room gripping their plastic cups of wine. And then, of course, there were the buyers. My people, my friends. I gave them a quick scan. Nobody like Libby or Kitty or John would be caught dead here, obviously. But I recognized some of the second tier.

"It's so hot in here," Gabe murmured beside me. I felt a flash of sympathy for him in those jeans. The shirt had short sleeves, though. He'd be fine.

Before casing the room for Isaiah Franklin, I looked around for Vienna, who, as the person who'd discovered him and funded him and helped him get here, should really be present. I'd been to a number of her other artists' shows, and she always showed up early and left late.

But she was nowhere to be seen. I pulled out my phone to text her. Vee, I'm at Isaiah's show, are you coming?

Once again, the three typing bubbles popped up immediately.

This time, I wasn't surprised when they disappeared without leaving any words in their wake.

I tucked my phone away, feigning lightness in my voice. "Well. What do you say we take a look?"

We grabbed our own glasses of wine from the plastic table in the corner. They came from a cheap bottle and were, I discovered after one sip, warm, which really brought out the plasticky undertones. If only I could wipe the taste from my mouth with a delicious pastry, like the guava and cream cheese Danishes I'd finally perfected last week at the bakery, but the only snacks on display were dry-looking cookies and brownies still in the plastic supermarket packaging.

Once I'd stopped grimacing at them in distaste, we took a spin around the room. Isaiah's work was eclectic and colorful, featuring abstract figures that were often contorted in ways that looked extremely uncomfortable even for somebody as well-versed in yoga as me. Many of his sculptures had sharp edges and protruding, razor-like juts, so the peacock wasn't out of character.

I stepped up to a cluster of people—buyers, judging from the quality of their clothing—examining a painting of a woman lost in what appeared to be a forest of dildos. Just in time to hear someone saying, ". . . had to ask Vienna not to come, unfortunately. He said that he so appreciated all she did, but he had to be able to sell his work."

My ears pricked. Isaiah had asked Vienna not to come tonight? The press had been that bad?

Oh God. She must be devastated. That was where I belonged tonight: at her side, curled up on the comfiest couch in her town house (the one in the den), wearing the extremely soft and plush robes I'd stolen from the Afton before I moved out, stuffing our faces with everything the bakery didn't sell that day, making increasingly drunken fun of all the accounts making fun of us.

Also, hello, the *hypocrisy* at hand. Isaiah could blabber on about how murder was art and yet not invite somebody tainted by it to his event. Unless . . . he didn't want her there because he'd done it and he didn't want competition?

It was then I realized I recognized one of the buyers. Her pained, frozen smile as she caught my eye from only a few feet away said she recognized me too. "Oh, Pom," she said, and everybody else turned to face me too.

What was her name? Peach? It couldn't be Nectarine, right? She was swathed in florals that would've looked overly frilly and feminine if not for the black combat boots beneath her skirt. Her white-blond hair, obviously but skillfully dyed, stood out against the fantastic tan that said she'd just returned from some glorious beach. I said brightly, "Hello! So nice to see you!"

Everybody in the group exchanged a glance. I withered a bit, but stood strong so that they couldn't tell. I recognized most of them—they were part of the in-group, but the second tier.

Peach said, in return, "So nice to see you as well. Here."

"I know, it's been too long," I said, though I knew that, from her emphasis on that last word, that wasn't what she'd meant. She'd meant that she was so glad to see me *here*, out in public, and of course by "glad" she meant the opposite, that she thought I shouldn't be *here*, I should be hiding my face after all that had happened.

I knew I should just smile and brush it off. Turn the other cheek and all that.

"When did I see you last?" I mused, tapping my chin. Turning the other cheek had never been my style. Bruising on one side was easy enough to cover up because you had something to match it to on the other; covering up bruising on both could make you look like a clown. "Was it that New Year's party on Lord Darby's yacht?"

If you hadn't been keeping a specific eye on it, you would've missed the split second her smile faltered. Because I had, of course, insulted her back. That party had been . . . maybe three and a half years ago? Back when we'd both spent lots of time partying, before her transformation into a "serious person." She sighed through clenched veneers. "Oh my God, that was a night, wasn't it? I'm glad I'm not in that headspace anymore; it was so unhealthy. Can you even remember everything that went down?"

Another insult—she was referring to how wasted I used to get. I tittered back, raising one hand to cover my mouth demurely and fighting the urge to give her the finger. "I remember enough." That, combined with the way my eyes flicked to her ass region, was metaphorically the finger. Once upon a time she was known for . . . well, I shouldn't get into it. That would be rude. But anyway, it was one of the reasons why she was still in the second tier.

Peach pursed her lips, practically admitting defeat. She knew that if she were to get more into it, I'd get more into it too. "And who's this?"

Gabe had clearly understood none of what had just gone on, because his smile was pure friendliness. My poor, oblivious, innocent man. Beads of sweat glistened on his tanned forehead and upper lip, where the faintest hint of stubble remained, enough to scratch me only the tiniest bit later, the way I liked. "I'm Gabe. It's nice to meet all of you. I'll have to get some of your stories about Pom one of these days."

Peach's smile turned pointy, sharklike. "Oh, are you her boyfriend? What's your last name?"

"Morales," Gabe said.

"Oh, really," she said. "How did you and Pom meet?"

Assuming she'd read any story about me in the past year, she knew perfectly well his mother had worked for my family. I couldn't let this go on any further. They'd tear into him, ripping out all his blood and guts and innermost secrets, and all the while he'd be smiling, no idea what was going on. Like my mom's C-sections, about which she was fond of telling Nicholas and me, "I was so numb I couldn't feel anything down there. It was like I wasn't even having a baby. You could be anyone's, really."

I'd almost forgotten about that. Something to talk about in my next therapy session.

I linked my arm through Gabe's, beaming at the group with all my teeth. "So great seeing you. We're going to keep circulating." And I towed him away, allowing him to get in nothing more than a quick wave over his shoulder, which, really, a *wave*? We weren't at a *carnival*.

I only let myself take in a full breath once we were out of earshot of the group, right next to a painting of what appeared to be a naked man with a knife in place of the penis. "My God."

"I know." Gabe glanced at the painting. "It's not very subtle."

"Not that," I hissed. "They hate me."

Gabe boggled at me. A group of people who'd clearly popped in for the free wine passed us, sniggering and pointing at the artwork. "What are you talking about? Weren't you guys just catching up?"

At least that validated me in my decision to drag him away, which made me look like a coward but saved Gabe from total evisceration. "We were engaging in a brutal battle of words," I hissed again. "Insulting each other the entire time."

Gabe's forehead creased. "No, you weren't."

"Yes, we were."

"No."

"Yes."

Before Gabe could keep arguing, I pulled out my phone and navigated to Vienna's "following" list. I typed in *P*, for Peach, but up popped the girl's photo under her actual name. Persimmon. Of course her name wasn't Nectarine. That would be ridiculous. I was already following her, too, but she wasn't following me. The insult. I wondered if she'd unfollowed me, or if she'd never followed me in the first place.

Now I couldn't unfollow her or she might realize I'd noticed, which was a faux pas. We were always supposed to pretend that you just didn't see or notice anything on social media. That social media wasn't real life.

Ugh.

As I scrolled through, I refreshed my memory. Persimmon Teacup Avalon Argent, age twenty-nine, the daughter of a thrice-married rock star who was huge in the eighties and his second wife, a former model twenty years his junior. She'd spent most of her childhood traveling around the world, then, after her parents' divorce, most of her teens and twenties partying before sobering up and making a hard switch into charity work and sitting on boards, mostly for museums and foundations that had something to do with music. And she was—I did a double take—apparently dating Kevin Miller. He had to be at least twenty years older than us, and he looked it, with his silvering hair. Daddy issues, clearly. She'd posted a pic of the two of them together at my gala. I had zero memory of this, which meant I hadn't acknowledged her there.

Well, that explained why she was being so snarky with me. Honestly, hard to blame her.

"Is that Vienna?" Gabe asked, mistaking my grimace at social media for a texting grimace. I couldn't blame him. The nuances were minute.

I tucked my phone away. "No." I sighed. "I really hope she's okay. I'm worried about her. It must have really hurt her to be asked not to come tonight. Considering she's not guilty."

"We'll clear it up for her," Gabe said. "And then they'll forget."

Yeah. Just like I'd forget about that thing Persimmon had done with her ass and the party host's collection of vintage elephant statues. And she hadn't even murdered anyone, just . . . well, no need to get into the gory details. "Sure," I said grimly, taking another sip of the terrible wine. It didn't erase the bitter taste in my mouth.

CHAPTER Nine

I let the party go on for a while, knowing that the artist wouldn't leave his own show, keeping my eye on how many empty plastic cups he handed off to friends and gallery workers and random guests. "Want me to sign it for you? It might be worth something soon," I heard him ask one. Ugh. How insufferable. But, on the bright side, it would probably be easy to get a DNA sample. If necessary.

Once the number of empty cups told me he was good and tipsy, I sidled over to him, arm in arm with Gabe. "If it isn't Isaiah Franklin," I cooed, taking my cue from him about whether he wanted to air-kiss or not.

He did not. He extended his hand for me to shake. I took it. His handshake was limp and a little clammy, like the condensation from all those plastic wine cups had soaked in. "So good to see you," he said. Some artists at their shows dressed like they wanted to blend in with the walls, keep all the attention on the art. He'd gone with the opposite tactic: become art. You couldn't miss him in his baggy banana-print sweater and his neon yellow skinny jeans. "Pomona Afton, I appreciate your presence. And I'm sorry, but what was your name again?"

Gabe extended his own hand. "I'm Gabe Morales, Pom's boyfriend. Your art is great."

Isaiah grimaced as he limply touched Gabe's hand for what might have been the shortest handshake ever. I had to fight back a grimace as well. *Your art is great*? Come on, Gabe. Squeaky could do better. "What he means is, the space is so great. We're loving how it reflects the themes of desolation in the pieces on that wall over there. It makes me think about how everybody is capable of terrible things, and isn't that what makes us human beings?"

I was rewarded with an eyebrow raise and a thoughtful nod, as if Isaiah was truly mulling over what I'd said. The great thing about art, as I'd learned in my art history degree, was that you could see pretty much whatever you wanted in it, which meant I could take exams on three hours of sleep and the aftereffects of whatever random pills my supplier had given me that week.

"Well said. I completely agree. It's one of the reasons I decided to let this gallery show my work—I felt like they truly understood what I was trying to say."

Sure, okay. Another thing I'd learned about artists both during and after my degree was they weren't that picky. Everyone was desperate for some recognition, and they'd show their work pretty much anywhere that wanted to, and also sometimes places that didn't. But I nodded as if what he was saying was 100 percent true. "Of course." I paused for a moment, letting the chatter of the room fill the air. "How are you feeling after the other night? I imagine it must be hard knowing that your artwork played a role in the death of another person."

A smug look crossed his face for a moment, just a moment, before it was replaced by an appropriately somber one. "Oh yes. Of course."

"But also a little thrilling," I said. "That's what really grabbed us and made us decide that we simply *must* own an early Isaiah Franklin. You know, since I don't know when the peacock will stop being evidence."

He preened. "An excellent decision. Though I'd talk to the gallery soon about your purchase. Everything's going fast."

"Of course," I said. "But we can't decide which one speaks to us the most. We were hoping you'd give us a brief tour. Talk to us about what each piece means to you."

He flashed us a cocky smile. "Come with me. I'll take you on a journey."

The journey lasted exactly two steps before he stopped in front of a large painting, maybe four feet tall. It captured a man with a blurry face and a knife protruding from the canvas where his penis would otherwise be. "I call this one simply *Violence*. It's a bit of a self-portrait. Man reckoning with his sexuality."

"I see," I said, nodding. The brushstrokes were strong, the figure both confident and unsure. The canvas was a little spare, the colors a bit unbalanced, but once he found his footing, I really did think (grudgingly) that Isaiah would be an artist to watch. "So knives seem to be a real theme in your work."

"They are." Isaiah gestured for us to follow him to the next piece. "A knife can be so many things. A friend, when it's used in the kitchen. A threat, when it's held to someone's throat."

"A weapon, when it's used to stab someone," Gabe said helpfully.

Isaiah rolled his eyes, but only part of the way, like he remembered halfway through that he shouldn't be rolling his eyes at people who wanted to buy his art. "Yes. A weapon."

The next piece he stopped in front of was the one with the woman lost in the forest of dildos. "Take this painting, for instance," he said. "It's also a self-portrait, in a way. How can you expect to find something real when all you know is plastic? Your own self can be a weapon."

"Absolutely," I said, nodding as if what he'd said made total sense. "If anything, your own self can be more of a weapon than a knife. A knife can only harm one person at a time. One person can harm many people at once."

Isaiah looked at me with newfound respect. Gabe looked at

me like I'd lost my mind. "So profound," Isaiah said. "If you don't mind, I might use part of that when I discuss this painting in the future."

"Use away," I said. "By the way, did you get any interest in your work at the gala?"

His face lit up before it carefully smoothed over into boredom. "Some. Mrs. Phlume had a lot of questions about the peacock. Before her husband fell on it," he clarified. "She wanted to know where the knives had come from, and what had inspired the arrangement. And Mrs. Jean-Pierre seemed really interested too." Cora Jean-Pierre—the woman who'd seemed vaguely familiar. "I kind of hoped she might show tonight, but no luck so far.

"Kevin Miller really liked the photo I showed him of that one." Isaiah pointed at a painting at the far side of the room, which showcased a variety of famous superheroes I recognized. They all wore their usual uniforms, but had brown paper bags over their heads. "I think that's why his girlfriend is here to see it in person. And Denise Ryan asked if I'd want to donate one to her foundation for her to auction off." He frowned. "Your mother was standing behind her and couldn't stop laughing."

I wondered why my mother had been so delighted by that. "That's great," I said. "It sounds like you received a lot of interest even before . . . you know, everything happened."

If I'd kind of been hoping that would spur us organically to discuss it, those hopes fell when Isaiah turned his back. "Indeed. I appreciate you inviting me. The next one—"

"You know, Vienna was the one who told me I should invite you to my gala," I said. It seemed important that he know that. "She suggested your artwork for display because she'd worked with you already. Just so you're aware."

He stopped in his tracks. I could see his Adam's apple bobbing up and down in his throat, as if he were swallowing hard. "I see. I'll have to make sure to thank her."

Yeah, by uninviting her to her own party. But I didn't need to drive the knife in any deeper. I formed my lips into a pleasant smile. "You were going to take us to the next piece?"

Isaiah showed us around to another few paintings before landing us in front of a sculpture. "This is another piece from the same series as the peacock."

We stared at it. It seemed that was all he had to say about this bird—some kind of long-necked seabird, I thought?—that was also constructed with knives. "I can feel the raw power," I said. "What was your inspiration for this series?"

"People aren't typically afraid of birds in most contexts," Isaiah said. "But birds are descended from the dinosaurs. They might not seem dangerous, but sometimes the things that don't seem dangerous are the most dangerous of all."

"So profound," Gabe said, taking Isaiah's own words and earning a grudging nod of approval. Then, of course, he ruined it. "It reminds me of what you said at the gala about murder being the truest art of all. The murderer as artist. It seems that, in order for everyone to truly understand the work, people would need to know what the artist did. If nobody knew he did it, what would be the point of that?"

Isaiah's cheeks went ashy, his lips pursed. But then he rolled his eyes. "Are you trying to tell me that you think I killed Conrad Phlume? Is that why you're really here tonight? To do your little interrogation act?"

Maybe Gabe could've been a *little* more subtle. But no point assigning blame. We couldn't go backward in time, and also I kind of didn't think I could listen to another pretentious explanation of human nature without throwing myself onto the knife-bird. I tossed my hair. "You have to admit, it's a tad suspicious that you tell us how much you want to murder someone for your art, and right afterward someone winds up murdered by your art."

My phone buzzed. I snuck a quick glance at it. It was Coriander with a question in my group chat with her and Millicent. I saw online that you're in Bushwick tonight at some art thing?? You didn't invite us? ☹️

Ignore. I slipped my phone back into my bag in time for Isaiah's answer.

"Right," Isaiah drawled, taking another sip of his wine. His hand was shaking the tiniest bit, I noticed. Could this really be it? We'd nailed the murderer with our very first interrogation?

We'd probably win some kind of award for this. Maybe the mayor would give us the key to the city or something. I could go anywhere with that. I'd always kind of wanted to see what lay beyond the grand oak doors of the private male-only club my dad and Nicholas belonged to. To learn if the rumors were true about the sauna.

Focus, Pom. I tossed my hair again, this time because the heat of the room was making it stick to my skin and I didn't want the celebratory photo of the night that would feed out to all the papers with news of our success to be plagued by misbehaving hair.

Isaiah continued—this was it! "Because that would be the smart thing to do. To tell people how murder is great art, and then immediately murder someone. I went to Harvard, you know."

I knew plenty of stupid people who'd gone to Harvard. It was easy, really—your parents just had to buy them a building or a sports field or something. But I got his point.

"You're here two days after the murder," he said. "Which means I'm probably the first person you're talking to. Is that right?"

I shrugged. Didn't want to give away all our secrets, but also didn't want to lie.

"Right," he said, taking another sip of his terrible wine, his hand still shaky. He'd been drinking a lot of wine, actually; we'd been noting it to see when he'd get tipsy. But I knew a lot of artists. I'd been to a lot of shows. They didn't usually drink this much during the event—they had to stay focused on schmoozing with buyers and networking with other artists and, if they were lucky, talking to the press. "Maybe I did do it. That's me, the ultimate artist."

Oh. I sighed, deflating as I did. My hair fluttered down to stick to the back of my neck, and I didn't bother trying to toss it this time. "No, you didn't. Are you okay?"

He took another long sip of his wine. No, not just a sip—he downed the entire rest of the cup. "Of course I'm fine. I am the ultimate artist."

"No, you're not," I said wearily. "You didn't do it."

He looked affronted by this, like, *How dare somebody accuse me of* not *murdering someone?* "You don't know that. Maybe I did."

"I mean, I wouldn't bet my entire fortune that you didn't do it, but I'm pretty sure," I said. Because I knew that drinking. I'd done that drinking. That was the kind of drinking you did when you were trying to forget. The artist was kind of a prick, but I softened toward him anyway, because plenty of people would say the same thing about me. "Have you talked to anyone yet? I saw someone after I found my grandmother's body who helped me a lot."

"I have three therapists," he said, still affronted, but then he lowered his voice and leaned in. "Do you still have nightmares?"

Gabe's hand found my lower back, rubbed gently in support. "Sometimes," I said, wanting to be honest. "But seriously, it really helps to talk to someone. Or three someones, if that's what you prefer."

He swallowed hard. "Thanks." He pulled back. "Or that's what I would say, if I was in need of your advice."

"Sure," I said. So Isaiah was a dead end. I probably shouldn't be surprised—it would've been awfully lucky of us to find the murderer our first time out. "But, like, out of curiosity, where were you at the time of the murder? Since you weren't in any of the alibi photos?"

His eyes shifted down. "Being an artist doesn't pay very

much," he mumbled. "I was in the corner, stuffing the leftover appetizers in my bag."

Ah. I made a mental note to see if there was anything my nonprofit could do for him. Nobody should leave a gala with deviled eggs leaking all over their wallet. "Anyway, how's tonight going? I'm sorry the people from the gala who expressed interest—who was it, the Jean-Pierres?—didn't show."

He snorted, the unimpressed-with-literally-everything mask falling back into place. "There's still time. Then again, they were recently involved in some scandal, weren't they? They might not want to be involved with an artist plagued by it." He appeared momentarily thrilled by the idea of being scandal-plagued.

"Really?" I said, trying to sound as casual as possible. The wife, Cora, was still nagging at me, because I *knew* I knew her from somewhere. That heart-shaped face, those catlike green eyes. And as far as I could tell, she hadn't been in one of the alibi-granting photos. Could she have been one of the people Conrad had harassed or wronged? "Do you know what happened?"

He shrugged. "I think her family was involved in some kind of scandal last year where they lost all their money. Her husband didn't like being associated with the icky poors. I heard he did whatever he could to separate himself and his wife from them. Maybe he didn't want more scandal."

A scandal where they lost all their money . . . catlike green eyes . . .

My breath quickened. "That family? Was her sister the one arrested for my grandmother's murder?"

Isaiah smacked himself in the forehead. Wine sloshed over the rim of his glass—well, plastic. "Yes. How could I forget?" He chuckled, tongue dulled by the alcohol. "Her husband's done a really good job keeping them away from all that."

Cora was Opal's older sister. Of course. It *was* all about me, after all.

Most things were.

CHAPTER *Ten*

With Cora out of New York and also actively avoiding us, our usual method of interrogation—taking a car somewhere nearby and asking questions—was not going to work. So we had to improvise. Namely, by taking a plane somewhere *far away* and asking questions.

"Nicholas is going to kill me," I said almost a week after interrogating Isaiah at the art gallery, lounging back in my seat and waving away the flight attendant with her crystal glass of sparkling water. "Hopefully we take off before he storms the airport."

The family pilot was like an uncle to me, except that I knew most of my uncles' last names. The family pilot had always just been Captain Ted. Captain Ted wasn't supposed to take the plane out without the authorization of the head of the company, who was technically my father (though in reality the temporary winner of the constantly shifting battle between my mom and Nicholas), but who could say no to the family's darling daughter when she came to you with a pout on her lips and big, sad puppy-dog eyes?

Captain Ted, that's who. The whole puppy-dog-eyes-and-pouting thing had worked a lot better when I was younger. It had taken a forged note from Nicholas and a whole lot of fervent praying that Nicholas wouldn't show up before takeoff.

"I still can't believe that this is just . . . how you travel." I was lounging, but Gabe was not; he was perched on the edge of the cushy leather seat, like he was afraid it might swallow him up if he leaned back.

"I mean, not *always*," I said. "I've flown commercial before."

"In first class."

"Obviously," I said. "I heard that back in coach they don't even have beds."

"The horror," Gabe said. I was glad he understood.

"Pom, we're ready to go." Captain Ted appeared out of nowhere, his blue pilot's hat sitting crookedly atop his thick blond hair. "ETA in four hours and fifteen minutes."

"Sounds good," I told him. The jet engines roared up outside the window. I sat back and sipped my iced tea as we took off. Bye, Nicholas. Hopefully he wouldn't need the jet for a business meeting while I was gone. I could only imagine the lecture I'd get if the company lost out on some deal because I had the jet. Though, really, wasn't what I was doing way more important? My work had life-or-death stakes. His work did not.

Once we were cruising thousands of feet in the air, I let out an exhale of my own. Nicholas couldn't stop me now. I turned back to Gabe. "It's been so long since I've been to a private island. I love them. You'll see."

Oh yeah. Did I not mention that? We were en route to a private island. Kevin Miller's private island, to be exact. It was a big part of his shtick: *I grew up poor and now I have a private island!* (I wasn't paraphrasing—that was the title of one of his books, exclamation point and all.) It was his fiftieth birthday and he was throwing a huge bash. The Jean-Pierres might be steering clear of scandal-plagued New York for a while, but we'd heard through the grapevine that they'd be down in the Caribbean for the party.

"A private island," Gabe repeated. "I never thought I'd be going to a private island." He'd been a little quiet so far on the ride. I thought he'd want to go over our plans for talking to Cora, or maybe do some more research than our googling last night (which hadn't turned up much; someone had scrubbed as much of the Internet as they could of any connection between Cora Jean-Pierre and the Sterlings—which was ironic, considering that, even though she was much older, she was the only sister to be a full-blooded Sterling), but so far he'd spent most of the flight looking out the window.

Poor guy. He must have been nervous for his first time. "A private island is just like a regular island, but better," I assured him. "More privacy. No dealing with the public on the beach. Usually not as well equipped as a resort is—if you're looking for specialty massages or face masks with any chemicals that need to be overseen by a doctor you're out of luck, so there are trade-offs." I wondered how the food would be. Last time I was there the desserts had been pretty basic, simple treats like chocolate mousse and cupcakes. Private chefs so often had a blind spot around desserts. Kevin would probably love if I popped down to the kitchen to consult on their pastries.

Gabe's face didn't move. "Private stretches of beach sound nice. Kevin must have a stretch somewhere on the west that's beautiful during sunset, right?"

"Oh yeah," I said, relieved he seemed to be coming around. "I've been there before, the last time a few years ago, when he wanted to talk to my family about branding one of his properties with the Afton name. He positioned his residence on the west side of the island so that whole stretch of beach is easily walkable and glorious in the evening." He nodded, his expression still grimly resolute. "We'll definitely get away one evening for a sunset walk."

He nodded. "Good."

I stared at him for an extra second, wondering why he was being so weird, but my phone buzzed. I grabbed for it immediately. It could be Bibi, who I'd finally reached out to in order to see what was going on with the building Conrad had promised me, though it probably wouldn't be Vienna, who was still avoiding—

It *was* Vienna? Pom, I'm sorry I've been MIA the last few days.

I've been dealing with a lot but I know you have been too. Can I come over? We need to talk.

I bit my lower lip. Gabe peered over my shoulder as I said, "I guess it's not too late to turn the plane around."

"You think so?" he said, and why was his voice so strangled? "We're already in the air. Once Nicholas finds out you took the plane, no chance you're getting it again for a while."

I sighed, settling back into my seat. "I guess you're right." I typed back, Babe we're in the air 🙁 Will be back next week. I'd wanted to stay longer, but Gabe had work. The compromises I made for this relationship. Can I call you?

I can't discuss this over the phone, she wrote back. It was just a relief at this point to have words pop up after the typing bubbles. Text me as soon as your wheels hit NYC earth.

Will do.

The flight flew by (pun not intended, but it pleased me). One of the flight attendants had brought some hydrating face masks, so I did one of those, then rested my eyes for a bit before reviewing the month's statements for the bakery. Gabe worked on lesson plans or grading or something. I had nothing to do for the nonprofit, which was weird, but then I realized it was because Lina wasn't here to give me papers and numbers and stuff. I'd need to find a new assistant ASAP.

Kevin Miller had cleared space for a long runway on his island to prevent himself and his guests from having to do the annoying move of having to land somewhere else and take a ferry over. It did kind of take away from the ambiance of the private island, I thought as we disembarked. When my family got a private island—assuming we didn't already have one; lawyers were still sorting through all my grandma's byzantine holdings—the maximum airstrip I'd want was one for small planes.

I told Gabe all this as we taxied to the resort. He looked faintly green, which was quite an accomplishment for someone who was brown. "I didn't realize you got airsick," I said.

"What?"

Just then the resort came into view. It wasn't technically a resort, I supposed—it wasn't like it was open to the public. But Kevin liked to call it a resort because it was as big and luxurious as one, although only for guests he invited: beautiful rooms with en suite bathrooms overlooking the sea; a private spa in the basement; multiple pools and a kitchen and bar that turned out food and drinks as good as any restaurant. (Aside from the desserts. The tropical ambiance was making thoughts of coconut conchas and pineapple upside-down cakes dance through my head.) "All my mother wanted was to vacation on the beach, but she spent so much of her adulthood working nonstop to provide for me," Kevin had said. "She died before she ever got to go on a plane. That's why I named the island for her."

Ann-Marie Island. The name made me think, with a pang, of Andrea, my childhood nanny and Gabe's mom. Had she ever gotten to take her kids on vacation? Or had all of her time away from home been about taking care of little Aftons?

Mental note: take Andrea on the best vacation of her life. Surely one of my friends could lend us their private island for a weekend.

Kevin greeted us himself in what was part lobby and part living room. "Pom, so happy you could come," he said. Instead of kissing both cheeks, as I leaned in to do, he reached out to give me a firm handshake.

"So are we," I gushed. "Happy birthday! You remember Gabe, my boyfriend."

Kevin turned to Gabe with a polite smile. "Of course I remember Gabe. One of my fellow regular people in this rarefied world. It's nice to have a comrade around who wasn't born into all of this."

"Right." Gabe shifted, looking uncomfortable even though I'd specifically given him some of the most comfortable clothes ever to exist: soft, supple leather sandals with loose white shorts and a pink silk Hawaiian shirt. "I was thinking maybe later—"

"Anytime." Kevin slapped him on the back, making Gabe stumble a full step forward. He nearly hit me, which would've been unfortunate, as I was wearing way less comfortable (and way less stable) cork heels. "Anyway, let me find someone to bring your things up to your room. You'll be in the Diane Suite, one of my favorites. I think that's where you stayed last time, Pom."

"Great. Thanks."

Kevin glanced around, saw nobody, then began to frown. I was surprised that, as someone who loved to talk about how normal and regular he was, he didn't offer to do it himself. Gabe did it for him. "Don't worry, we got it."

By that, of course he meant that *he* got it. This ultrasmooth gemstoned manicure was not made for carrying my own bags. By the time he'd lugged all of our luggage—okay, by the time he'd slung his one small bag over his shoulder and then lugged all of *my* luggage—up two sprawling flights of stairs and into the Diane Suite, he was breathing heavily, beads of sweat sparkling on his broad forehead.

The king-size bed was soft and plush, covered with a peach-colored feather blanket and a seafoam-and-periwinkle quilt that might have looked homemade but that I recognized from Gilda Traynor's 2021 collection. Various depictions of the sea, from stormy to pastoral, hung on the walls, and the sliding glass door on the far side of the room that led out onto a private balcony showed off the real sea, which sparkled merrily beneath the sunlight. It was warm enough here that I'd have to go in for a dip later. We were here to investigate a murder, of course, but that didn't mean we couldn't enjoy ourselves too.

I turned away from the view as Gabe said, "Wow." For a moment I thought he, too, was admiring the view—of me from the back—until I realized he was looking at something sitting atop the room's desk. A book. A Bible? The Afton had phased out leaving Bibles in every room—they kept getting stolen, which was ironic.

But no. Or maybe it was a Bible, just of a different sort: Kevin's famous first memoir, the one that had catapulted him to the late-night shows and TED Talk stage. A version of our host from ten years ago, one with fewer silver hairs and somehow looser skin on his jaw, grinned up at us, arms folded across his chest. I snorted. "He really thinks a lot of himself."

Gabe stared at the photo for another moment. "You know, at the gala, he cornered me for an interrogation."

"Interrogations are a lot more fun when you're the one giving them," I said. "What was he interrogating you about?"

"He wanted to know about where I'd grown up, that kind of thing. He'd heard that my mom had worked for your family and wanted to know if it was true, then wanted to know if I'd be working for the family business."

I'd never thought about it before, mostly because there was no way anybody would accept him working for the family business unless he changed his last name to Afton, which, actually, why not? Feminism and all that. Men could change their names too. I certainly wasn't changing mine. "Do you have any desire to work for the family business?"

"Not really," Gabe said. "I don't know anything about hotels, except that I don't usually like them. They always smell weird."

"You could be the Afton's chief officer in charge of smells."

"Thanks, but I think I'll pass," he said dryly. "When I told him that, he lost all interest in me and made an excuse to get away."

"Probably it wasn't an excuse," I said.

"It was 100 percent an excuse," Gabe replied. "He said he wanted to grab one of the gazpacho shooters. Who feels that strongly about cold soup?"

I shrugged. "Well, we're not here for him. We're here for Cora."

Gabe took a deep breath, shaking out his shoulders as if he was nervous. "Right. Of course. That's what we're here for."

Something about his tone struck me as weirder than the smell of some random hotel. "Is everything okay?"

"Of course," he said, but his voice was just a little bit too loud, his eyes just a little bit too jumpy. He'd never been this nervous before an interrogation before.

"We don't have to go down right away," I said. "We could hang out up here for a little while. Take a relaxing bath." I knew from experience that the tub was great—not only did it overlook the sea, but it had about a thousand jets and was lined with at least ten different bottles of bubble bath scents, from lavender to bacon (which I was almost intrigued enough to try).

He shook his head, already moving toward the door. "Let's go down. Don't worry about me."

I hadn't worried about him. Not until this moment. Which was really selfish of him to make me do right now, honestly!!! We had a murder to solve and multiple reputations to save. How was I supposed to do those things when my stomach was twisted into a full-on knot?

CHAPTER Eleven

If there was one thing I was good at, it was my fake smile. And also choosing the perfect outfit for an occasion. And also solving murders. Okay, I was good at a lot of things, and they were all relevant as I picked my way down the stairs of Kevin's private resort, clad in the perfect flowy white sundress that screamed *innocent young woman* and the bright yet calm smile that screamed *innocent young woman who you really want to spill secrets to.*

A quick scan of the stretch of beach behind the resort showed that Cora and her husband were not yet among the few people hanging out enjoying the view—it was getting close to sunset—or sipping a drink by the bar. Gabe and I decided to divide and conquer—I'd chat up a few of the people near the bar, while he'd go down to the sand. We recognized some of the guests from my gala, though most had alibis from the photos; still, maybe someone would be able to tell us something useful. "Don't get too sucked into anything," Gabe told me before heading off. "I really want us to go for a walk on the beach at sunset."

I didn't have much time to worry more about how weird he was being, because I was accosted by Denise Ryan the moment I wafted over toward the bar. She was nearly at the bottom of something fruity; at least three cherries floated in what was mostly ice by now. "Pom," she said, smiling. Her teeth were tinted pink. "I didn't know you were coming."

"Oh, it was kind of a last-minute thing," I said. "But it's so nice to see you!"

"Is that handsome hunk of yours here too?" She said it with a self-conscious grin, making fun of herself. At least partially. Or maybe she wanted to take a bite out of my handsome hunk.

"Yes, he's down at the beach. He wanted to rest for a bit by the water."

"Can't blame him," Denise said, taking one last sip of her drink. The ice rattled as she set the glass down and pushed it away. I looked longingly at the cherries. "So annoying to take a ferry ride after a flight."

I blinked. "You didn't fly direct to the airstrip?"

"He has an airstrip suitable for a jet?"

I nodded. Poor Denise. Her assistant was totally going to get fired for this. "You'll have to tell your captain to pick you up from here directly."

"Oh my, I definitely will." She raised her hand, signaling the bartender for another drink. I raised my hand, too, indicating that I'd have whatever she was having. It looked good, in that I liked my alcohol to contain a surplus of cherries. "Anyway, Pom, how are you? I've been thinking of you, after everything that happened." She gave me gooey eyes. I had to look away so I wouldn't get all sticky with her sympathy. "Your very first gala, and there's a murder. It's enough to make you never want to be charitable again, huh?"

That was an odd thing for her to say, considering she'd made it her life's work to give away all the money she'd gotten from her ex-husband. But I didn't want to ruffle any feathers, at least not when they weren't filling out a gloriously soft mattress. "For real," I said. The bartender slid our drinks in front of us. To my great pleasure, I saw he'd put not one, not two, not even three, but *four* cherries in mine. "Not going to lie, I've had a hard time with it. But not as hard a time as the people who loved Conrad Phlume, right?"

Denise barked a laugh. It had an edge hard enough to leave a bruise. "*Was* there anyone who loved him?"

Probably a callous thing to say about a murder victim, but also probably true. "Maybe a mistress or two?"

She cackled. "He used to 'tease' me for being a former bartender, and by 'tease' I mean he'd constantly bring it up as a way to invalidate whatever I had to say. Funnily enough, it was never in front of my ex-husband. Not like it mattered." Something dark glittered in her eyes. "It wasn't as if my ex ever reminded people that the reason I'd bartended was so that he could focus full-time on his start-up that wasn't making any money."

Old Pom would've just asked, with genuine puzzlement, why their parents didn't help them out. New Pom nodded sympathetically and wondered if she could drop a hint about how, if Denise had been able to take advantage of a living grant from the Pomona Afton Foundation, she wouldn't have had to work two jobs. It would probably be crass.

But what the hell. My reputation had taken a dive into the toilet anyway. "By the way, we never got to finish our conversation from the gala. These kids deserve the world, and you can help give it to them."

"Of course they do," she said. "But, Pom . . ."

"What?" I tried not to snap.

"To be frank with you, my ex-husband and I are locked in a battle of reputations. If I'm involved with anything that has even a whiff of scandal attached to it . . ."

"Of course," I said flatly.

"I'm so glad you understand," she said, taking another sip of her drink. The bartender had somehow refilled it without my even noticing. A true genius at his craft. "But come now, we're at a party. We're supposed to be having fun." She leaned back, so now I was flooded with the smell of salt and sand, brine and ocean. Music strummed softly in the background. I thought it was a speaker, but then I noticed the trio of string players set up on the beach. "You and that handsome hunk of yours, when are you getting married?"

Was this her trying to feel out how serious we were? "We've discussed it," I said vaguely. "It's in the cards."

"Oh, really?" The response hadn't come from Denise; it had come from behind me. Freaking Peach—no, Nectarine—no, *Persimmon* sashayed around me, all dolled up in a floral maxi dress that was appropriately floaty for the occasion but whose pastel colors washed out her pale hair. "Then where is he? He didn't have to stay home and *work*, did he?"

"He's around here somewhere." I spoke through clenched teeth. I really wanted another sip of my drink, but I wasn't sure the liquid would make it through. Besides, I was getting enough ice from my new nemesis that I might end up with brain freeze. "I didn't realize you knew Kevin." I did, of course, but considering I'd learned it through social media research, it would be a faux pas to admit it. Besides, I didn't want her thinking I'd looked her up.

"You don't realize a lot of things, it seems!" she said, and tittered, though we both knew she wasn't joking. She slithered her way neatly between Denise and me to signal the bartender for a drink of her own. Denise took the hint and wandered off to another cluster of people closer to her age. "I was Kevin's date to your gala. I'm sure you were so busy, you didn't even notice me."

She sounded kind of hurt. Though, to be fair, she could have made sure I noticed her by, like, saying hello to me or something? This definitely was not entirely on me. "So he's your . . . boyfriend?"

She tittered again, covering her mouth with one dainty hand. Orange polish gleamed on her fingernails. "You could say that. I do hate the word, though. 'Boyfriend' sounds so . . . juvenile, wouldn't you agree?"

I might not remember her at the gala, but I did remember introducing Gabe as my boyfriend at the art gallery. I didn't let my smile falter. "Oh, I'm sorry. You wouldn't want to be juvenile when you're dating such a . . . distinguished fellow." Aka old man.

She didn't let hers falter either. "We've been discussing marriage. That's one perk of seeing someone older—they don't want to waste any time." Ouch, that was a dig at me. "I haven't decided how I want him to propose yet. If I want something small and intimate, like a dinner flown from my favorite restaurant to a remote mountaintop, or something big and splashy, like a surprise yacht party."

That was also a dig at me. And Gabe. That I was dating a poor.

But there was no chance I was going to let her think she'd won. Besides, grimacing gives you wrinkles, or so said the part of my internal monologue that sounded scarily like my mother.

"You know, we've also been discussing it," I lied. "I've always dreamed of a proposal on my favorite private island. Not one in the Caribbean—there's nothing wrong with the Caribbean, of course, but I feel like I'm here so often it's not special." Hopefully my host wasn't in earshot. I had no grudge with the Caribbean, I just had something against Persimmon. "A family friend has an island in the Maldives that's the most spectacular place I've ever been. I'm imagining us going snorkeling on our private reef and that's where he's hidden the ring. He proposes at sunset, while the water is sparkling with the colors of fire—not on one knee, of course; the coral will shred your knees and also it's bad for the environment to touch it—and then we swim back to the island only to find that all of my friends and family are there for a giant party and they've actually seen the entire proposal from afar, with a professional drone operator having taken photos and video from above."

Persimmon raised one perfectly sculpted eyebrow. "Sounds lovely. Though I imagine you can't hide a very big ring in there."

That wasn't what she was saying, unless she knew absolutely nothing about coral. She was shading Gabe—*I imagine your teacher boyfriend can't afford a very big ring.*

I tossed my hair, throwing all caution into the wind along with the perfume of my new favorite conditioner, which smelled of an oil extracted from a flower that only grew on a vine in a tree somewhere in the Andes cloud forests. I hoped it hit her smack in the face. The scent, not the hair. Though I wouldn't be mad if the hair did too. "Actually, you can hide a ring of any size in coral. At least any size that fits on a human finger." I raised my eyebrow, which was, honestly, not quite as sculpted, back at her. I'd simply been too busy with the whole murder thing to worry about making a threading appointment. "And, while I haven't seen the ring yet, I'm pretty sure it's going to make it hard to lift my hand. Because it's so heavy. And big. I wouldn't be seen in anything less. What would *all* of my followers say? You're lucky you don't have to worry about disappointing so many people."

Nailed it. She wrinkled up her nose like I'd accidentally purchased the conditioner made out of the oils extracted from the fur of a small marsupial that lived in the remote Australian outback (while I've heard the smell is not great, it does apparently leave your hair the softest and shiniest it could possibly be). "I'm sure."

Someone cleared their throat delicately behind me. I girded for battle with one of Persimmon's friends—Plum? Pineapple?—but, to my surprise, turned and found Gabe standing there, all dewy in his salmon Hawaiian shirt and white shorts, an outfit that positively screamed *balding douchebag on a golf course on his third divorce*. It was shocking how well he was pulling it off. "Oh, hey," I said. "When did you come over here?"

"Just now," he said. Good. Hopefully he hadn't heard any of my lying. He liked to get on me about lying. *It's wrong, Pom.* Okay, sure, Gabe, *you* tell me a better way to get out of things you don't want to do without hurting anyone's feelings or causing any international incidents. "Persimmon. Hi. Nice to see you."

He sounded a little like he was being strangled, which, understandable.

"Oh, you, too, Gabe," she purred, literally batting her eyelashes. "I was hearing the most—"

"We've got to go," I broke in, tucking my arm through Gabe's elbow. "I see our friend over there. Nice seeing you, Persy!"

From the way her face darkened, I would definitely be paying for that off-the-cuff nickname later, probably through her telling her boyfriend to pay someone to hammer stuff all night in the room below us and toss bowling balls on the roof above. But that was okay. I had great earplugs. I steered Gabe away from the bar toward the beach, leaving my drink behind.

It was cooler on the beach, with the breeze coming in off the water. Damp sand squished between my toes. I'd always loved sand: building castles out of it; digging up little crabs; lying down on it during a hot day and soaking in its warmth. I even liked shaking off the dried bits that clung to every part of me after a long day at the beach—it was like bringing home a thousand little reminders of the beautiful outdoors. And I liked listening to the rattling it made when my former housekeeper (and current employee of the foundation), Lori, would vacuum it up the next day.

I had time to get through all that in my head because I was waiting for Gabe to ask who I'd seen, but he must understand enough of my interactions with girls like Persimmon by now that he realized I'd been making it up. Right?

Quick glance over at him. He was staring up at the sky in the direction of the setting sun. That wasn't great. He wasn't even wearing sunglasses. "Hey, Gabe," I began, but his eyes widened. That was even less great.

"Isn't that Cora?"

I spun around, the health of Gabe's eyes forgotten. Glasses existed. He'd be fine, as long as I made sure he got frames that suited his face. "Oh! Yes! Okay. Good. Do we have a strategy?"

He didn't respond. He was looking at her off in the distance. Irritation tickled my stomach. "Hello? Gabe?"

"Right. Sorry." He scratched the back of his neck. "Do you want to handle her on your own? It's probably best for . . . optics and things."

Optics and things? What did that even *mean*? (Yes, I knew what both the words "optics" and "things" meant, so don't go running and submitting any blind items about how stupid I am.) In this *context*. I was about to confront a potential murderer who, even if she hadn't murdered the victim in question, probably wanted to murder me. You'd think my loving boyfriend would want to be there to throw himself dramatically in the path of the bullet or the knife or whatever. Maybe he'd think he was dying, even though obviously he would only have been grazed, and realize there, lying on the floor all bloody and sexy, that he wanted to give me everything I wanted (an autumn wedding in Tuscany).

Because nobody else ever chose me like that. My family made it clear often how they were stuck with me. Andrea had been paid to raise me. Opal had been a secret murderer. Gabe was . . . Gabe was . . .

Gabe was gone. I blinked. On my right there was only surf and sand, on my left a growing crowd that did not include my boyfriend.

I hadn't even seen where he'd gone.

Okay. Fine. Whatever. The best state of mind to conduct an interrogation was a fragile and slightly panicked one, right? Right. It was probably a great sign that I was answering my own questions. I squared my shoulders and forged off across the sand, strong and resolute, except not strong or resolute at all, really. Unless "strong and resolute" meant "wanting to cry," and yes, anonymous leakers, I knew it didn't.

CHAPTER Twelve

Like a predatory bird zeroing in on a mouse in the forest, I swooped down on Cora while she wasn't paying attention. Only she wasn't nibbling on an acorn or something, she was smiling politely at a group of people by the side of an older man who, according to the photos I'd googled on the way here, was her husband, Marc Jean-Pierre.

It had taken a few deep breaths on the walk over to push down that fragile, panicked feeling Gabe's departure had given me. Honestly, at that moment, I'd kind of wanted to fly off into the sunset like an actual predatory bird. *You need to do this for the kids*, I reminded myself. *You just saw with Denise—nobody wants to work with a foundation tainted by death and scandal.* And a whisper of the reason I didn't even want to admit to myself. *You need to do this to make sure all your best friends aren't murderers.*

"Hi!" I said brightly, interrupting the conversation and touching Cora's bare, dewy shoulder. The old men in my new circle looked dour at the interruption. I would've expected Cora, as a suspected murderer, to panic at the thought I might be onto her, or at least wrinkle her face with annoyance at her proximity to the person who'd put her (half) sister away for twenty-five years to life. On the contrary, her lips parted in a friendly sort of way, and her eyebrows lifted in a welcoming manner.

These old men must have been *really* boring.

With that in mind, I chirped, "Fascinating stuff. Cora, can I talk to you for a minute? Girl stuff. You know, tampons. Shoes. Blah, blah, blah."

These men were of an age where being grossly sexist was still socially acceptable, so any whiff of interest in us two young women withered away. Cora's face was a blank slate, but after that tableau, she couldn't say no. And besides, she had to be at least a little interested in what I wanted. I pulled her off to the edge of the crowd, to where the sound of waves lapping at the shore overtook the music, but not too far off the edge, just in case she was feeling at all murderous tonight. Flashed her my most winning smile. "Sorry if I'm being presumptuous, but you looked like you could use a rescue."

"Sorry if I'm being presumptuous for assuming that you didn't know the word 'presumptuous,'" she deadpanned.

Well, that was kind of mean. But it was far from the meanest thing I'd heard this week. Maybe that was one thing I could be grateful to my mom for. And the press. And also some of my former modeling colleagues, who lived in a permanently hangry state that gave everything they said an extra-vicious edge.

But before I had to figure out what to say back, she cracked a grin, one that rocked me a little bit, because I was so used to seeing it on Opal's face. When I told her I'd dare go to her favorite restaurant to try the new sashimi she was obsessed with (some kind of tuna that lived only in deep rock pools off the coast of Mombetsu), even though its oysters had once given me a fiery case of food poisoning. When she'd told a particularly clever joke (they usually involved calling Coriander by a different herb, which often fell flat because we actually had other friends named Basil and Parsleigh) and was pleased with herself.

The stabs of sadness and betrayal came less often these days, but they still did come.

Cora went on, "I'm just kidding. You know that, right? You

made that 'presumptuous' joke yourself when we went out for Opal's twenty-first birthday."

That entire night—that entire year, truthfully—was kind of a blur, but I nodded anyway, relieved that my suspect wasn't on the offensive. That was *my* job. "Was that the last time we saw each other?"

"Maybe," she said. "Honestly, I can't remember. Opal and I were never super close; I was so much older. I think it was right after that I got married and moved out to Cali."

"Right," I said, like I hadn't refreshed my memory with Google on the plane. I drew in a deep breath of salt air, sparing a moment to hope that the breeze would give me glorious beach waves and not frizz. "How old are your kids now?"

She told me all about Sloane (age six), Harrison (age four), and Frances (age two). I was only half listening, because I was busy noting her cheerful manner—so different from her manner at the gala, when she'd barely spoken to me and had pretty much run away without even telling me who she was. "I'd love to have another, but you know, my husband is a bit older." I wasn't sure you could characterize fifteen years as "a bit," but whatever. "And he doesn't want to be sixty years old with a baby, which, you know, I understand."

If her husband was anything like the other men his age I knew, the most care he did for his baby was showing off pictures of them to clients. But I nodded sagely, because it wasn't like Cora was probably doing all that much work either. Those elegantly manicured, ring-covered fingers likely didn't change very many diapers. That was what nannies were for. "Of course," I said. "Hey, thank you for attending my gala and supporting my cause."

"It was the least I could do after . . . you know." She winced, the expression an echo of her same one that night. "Look, I should apologize too."

I held my breath. Was it too much to hope for that she was

going to apologize for killing Conrad Phlume and ruining my big night?

Yes. "I was rude the night of your gala. You came over and gave me the same smile you were giving everybody else and introduced yourself like you'd never met me before, and my feelings were hurt. I didn't want to say anything and make you feel bad on the evening of your first gala, so I just excused myself abruptly. My husband told me later that I'd come off as impolite, and I didn't mean to, so I'm sorry for that."

Well. That explained her weird behavior there. "No, *I'm* sorry! And I did recognize you; that's why I was trying so hard to place where I knew you from. I definitely remember you. It'd been so long since I'd seen you, though, and—"

"I know, I know." Her wince reminded me of Opal, too, though I hadn't seen it often on her face. That would've required a modicum of self-awareness. "I realized later how petty I was being. Of course you wouldn't recognize me. It's how many years and how many kids later? But I didn't want to bother you with an apology, not after what happened. I figured you had way more pressing issues to worry about."

"Of course," I murmured. A burst of laughter from the other side of the crowd arose, followed by the squawk of some seabirds. I wasn't quite ready to let her off the hook yet, though. She'd said something earlier that had piqued my curiosity. Also, I didn't want to have to tell Gabe that I'd cleared the entire reason we'd come here in about thirty seconds with a conversation that could've been a phone call. "Hey, you said earlier that supporting my cause at the gala was 'the least you could do.' What did that mean?"

Cora's face dropped into such a cartoonishly somber expression that it was almost comical. Also incredible, since most women her age I knew had started on a pretty intense Botox regimen. "After everything my sister did. Pom, I'm so . . . so . . ." Those green eyes filled with tears, turning into the sea. "I'm so sorry! She was clearly troubled, and I wasn't there for her. Maybe if I'd called her more, if I'd done my duty as the older sister . . . she wouldn't . . . she wouldn't have . . ."

The tears overflowed, spilling down her cheeks. A true pro, she'd worn waterproof mascara for the beach, which meant her makeup didn't smear. Still, I tucked an arm around her, more to turn her away from the crowd than for emotional support. Though the reason I was turning her away was because I didn't think she'd want the crowd to see her crying, so maybe that was a form of emotional support? Either way, I was doing a good deed. "It's not your fault," I told her.

She sniffled. The tip of her nose was turning bright red. "It feels like it is. I'm so sorry. Because I wasn't there for my sister, she took away your grandmother, and I feel like I'll never stop being sorry. Donating to your cause was the absolute least I could do. I'd do more, I would, but the money is mostly my husband's family's, and they already have their own causes . . ."

I'd gathered from my trusty informant Google that the Jean-Pierre family's main cause consisted of a museum bearing their name and holding their art collection that served primarily as a tax shelter. But I nodded sympathetically. I imagined it had to be hard to be beholden to your partner for all your money, to feel like you're the less influential half of a pair. Like Gabe?

But this wasn't about Gabe. It was about me. "So you were trying to help me?" I said. "I thought you'd be mad at me. For turning Opal in and getting her locked up."

Cora's eyes widened. "Mad at you?" She shook her head. A tear flew off her cheek and landed on mine. I had to fight the urge to wipe it off. "No, Pom, of course I'm not mad at you! You didn't frame her or falsely accuse her of something. She did it; she confessed. She killed someone. It was right that she should go to prison."

Her words rang of truth. Not that I knew the tone of truth so well; Opal's words had also rung of truth when she was tearfully telling me she'd been acting weird because of "family stuff" and not because she was a cold-blooded killer. But my intuition was probably way better than it was back then, now that I'd actually solved a crime, so I assumed I was correct. "It's not your fault, Cora."

"Part of me knows it, but another part of me still thinks it is." She swiped her cheek with the back of her hand. A point against her: while her mascara was waterproof, her rouge was not. It smeared into a patch under her eye that looked eerily like blood. "So I wanted to help. And money wasn't enough. I saw what was going around online about you, and I wanted to clear your name."

She pulled out her phone. I braced myself to smile politely at photos of her kids and tell her how cute they were even if they looked like the hobgoblins in *Labyrinth*, but, instead, she showed me a screenshot with a bunch of numbers in it, which was less appealing than a tiny hobgoblin. "What is this?"

"It's a financial statement," Cora said. "Don't ask me what kind or what all the numbers mean." She pointed to a line with a name on it. *Vienna L. Soo*. "All I know is that it shows your friend taking money from Greystone Inc."

My mouth dropped open. Greystone, the evilest of evils in the finance world. "Vienna would never."

"Numbers don't lie," Cora said. "It's dated a few years back. It looks like she accepted an enormous contribution from the corporation to start up her charitable foundation, but she never spoke about it publicly."

"Or privately," I said, still shocked. Vienna had always told me that she'd started up her nonprofit solely using funds from her trust and her family . . . but, you know, I'd thought in passing, having started up my own foundation, that she must have received a *lot* of money from them. Because my family was wealthier than hers (not trying to brag or anything; it was just true) and mine was still slower going. She'd entered the scene with an enormous splash and hadn't stopped since. "Are you absolutely sure? How do you know this wasn't forged?"

"I mean, I can't give you a notarized statement from Vienna and the CEO of Greystone," Cora said. "But I overheard something at the gala between Vienna and Conrad that made me suspicious, and then later when Conrad was murdered and the public was trying to pin it on you . . . well, I followed my suspicion and went digging in hopes that it would help you. My husband works a lot with Jack Wohl, whose hedge fund works with Greystone, and he was able to find this statement, which tracked with what Vienna and Conrad had been saying to each other. Between this and the earring, maybe it'll be enough to get people off your back."

She must also have overheard their heated discussion in the corner—maybe she'd been standing closer than me and could hear more, or she'd gone by at a different moment. Or who knew? Maybe Vienna and Conrad were having heated little discussions the entire night. "So somehow Conrad found out that she'd taken money from Greystone, which is super sketchy and definitely evil, to start her foundation," I said slowly, piecing it together in my mind. My toes curled, sand catching sharply in the bends. "He said in his speech that he knew someone's secret, and Vienna looked like she was going to puke. Could he have been blackmailing her?"

"I don't know," Cora said. "I'm just trying to help you by sharing the few details I have."

I felt a little bit like a large frog had taken up residence inside my chest. If the police had this information, too, no wonder they thought Vienna did it. Between the altercation at the gala, and the earring, and the fact that the victim had been blackmailing her and threatening to expose her unless she . . . what? Did it matter?

Well. She looked awfully guilty.

The frog was so heavy. It couldn't be Vienna. It just couldn't. I went to turn to Gabe for comfort—even if he didn't agree with me, he'd tell me he did to make me feel better—but of course he wasn't there. *For optics and things.* I felt his absence like a wound.

Honestly, it made me want to drink. So I did. I waved over a passing waiter and told him to give me whatever was on his tray. He did, because I was the guest and guests were always right and so *I* was always right, right? I took it without a thank-you, because I was a guest and he was paid to do this and I—Old Pom was starting to poke her head out again.

"Are you okay?" Cora asked. I took a long sip to silence both her and Old Pom, or maybe the drink was feeding Old Pom. It was terrible, honestly. The drink. It had clearly been going to some old man, because it tasted like medicine and was at least 90 percent alcohol. I didn't gag or grimace as it went down, though. Because I was a professional.

Or I used to be. A professional partier. It seemed those skills didn't go away, even though I specifically hadn't used them in over a year. *What will people think?* whispered New Pom. I'd get judged so hard. Though right now I was just drinking. Not partying. I firmly told my shoulders to stop shimmying to the beat of the players on the shore. No dancing. What would people think?

I really needed Gabe. I took another long drink—God, that burned—and smiled. The air felt so cold on my teeth. "I'm fine. Can you send me that statement?"

"Of course." Cora immediately texted it to me. I couldn't believe she'd saved my number after all these years. I used to make Lori do yearly refreshers of my contact list to get rid of all the randos. "Pom, are you sure you're okay? You're looking a little green."

That gave me the perfect opening to excuse myself and go

looking for Gabe, to nestle into his arms and let him tell me I wasn't a total failure.

But why should I? He'd ditched me here. So I didn't take it. Instead, I stretched my smile wider. I was out of practice with my slightly deranged infectious party smile, but it worked. Cora smiled back at me. "Nothing another drink won't solve."

CHAPTER Thirteen

The plane ride back the next day was quiet and subdued. My conversation with Cora had finished soon after her texting me the financial statement, with her promising to get back in touch if she learned any more intel and also to keep patronizing my nonprofit—that was a plus, I guess, that not *everybody* would abandon me. Maybe Vienna would be sent to prison but transfer all of her ill-begotten funds to me to use for my foundation. Something something, silver lining?

Anyway.

After learning what I had from Cora and provisionally clearing her from the suspects list, I hadn't felt much in the mood to spend the rest of the weekend hanging out with people I didn't care about and didn't even suspect of murder. Once I'd gone looking for Gabe, only to find out he'd gone up to our room with a headache, the decision was easy. I begged off early the next morning with profuse apologies to Kevin instead of leaving later that evening as planned. I even spared a polite smile for Persimmon, who was hanging off his arm, dressed in what didn't amount to much more than a scrap of silk. She looked fantastic, actually. If her hope was to make me jealous of her man, she'd failed, but I was now super jealous of her waist-to-hip ratio.

"Don't worry, of course things come up," Kevin said solicitously, patting me on the arm. I'd told him my dad had summoned me back to the city to help him manage an urgent business matter. (If you're going to lie, why not lie big, right?) "Perhaps we can all go out to dinner when everything is resolved and Persimmon and I are back in the city. I'd love to hear more about your work."

I glowed, choosing to believe he was talking about my nonprofit and not my pretend work for the family business. "Absolutely."

"Speaking of which, do you have a seat on the Afton board?" he asked.

So much for that hope. I smiled enigmatically, because I didn't actually know the answer to that question. "Why do you ask?"

His own solicitous smile disappeared, and it took me a second to realize it was because he thought I was being difficult with him, not difficult with myself. "I'm considering making an inroad into the hotel business. As you probably know, office real estate is slumping, and that's where a lot of my portfolio is. I think boutique hotels are the future."

Afton Hotels were anything but boutique, so I wasn't sure why he wanted to talk to *me* about this. "I see," I chirped, stretching my own smile super wide in hopes I wouldn't look difficult. "Well, I'm happy to connect you with my brother. Or my dad. They're really the ones who are focused on the business."

"I appreciate it," he said. "Let's connect soon." With that, he let me board the plane, where Gabe's headache was still in effect; he was slouched in one of the window seats and served me one-word answers whenever I asked him questions. He did raise his head, however, when I pulled out my phone to share the statement Cora had sent me. "So it probably wasn't Cora. But—"

"She just felt guilty for what her sister did and wanted to help me," I hurried to say before he could bring up Vienna. I frowned out the window as we flew over the crystal clear, sparkling ocean back toward New York.

I'd woken up to a furious text from Nicholas. Pom, did you

hijack the jet? Sure, it might not have sounded furious to a casual observer, but I could sense the anger beneath my brother's words. I'd texted back, *Yes, I held Captain Ted at stiletto-point and forced him to take off.* Hopefully Nicholas would be so outraged at my making light of the deadly shoe that had killed our grandmother that he'd forget how angry he was about the stealing-the-jet thing.

I continued, "Honestly, I kind of get it." Or so I'd decided as I lay awake last night, staring at the crack running down the plaster of our ceiling, unable to sleep. If I up and left Nicholas at a time when he was troubled and then he snapped and killed someone, I'd probably wonder if my presence could have stopped him. Likely yes—I'd been told that I had an incredibly soothing aura. "I felt bad for Cora. Though hopefully I didn't comfort her enough that she'll decide I'm right and she doesn't need to donate a bunch of money to my nonprofit."

Gabe made a noncommittal "hmm." "But this other thing, Pom," he said. "You've got to admit it's making Vienna look more . . ."

I was grateful he didn't finish his sentence, but I didn't think it was out of any consideration for me—it was because the flight attendant made an appearance to check on us and see if we wanted anything to eat or drink. "I'll take a bellini," I said, then reconsidered. I had a little headache of my own. "No, I'll take a water. Sparkling. With lime. Not lemon." The flight attendant nodded and made it a bit down the aisle before I remembered to add on, "Please."

I turned back to Gabe, my stomach rolling, or maybe it was just turbulence. "I know how it makes Vienna look. I don't want to, but maybe we do have to consider her as a possibility."

"What do they say?" Gabe said. "Sometimes the most obvious solution is actually the solution."

Whoever "they" were, I kind of hated them right now. "I have to talk to Vienna," I said. "She wanted to talk while we were flying here. Hopefully she still does." I grimaced. "I can't interrogate her, though. Not my best friend. I'll ask her to help me with something nonprofit-related. That should help her let down her guard."

"Smart." Gabe turned back to the window. We were leaving the ocean behind, coming up on the Florida coast. I wondered how my cousins, Farrah and Jordan, were doing down there and mentally waved hi. "I might close my eyes for a little bit."

I took a deep breath. "Gabe?"

"What?"

My stomach was still swimming unpleasantly, and of course it wasn't turbulence. Captain Ted would be offended by the very thought. His flights were smoother than my mother's forehead. "I love you."

"I love you too," Gabe said.

Well, that was a relief to hear, at least. "Is . . . is everything okay?" He didn't respond. Not to be dramatic or anything, but I had to fill the silence or I might die. "It's just that you were behaving kind of weirdly last night, and now today with the headache, and . . ." I trailed off, because I wasn't sure exactly where my speech was heading. "I just . . . Are you okay?"

The flight attendant chose that moment to come by with my sparkling water and a winning smile. "Let me squeeze your lime for you." Gabe and I sat there awkwardly as the flight attendant juiced that lime to its last dying breath. I kind of wanted to wither up with it. Or maybe jump out the window. No, we were above Florida. No way was I dying in Florida. "Anything else I can get you?"

"No," I said abruptly. "Thank you." She retreated, leaving me and Gabe alone again. Suddenly I wanted to call her back and ask for lemon.

It took him an excruciating seventeen minutes to speak, or maybe that was just what it felt like. "Yeah," he said, and paused.

I definitely aged at least a year in his pause. "Yeah, no. Pom, am I enough for you?"

"What?" I said, offended by the question. "Yes. Of course. Like I would waste my time with somebody who wasn't."

He didn't seem convinced. "I'm worried that maybe I don't . . . I don't quite belong in this world. Like you want things from me that I can't give you. Like everybody around me is always laughing at me. *Look at him, what is he doing here, acting like he belongs?*"

"Aw, Gabe." I'd felt exactly the same way when I'd been launched from my penthouse into his tiny little apartment. I knew I didn't belong in that world of waiting in line and holding the subway pole and taking the stairs. My heart went out to him. "You belong because you're here with me. If anyone has any thoughts about you, they can bring them to me, and I'll take them down."

He raised an eyebrow. "You're going to beat them up?"

"No," I said patiently. "I'll start rumors that they ate baby penguin on their trip to Antarctica or made a coat out of baby giraffe skin."

"Won't your world see that as a fine thing? I mean, Jack Wohl is still invited to every gala, and everybody knows he burned down that homeless shelter for the tax break."

"Yes, those were people," I said even more patiently. "Nobody cares about people, but *everybody* cares about baby animals." Then what he'd said before struck me. "What could I possibly want that you can't give me? You are *everything* to me. What's mine is yours. My world is your world."

Gabe snorted. "This will never be my world."

It was like a fist had grabbed my heart and squeezed. We were a unit. A couple. What was mine was ours, and all of that. And once you were married, you were *legally* one unit.

If this was never going to be his world, then did that mean he didn't want to be one with me and everything? Did he not want to marry me after all?

I cleared my throat. I would do this new thing I'd been trying called "asking" instead of "assuming." "What do you mean by that?"

In the corner of my eye, I could see the flight attendant hovering behind the curtain that separated the staff area from my area. Eavesdropping, or waiting to see if she needed to bring tissues and a chocolate croissant (sourced from my bakery, of course)? Either way, she was being unprofessional. She should have been out of sight. When I told Captain Ted about this, she'd be fired.

No. She didn't deserve to be fired for making one mistake. I'd make sure to tell him to have her be more careful in the future. That was what New Pom did. Old Pom wouldn't have cared, but New Pom had a heart for all the little people.

Gabe cleared his throat in response. "I don't know, Pom. Sometimes I hear you talking about things and it's like a foreign language to me. Like I've never even considered the things you're talking about, and not in a good way. It's like you're fluent in Swahili and I'm trying to muddle along in English. I feel like everybody's laughing at me behind my back all the time because I don't know all these secret rules that you apparently learned in prep school while I was in algebra figuring out what *x* was."

I didn't think I'd ever figured out what *x* was. An eternal mystery. "You'll learn," I assured him. "Just look at Kevin Miller. He's one of us now. And Jessica, she's getting there. It's been a really long time since she told anyone she bought whatever she was wearing on sale like it's some kind of achievement. It takes some time, sure, but you're with me, and I'm a master."

Gabe was quiet for a moment. "But what if I don't *want* to be one of you?"

It was my turn to blink, uncomprehending. "Why wouldn't you want to be one of us? Gabe, we're flying in a private jet right now, returning from a private island. Why would you want to be anything else?"

Checkmate. But he shook his head. "You just said it before. How you'd make up a rumor about baby animals because nobody in this world cares if someone did something terrible to human beings. It's like wealth at this level . . . warps you."

"I don't think that's unique to us," I told him, a little offended, honestly. "I think there are people all throughout society who care more about bad things happening to baby animals than people."

"Still," said Gabe. "I became a teacher because I cared about these kids—regular, public schoolkids—and what they're going through. They're in a different stratosphere from this . . . society." He was quiet for a moment. "I don't want to stop caring about them."

"Oh, Gabe. I don't think that's a money thing. I think that's a you thing."

"I don't know." He cast his eyes at me, and I couldn't help but wonder what he saw. Did he think I was "warped" by my money and my position? I probably would have agreed with him before everything that went down last year, but I'd changed, hadn't I?

The curtain at the back of the plane fluttered. The flight attendant appeared, her feet quiet on the soft plane carpet. "We're about to start our descent. Would you like anything to eat or drink before we land?"

I *had* changed. I didn't need Gabe to validate that for me. Old Pom would've gotten the flight attendant fired without ever thinking about it again. New Pom just said softly, "No thank you."

CHAPTER Fourteen

As soon as we landed, Nicholas texted me that I was grounded. I would've been tempted to respond with something like, *You're not my dad*, except that I knew he meant it literally, as in, I was stuck on the ground because I was no longer allowed to use the jet. That didn't mean I was trapped, though—I could still fly commercial if I really wanted to go somewhere. I announced that to Gabe as we disembarked, feeling proud of myself for stooping to that level. Surely that was proof I hadn't been warped by money.

He did not look overly impressed.

My parents had texted me too. My mom: What were you doing on Kevin's island? I was surprised the two of them hadn't been there, honestly. I mean, it would have been the most unpleasant surprise, to be working on an interrogation and see my mom's face pop up over Cora's shoulder like the world's worst jack-in-the-box. But they were fairly tight with Kevin and Jack and all of their crowd (which, yes, was hypocritical given my mom's attitude toward Jessica and Gabe the money-grubbers, but my mom loved an opportunity to be a hypocrite), so it was strange they didn't show for his big birthday bash.

I texted back, Had a party! The best time! Too bad you weren't there.

The second thing I did—well, third, after booking a spa sesh for the next morning, because, after the stress of this plane ride, I really needed a Himalayan pink salt soak and one of those face masks made out of eel slime—was call Vienna. "I'm back," I said as soon as she picked up in lieu of a hello. Time was too precious to allow for hellos. "Let's talk."

"When are you free?" she said, voice flat. My instincts had been correct; I couldn't rely on getting real answers out of her with just a face-to-face conversation. I had to show her I still valued her. Get her distracted by doing some kind of work.

"Can you meet me at the Chelsea building tomorrow after lunch?" I asked. "I want to keep working on it. My kids shouldn't have to wait until this investigation is done for their refuge." I hadn't heard back from Bibi about whether my foundation could still use the building, which was hopefully a good sign. Surely if she was going to take it from me, she would've made that clear already. In the meantime, maybe continuing to work on it would show her how important it was to me.

"Sure," Vienna said. She sounded tired. A little depressed. Not that surprising, I supposed. "What will we be doing?"

"I don't know, exactly," I said. Whatever Lina had left for me. "Appraising the site. Some interior design. Cleaning out some files."

"You're going to clean?"

"Of course," I said, trying to sound breezy. "I've cleaned up trash plenty of times before." If you counted the hours it was court-mandated (I'd actually looked great in orange).

"And the building still belongs to you? Even after—"

"Of course," I chirped, even though I had no idea. "See you then!"

I hung up before she could interrogate me further. "Okay," I told Gabe. "We're on for tomorrow. You ready?"

He gave me a funny look. "No, Pom. I'm not ready. Tomorrow's Monday. I have to work."

"Oh," I said. "Well, can't you call out sick or something?" I could certainly text Ellie and Sage to let them know I wouldn't be at the bakery, though I understood that was because I owned the bakery and could do whatever I wanted, unlike Gabe. Surely solving a murder took precedence over tutoring kids, though. No matter how important teaching was! Teachers are important! They should get paid more! Like, a lot more. Then maybe Gabe and I wouldn't have this weird money-related tension between us.

"No, Pom. I'm not going to call out sick."

"But you were going to call out sick if we got stuck on the island."

"We're not stuck on the island," he said. "And that would've been an emergency situation. My AP kids have their test coming up soon, and I have to help fine-tune some bonus college essays for kids hoping to get off the wait list. I need to be there for them."

He'd always been a stickler about not calling out of work, even for investigating a murder. Back when we'd done our very first interrogation together (of Fred, the Afton CFO), he'd called out of work for me. I guess it had been charming, then.

Or maybe this was what he'd been talking about. Because I'd gone ahead and made my spa appointment for the morning without consulting him. He had his tutoring sessions in the afternoon. If I'd planned my chat with Vienna for the morning, he probably would've been able to come, but instead I'd just steamrolled ahead without even asking.

"Of course," I said. "Your job is so important. The kids need you. I can handle this on my own."

Far from his eyes welling with tears of love at what a kind and compassionate girlfriend he had, he tensed his jaw. "I don't need your sarcasm."

For a moment I was oddly touched that he thought I was being sarcastic, considering that the *New York Post* had once said I thought sarcasm was a new perfume. Then I just felt bad that he'd misinterpreted what I was trying to say. "I'm not being sarcastic, I swear. Go be there for your kids. I know that what you do is important."

He stared at me warily for a moment, as if not quite sure I meant it. He turned away before I could be sure he was.

• • •

As far as I was concerned, the Chelsea building was ours until someone in a uniform or with the last name Phlume told us it wasn't. I mean, I still had the key, and the security code for the alarm still worked. I didn't realize I'd been holding my breath on that until the keypad beeped green.

Our building had once been a grand Chelsea town house. It had housed some presumably very wealthy, prominent families for years after it was built in the 1800s before being subdivided into apartments in the seventies or eighties and then falling into disrepair in the nineties. The building had to be worth millions and millions now, but the state of the inside was, to put it mildly, not great. I was pretty sure Conrad's plan had been to let us clean it out and do basic renovations on it while collecting generous tax breaks and then, in ten years or so, use that money for a gut renovation before putting it on the market and profiting handsomely. But who knew what Bibi would want to do?

As soon as the door shut behind me, leaving me in the slightly musty-smelling, dusty foyer, my phone buzzed and buzzed and buzzed. Someone calling me—hopefully not Vienna telling me she couldn't make it, not after I'd come all the way down here.

Nope. It was Nicholas. I picked up. "I know, I know, I'm grounded, and I'm a terrible person for stealing the jet," I said, hopefully preempting any yelling. "Is that it?"

He was quiet on the other side. I loved it when I got to shock people by showing them I understood more about the world than they thought. "No," he finally grumbled. "It's not it. I wanted to talk about your . . . building."

"My building? The one Conrad gave me?" He grunted assent. I turned in a little circle around the foyer. Better not mention that I was here right now, just in case. What if I wasn't supposed to be and he told Bibi out of revenge for me stealing the jet? "What about it?"

He gave a disgruntled-sounding cough. "I was thinking that it would make an excellent little boutique hotel. You know that we don't have anything in the Chelsea area, and a big building right now might be . . . well. Too much. But a small, exclusive hotel . . ."

"You know when I said Conrad was giving me the building, he wasn't really *giving* me the building, right?" I said. "It's an exaggeration, like if someone said I stole a jet when really I just borrowed it from a family member for a couple of days without authorization." I paused to let that sink in. "He was going to lease it to me for a very low rate for a long period of time."

"Yeah, but you can do whatever you want with it once you sign the contract, right?" Nicholas said.

"Yes, because accepting a building for use as a hub for my nonprofit and then immediately turning around and using it as a for-profit hotel for the family business would be fantastic for my image," I said. Weird that two people in two days had mentioned doing the same thing with Conrad's building. Greedy vultures. "I'm not signing it over to you for a hotel. If it's even going to be mine now that Conrad's dead. The whole thing's up in the air. Okay? I have to go."

Like a coward, I hung up before he could argue with me. Took a deep breath. Shook myself out a little. Like I would jeopardize my nonprofit, the thing I was investigating a murder to save, for anything, but *especially* for the family business. Come on, Nicholas.

Now. Where was I?

I'd beat Vienna here, and I needed to cool off from my annoyance over Nicholas's call, so I used the time to take a look around. I hadn't been here in a while, but my old assistant Lina and her team had been working on it in the weeks before the gala, as had the contractors I'd hired to rip up moldy carpet and fix a cracked toilet and paint some walls. It was looking much better, though the smell of paint was making me a little woozy; the interior was cleaner and brighter, with a lot of the old wall detailing and crown moldings still intact. The peeling wallpaper revealed scrawled writing and graffiti on the walls themselves. I wondered idly if we'd find any treasure under the floorboards. Images filled my head as I poked it around corners: a couple of housing-insecure students sleeping in this nice, quiet room overlooking the air shaft; Lori cooking up some healthy packed lunches in the big top-floor kitchen; kids studying on free laptops in one of the living rooms, with shelves of donated books lining the walls.

By the time I heard the doorbell downstairs, I was feeling really good about the space. Too good. To the point where I'd almost forgotten why I was here in the first place. My mood plummeted the way I did when I went bungee jumping off the top of the Burj Khalifa (very illegal, but nothing is too illegal to be done when you're in the company of a Saudi prince).

"Vee!" I said as I flung open the door, pulling her in for a hug and some cheek kisses before I could even really see her. Our hug ended quickly so that I could usher her inside before anyone on the street could snap a picture.

There, I drew back and bit my lip before I could blurt something unfortunate about her unfortunate haircut. Last year, post our temporary friendship breakup, she'd chopped her long hair into a sleek bob. Now, perhaps reflecting even greater stress, she'd chopped it into a pixie cut. She did not have a face for a pixie cut (to be fair, very few people did). "You look great," I lied. Even beyond the haircut, she did not look great. Her eyes were hollow, and her fingers wouldn't stop tapping against the banister of the steep staircase.

Her laugh was as hollow as her eyes. "Sure. Okay. Thanks." Her voice was raspy, probably from all the talking she'd done with lawyers. I knew from experience that they'd ask you to tell your story over and over and over, ask you the same questions over and over and over, to see if they could trip you up. Or maybe it was from all the crying. I knew from experience that speaking with lawyers often came with a lot of crying too.

She cleared her throat, which wouldn't help with the raspiness. I made a mental note to send out my assistant to pick up some honey and tea with lemon for her—oh, wait. I made a mental note to order it in. I really needed to hire a new Lina, but it would have to wait till I solved the murder. "Pom," she said. "I just wanted to apologize."

My breath caught in my throat. She couldn't really be apologizing for the murder, could she?

Of course not. She continued, "I've been a bad friend lately. You're going through a lot, too, but I've been selfish. I've only been thinking about myself."

"You never have to apologize to me for being selfish," I said. It wasn't like I hadn't spent almost the entirety of my adult life being the most selfish person imaginable. "And trust me, I know what you're going through. I've been there." I took her hands in mine. They were freezing. "Let me help."

She blew out a long exhale. "I don't know what else there is to do, honestly. I've hired the lawyers and they're doing their thing. I didn't kill the guy, so the other side isn't going to be able to prove that I did unless someone is trying to frame me."

"I imagine the earring doesn't help," I said in what I hoped was a soothing way.

She shook her head grimly. "No, that doesn't help. But it's not like someone stabbed him with it. He was just holding it."

"Right," I said. "Of course."

She sighed. "And all this garbage online isn't helping."

"Don't look at it," I said, and she gave me a deadpan look

back, probably because she knew 100 percent that I regularly disobeyed that advice. I had in fact, just that morning on the car ride here, spent some time scrolling through a series of posts using the hashtag #PoMoanA, I guess because I bitched and moaned too much about the murder happening at my gala, even though I hadn't done any of it publicly? Or maybe it was a reference to the rumored sex tape that would remain a rumor because of the enormous payoff I'd given my ex? I didn't know. "Anyway, want to stop thinking about online garbage and think about actual garbage?"

"Not really," she said.

"That's the spirit," I replied. "According to the notes my former assistant left me, we need to go through all of the boxes in the basement by hand. Apparently they're full of records from all the people who have lived here previously, and there could be something interesting and/or valuable in there."

"Valuable?" She wrinkled her nose. "Like what?"

I shrugged. "I don't know. She was convinced, though."

The basement was, unfortunately, a typical basement: chilly, damp, musty. Cobwebs draped themselves in luxurious scarves from the ceiling. A sizable space had been cleared out already, exposing a bare concrete floor, but there were still stacks of boxes along the walls: some old, disintegrating cardboard, and some wood. A few file cabinets also stood against the far wall. "Those file cabinets look locked," Vienna said from behind me, still up a few steps. "Oh well. I guess we can't go through anything and we'll have to go upstairs where it's nice and clean and have tea."

I made my way toward the file cabinets, grimacing as I sidestepped a clump of something that was either dust or the remains of a dead mouse from before I was born. Indeed, a lock chained the drawers closed. I leaned in to examine it.

"It's too bad there are laws against removing padlocks," Vienna said cheerfully. "I guess we'll just have to—"

She broke off, interrupted by the sound of me smashing the

lock with my foot. "There," I said, regarding it with satisfaction. The old metal had been so brittle it hadn't even taken that much force. "There aren't any rules against opening something that's locked if the lock is already broken when you find it." I actually had no idea if that was true, but whatever. "And it was already broken when we found it, right?"

I looked over my shoulder just in time to see her wince. For a moment I was relieved: Surely, someone so concerned over breaking a minor law would never break a major one, like the ones forbidding murder. But then she said, "With everything going on, I really can't handle any kind of run-in with the law. I'm under a microscope right now."

Of course. "Don't worry," I said. "If the law comes after us for this, I'll take all the blame."

Lina had brought down an old chair to sit on while going through the items. I took that while Vienna perched on a wooden box, pulling a couple of drawers from the filing cabinet and setting them on the floor before us with a clang. "Okay. Let's get this over with."

As it turned out, doing this was extraordinarily boring. As in, more boring than you'd think going through boxes of musty outdated records in a basement would be. My eyes glazed over at all the names of people who'd lived here back in its brownstone era and the various things they felt necessary to hold on to. Copies of complaints to the city about pigeons crapping on her stoop from a Catherine Craig. Doodles of superheroes from a William Melrose. A short story about a brownstone mouse who fell in love with a city rat from an Erwin Roost.

Nothing better to break up something boring than something terrible, right? "So, anyway, Vee," I said, clearing my throat. That wasn't a cobweb stuck in there, was it? "How are you doing? Really?"

Her eyes were trained on the yellowing sheaves of paper she was flipping through. "*Really?* Fine." I stared at her the same way I did when trying to will Millicent's tiny dog to drop the sapphire pendant or silk scarf it inevitably tried to eat whenever she'd brought it to the hotel.

She must have felt my eyes burning into her head and sighed, sending half a sheet of paper crumbling into dust. "Okay. Not so fine."

"You texted while I was up in the air and wanted to talk," I said gently. "What did you want to talk about?"

She sniffled, and for a moment I thought she might cry, until she wiped a cobweb off her nose. I should've known better. Vienna had tear ducts of marble. "I wanted to tell you the truth. In case it comes out publicly."

"What is it?"

She bit her lip. "Conrad Phlume was blackmailing me."

So. There it was. I was glad I didn't have to get the financial statement out and confront her with it. "Because of Greystone?"

She startled at the sound of the name, dropping a packet of papers on the floor. The bare bulb overhead flickered, but I didn't think that was related. "How did you find out?"

"The public doesn't know yet, if that's what you're asking," I said. "Someone at Kevin's party who was connected to Greystone asked me about it." I paused for a beat in case she was going to push back or get more upset, but she didn't move. "Why did you take money from them?"

She wiped her hand over her cheek, but it came off stone dry. "It was because of you."

"Me?" I cried. "Don't blame this on me."

"No. I'm sorry. I didn't mean it like that," Vienna said. "It was because of how I *felt* about you. It was right after our big fight."

I nodded her on. She didn't have to rehash it to me—I'd never forget the day when she told me she felt like we were wasting our lives and all of the privilege we'd been granted by virtue of our birth, that she was tired of spending her time partying and sleeping in, that she wanted more. I'd taken it as an attack on me, which it kind of was, but only because she was attacking the both of us. She split and started her foundation and became the artsy, sophisticated Vienna Soo that everybody now knew, while I partied for another year before my fall from grace.

She continued, "I left our fight all fired up and ready to make a change. I immediately went to go start my foundation with money from my trust fund, but . . . well . . ." She hung her head, hopefully because she was embarrassed and not because she was trying to see if a mouse had run over her foot. "It turns out that it wasn't as big as I'd thought it was, and a lot of what I did have liquid and ready to go was tied up in red tape. I knew I needed to make a splash if I really wanted my life to change so quickly, and I needed money for that, but I also didn't want to, well, downgrade my quality of life."

"Understandable," I said. Not going to lie, I was feeling a little bit smug, because I *had* downgraded my quality of life in order to start my foundation. Not, like, horribly so, but I'd learned when I went hunting for the apartment I eventually bought that I totally could've afforded another couple of bedrooms in my unit and a second swimming pool in the building if I weren't such a charitable person.

"I'd made such a big, public declaration of what I wanted my life to look like, and I knew that if I didn't get it moving right away, it might never happen." Little spots of red bloomed on her cheeks. "And I was afraid of what you'd think. If I'd just sacrificed our whole friendship for nothing. My dad had done a little work with Greystone, and I picked up the CEO's business card, and then . . . well . . ."

"So you took their money," I finished. "Honestly, Vee, it's not *that* bad."

"That's not how people are going to see it," she said. She paused, cocked her head, considered. "Unless we start the PR spin right away. Put it out there that I was naive, that I had no idea who they were, that I was just so desperate to do good . . ."

"And that you took their evil money and did good things with it," I said. "It could work."

"It could totally work." The color was coming back to her face, some of the spirit to her eyes. "Okay. Okay, so my life isn't over."

"Not like Conrad's." We shared a mirthless grin. "So he found out somehow and was blackmailing you? You weren't having an affair?"

"An affair? With him?" She scrunched up her whole face like I'd tried to feed her the rotting mouse corpse in the corner. "God, my God, no. *Gross.* Ugh. How could you even think that?"

"I didn't think that. My mom's friend apparently saw you out with him and decided that's what was going on."

"Ew, gross," she repeated. "No. I barely knew who he was until he asked me to lunch. I figured, why not, maybe he'd invest in my foundation and I'd get a good lunch out of it. But he told me what he'd found out and that he wanted me to pay him to keep it secret."

"How much? The man has more money than God; why did he need yours?"

Her face turned somber. "He didn't want money. He wanted me to pretend to date him. I guess there were cracks in his marriage? He thought his wife might be having an affair and he was afraid she'd leave him and he'd be this old man alone with his money."

Hmm. Bibi was cheating on him? I filed the information away for later. That would explain the timing of him coming to me with his building donation. I'd get him back into the social scene he'd been pushed out of. And a pretty young thing on his arm . . . "Why wouldn't he just hire an escort to pretend to date him, then?"

She shook her head. "I asked the same thing. What he wanted

more than anything was his social capital back. Having a hot escort pretending to be in love with him on his arm might score him points with other creepy old guys, but not anyone else. He needed to date someone everybody knew, someone everybody liked and admired, someone who'd get him through the doors that had closed in his face. And I was just the lucky girl whose incriminating information turned up first."

"I see," I said slowly. "So when you two were arguing in the corner at the gala . . . ?"

She full-body cringed. "Ugh, you heard that? I was trying to stall for time to figure out how best to handle him. I told him I didn't have the stomach yet for what he was asking of me. I guess Bibi must have overheard us too. I assume I'm the 'skank.' I followed her out after to try and explain, but she wasn't interested in talking; she just pushed past me on the way out of the bathroom and stormed off." She sighed. "I think my earring fell off when she pushed me, because when I checked myself out in the mirror after leaving the stall, it was gone."

"I wonder how it ended up in Conrad's hand," I said.

He could've found it on the floor in the hallway and innocently picked it up, figuring that someone would be looking for it. Or somebody else could have found it. Someone who'd seen the interaction between Vienna and Conrad and thought that, maybe, it could be useful for whatever they were planning.

Or maybe it had ended up stuck to Bibi somehow as they were pushing past each other. And then Bibi went after Conrad, newly furious about him and his "skank." Only, if she'd been cheating on him first, would she really get that mad about him cheating on her?

Before I could voice any of those thoughts to Vienna, a creak sounded overhead. Then another. "Did you hear that?" I asked.

She glanced upward, as if she'd be able to see whatever had caused it through the ceiling. "It sounded like—"

Thump. "Footsteps," she finished with a whisper.

CHAPTER Fifteen

We should not be hearing footsteps right now. Nobody else was supposed to be in the building. If Gabe had changed his mind and wanted to come meet me, he would've texted to let me know. I checked my phone just in case he had and I'd missed it, but I didn't have any signal down here in the basement. I telepathically asked Vienna if she had any, my eyes flicking down to her phone in her hand. She glanced down, pursed her lips, shook her head. No.

The footsteps grew louder. *Thump, thump, thump*. Big and heavy, like they were coming from a large man wearing work boots. I froze, holding my breath, as if he'd be able to hear the air moving in and out of my lungs.

Calm down, Pom. Maybe he was wearing work boots because he was here to do work. Maybe Lina had booked someone to work on the plumbing or whatever before she quit and had forgotten to let me know. Maybe Bibi had sent someone over to assess the property.

A voice filtered down the stairs, through the cracked-open basement door. Definitely male. "Where aaaaare you? Where are you hiding?"

Okay, scratch those theories. I gasped. It didn't matter if the intruder heard it—he already would've been able to track me by the sound of my heart pounding the walls of my chest. "What do we do?" I said frantically. Vienna always knew what to do. She would know what to do. Right?

Wrong. Her eyes were as wide as those on one of Damien Hirst's famed diamond skulls, and she had to swallow three times before squeaking, "Run?"

We stiffened again as the footsteps ranged overhead, pausing every so often as if the intruder were looking inside closets and checking under couches. "He might see us," I whispered back. "And I don't think we want him to see us."

If only there was another way out of the basement than the stairs back up to the—oh. There *was* another way out of the basement. Old New York City buildings like this had exits from the basement directly to the street for the servants back in the old days, so that the home's residents wouldn't have to see them going about their work. I scanned the basement. Not there, not there—oh, there. I pointed. Vienna followed me as I bolted over to the cobwebby door, leaping not-very-gracefully over a wooden box so that I wouldn't hit it and make a noise.

We were both pulling at the door together, our Pilates-toned arms bulging at full strength, for what felt like an hour before we had to admit it wasn't working. It was either locked or totally jammed. Crap. Crap, crap, crap. "Okay," I hissed. "When we hear the footsteps get faint, or if we hear him go up the stairs to the second floor, we wait a minute and we run for it."

Vienna nodded quickly, jerkily, like a rabbit. "Who knows we're here? Were we followed?"

We both held our breath as the intruder repeated his questions from before, the words filtering eerily through the crack in the basement door. "Where aaaaare you? Where are you hiding?" Then something new, a note of menace hanging heavy in his tone: "When I find you, I'm going to rip you to pieces. Nobody's going to know you ever existed."

My blood turned to ice in my veins. Which was probably a

good thing, because it kept me from melting into a terrified puddle of goo on the floor. Anyone could know we were here. The killer, or someone associated with the killer, or someone who just didn't like me, could've been keeping an eye on my building and/or this building. It was a matter of public record that I owned my apartment in the first and was involved with the second. And it didn't have to be someone watching us: People snapped photos of me on the street and posted them on social media all the time. "Who wants us *dead*?"

The footsteps thump-thump-thumped overhead. My heart pattered frantically. I went to whisper again to Vienna, but then stopped. They sounded close. Too close. Like they were right—

Light flooded the staircase as the basement door creaked open. Vienna and I scuttled backward toward the wall like cockroaches.

The intruder's voice crooned down the stairs. "I bet you're hiding down here, aren't you? I bet I'm going to find you all tucked away neatly in a little box, waiting for me."

My legs were shaking so hard I swore I could hear the bones rattling. I'd drag raced on the Autobahn with no speed limit in a car that didn't have seat belts. I'd popped a random pill from the stash of a man who claimed to have spent a year in the north of Canada living with polar bears that made me believe I was half-mermaid and that I could breathe underwater. Those near-death experiences would have, at least, made for obituaries that were both cool and not embarrassing.

This one? *Pomona Abigail Afton, twenty-nine, was found sliced to ribbons while hiding in a cardboard box in the basement of a dilapidated town house in Chelsea. Her murderer will most likely never be found, as the mind most talented at hunting murderers died with her.*

No *way* was I going to let the *New York Post* print that alongside what would surely be the most unflattering photo of me they could find (probably from the year I let a psychic convince me that waxing was bad for my aura). I girded my shoulders, fists balling, as a footstep thumped onto the top step, a very long, very broad, shadow falling down them. Another step, then another, and I could see glimpses of him. Not that it helped, because he was wearing a black balaclava over his head.

Quick. Take stock of what I had. Pepper spray, but that was, helpfully, in my bag that I'd left upstairs. Lots of papers, but those weren't useful for anything besides giving the intruder some paper cuts. The drawers from the filing cabinet, which were sharp at the corners and heavy enough to hurt when hit, but not too heavy for a woman with toned but not too muscular arms to pick up and swing.

Jackpot.

I slid one of the drawers out as the intruder's feet landed at the bottom. My goal had been to keep it on the down-low, but it made a horrible screech as I pulled it from the cabinet. Vienna let out a gasp that sounded as if she was choking.

Well, so much for the down-low. Before my brain could convince me this was a very bad idea and we'd be better off sinking to our knees and begging for our lives, I forced myself to lunge forward. "Aiiiiiaaaaaahhhh!" tore itself from my throat.

The intruder shouted something incomprehensible at me as I lunged at him, fully expecting that, any second, he'd grab me by the waist and snap me in half. But he didn't. Somehow the power of surprise was on my side, and I was able to bash him in the head with the filing cabinet drawer before he could react.

It wasn't hard enough to kill him or even knock him out, I realized right away. Curse my mother for spending my entire young adulthood telling me that if my arms got too bulky, nobody would ever love me. But I did hit hard enough to send him reeling to the side, where he smashed into the wall and went reeling again.

I didn't spare a second. "Run!" I shouted at Vienna, already moving toward the stairs. I was halfway up before I heard him lumber back to his feet. God, I hoped Vienna was behind me.

She was. She'd barely cleared the doorway behind me before I slammed the basement door shut and threw the dead bolt. As I pulled my hand away, I realized how hard it was shaking. "Oh my God, we almost died," I breathed, the shock hitting me now. I expected the shock to hit the intruder, too, for him to roar in anger or pound on the door, but nothing. Maybe he'd passed out. Or he was lifting one of the big filing cabinets up to heft on his shoulder and use as a battering ram.

Well, I wasn't going to stick around and find out. "Call 9-1-1," I directed at Vienna as we hustled as far away from the basement as we could. My purse! It had been dumped from where I'd left it sitting on a side table. And not like he'd bumped into the table while walking by: It had clearly been lifted and turned fully upside down so that all of its contents tumbled out and splayed across the dirty floor. Thank goodness my phone and wallet had been in my belt bag. My poor shattered makeup compact and wireless headphones and 100 percent organic Sea Island cotton tampons. I left those behind, but stooped for my pepper spray.

I didn't feel like I could take a full breath until we made it outside, and it was not a very enjoyable full breath, considering that downtown in summer smells like urine-soaked garbage baking in the sun. Vienna was hanging up the phone, having described the situation to the operator. "What now?" she panted. Her pixie cut was no longer as sleek as it had been before, little strands of hair raising around her face as if she'd been electrocuted.

I glanced around. Our building was on a residential side street of brownstones, which meant that foot traffic was minimal, especially considering that most of their owners would be off summering somewhere that didn't smell like urine-soaked garbage baking in the sun. "We need to be close enough to talk to the police when they show up, but I also don't want to be right here in case he manages to get out of the basement and he's even angrier that we hit him in the head and got away."

"How would he get out of the basement?"

"I don't know." I chewed my lower lip. "But he got in. Maybe he could bust out."

"I think there's a coffee shop a couple of blocks down."

We skedaddled, glancing over our shoulders the entire way to the point where my legs got tangled in a dog walker's leash web. I managed to extricate myself without stepping on any paws or slipping on a puddle of beagle slobber (now *that* would be an obituary the *Post* would love) and make it into the coffee shop without further incident. Both Vienna and I faced the door. "There's a back exit, it looks like, if we need to run," I said, but I'd let myself relax a little. He wouldn't come here, into this crowded coffee shop, with a mask on his head, to finish the job.

We were both jittery enough without adding coffee into the mix, thank you very much, so we ordered a sampling of baked goods. They were dry, or maybe that was just my mouth. I tried to distract myself by thinking about ways I could improve them—piping a fruity jam filling that would moisten one of these too-flaky croissants?—but I was too jittery, too occupied with watching the door.

Fortunately, it wasn't long before the police showed up. They met us at the coffee shop, because I was Pomona Afton. "Are you ready?" asked the older one, a man whose name I'd already forgotten.

I paused a moment for dramatic tension, then nodded. "Let's nab him." The other cop rolled her eyes, but I ignored her. She clearly had no instinct for the stage.

We backtracked the few blocks to our building, me and Vienna recounting our tale of woe the whole walk. Well, mostly me—Vienna seemed to have gotten laryngitis upon being in the presence of the police, and couldn't let out more than a few croaks affirming things I said. Luckily, I can talk enough for two people.

We'd almost finished by the time we approached the building.

I took a deep breath, my stomach dancing either with nerves or with the flakes of the coffee shop's mediocre croissants. "Okay. Let's see who this guy is." If we were lucky, he'd be the murderer, and we'd kill two birds with one princess-cut, five-carat, precious stone, which Gabe would promptly then use to propose to me.

CHAPTER Sixteen

We were not lucky. (On either count, but who's counting?) As soon as we got close to the town house, I realized something was amiss, but didn't realize what it actually was until the officers were climbing up the stairs. "Oh. That door." I gestured at the servants' basement door, which was down a flight of stairs and usually shut tight. I'd never actually seen what it looked like open.

Now I did: a yawning black hole. My stomach plummeted to my feet. "Oh no."

"Oh no," Vienna echoed, staring at it with dismay.

The officers did their search, but came out alone, which was what I'd expected as soon as I'd seen that open door. "He must have gone out that way," the younger one said. I hoped it wasn't my pause for dramatic tension that had given the intruder the crucial moment to escape. "We can check if any of the surrounding homes have cameras so we can see which way he went. He must have removed his mask at some point. Maybe we could get a glimpse of his face."

I'd seen enough WANTED posters featuring photos from those cameras, all blurry and half-formed snatches of forehead or cheek, to know how that would probably go. Still, I nodded, because who knew?

The police left. I called my car. As we waited for it on the sidewalk, our backs up against the side of a stoop so that nobody could swoop in and stab us from behind, I asked Vienna, "You didn't recognize his voice, did you?"

"It sounded vaguely familiar," she said. "But I couldn't pinpoint it."

I thought back. The sound of his voice was already fading from my memory, but I could swear I'd heard it before too. From someone at the gala? I imagined myself walking around in my gown, smiling and nodding. What would that voice have sounded like telling me how impressed they were by all I'd done?

It was no use. Not to recognize the voice, and not to will any nights like that back in the future: I was so hoping the attacker would still be there not just because he'd already tried to hurt us and might do it again, but because his capture could bring this whole nightmare to an end. But no. My nonprofit and all the kids it was supposed to help were still in jeopardy.

The black car pulled up, and we piled in after only a brief hesitation to make sure my driver's voice wasn't the same as the intruder's. Once safely locked into the back seat, a bottle of sparkling Balian water in my hand, I let myself exhale. "Why would somebody want to kill us?"

Vienna was silent for a moment. "You've been investigating again, haven't you?"

I wasn't going to lie to my best friend. "Yeah."

She was silent for a moment. "It has to be connected. It must mean you're getting close."

"I was going to look into Bibi next, but that obviously wasn't Bibi," I said. "Still, everything you told me was suspicious. And she could've hired someone to come after us."

Vienna was silent for another moment. "You know, there was one thing she said. I didn't think it was relevant if you weren't investigating, but . . . I did tell the police." She snorted, rolling her eyes. "Not like they can do very much without a confession or her blood under his fingernails. She has so many lawyers running interference."

I nodded, understanding. Of course the police would've questioned Bibi, like they questioned most of my family members after my grandma's murder. But that was where it stopped unless they had cold, hard evidence to take it further, because mistakenly arresting an Afton or a Phlume could have dire consequences for them.

Vienna continued, "I thought she was on the phone while we were passing each other going in and out of the bathroom, but she might have been talking to herself. All I know is that she said, 'I can't believe tonight is going to be the last time I see him.' I didn't think anything of it at the time. But, obviously, after Conrad's murder . . ."

"She knew he was going to die," I said slowly. At least, probably. I didn't entirely discount the idea that she could've been talking about another "him." But it was awfully convenient that she said something like that after having a fight with her husband and then her husband went and died. "She knew."

"She knew," Vienna confirmed. We sat there in silence, letting the words roll around our heads, until the car dropped her off.

• • •

At home, I relayed the whole thing to Gabe, who'd just gotten home from a tutoring session. As soon as I got to the break-in, he leaped up from where he was sitting on the couch, disturbing Squeaky from where he'd been rubbing against his leg. "What?" His fists were clenched as if he were about to punch someone, and I wasn't sure I'd ever seen his face darken with fury like this. Not going to lie, it was kind of hot. If the intruder were here right now, I'd bet Gabe would rip *him* into pieces.

But, as quickly as the anger had taken over, Gabe wilted, shaking his head, clenching his jaw with frustration. "I should've been there. What if . . ." He couldn't even finish the thought.

"Nothing happened to me. I'm okay," I said. Yes, it was traumatizing that someone had tried to kill me. Yes, it was even more traumatizing that they'd probably be back. But I'd already contacted private security firms for me and, just in case, for Vienna. Armed guards following us around should dissuade any future people trying to cut us to pieces.

Shudder.

"So we need to figure out a way to get to Bibi," I continued. "I've already emailed her about the house and she hasn't gotten back to me. I don't want to come on too strong—can I rock up at a grieving widow's home to chat? Do people still bring, like, casseroles to grieving widows?" I stopped and considered. "Also, what exactly is a casserole?"

"Don't tell me you've never had a casserole."

"It sounds . . . French?"

Gabe sighed. "Okay. I'm not even going to start."

Before we could solve that mystery, my phone buzzed. An unfamiliar 212 number. I always picked up 212 numbers, whether I knew them or not. Yes, some of them were spam. Yes, other ones were reporters trying to get some kind of comment about how I felt now that Opal was in prison for twenty-five years to life. But others were calling to offer me roles on reality TV shows. I'd love to go on *Celebrity Survivor* again. The other contestants had underestimated me all the way to the finals, because while I was terrible at the actual tasks of surviving, like making fires or catching food, I was excellent at turning people against each other and making my teammates hate someone else on our team more than me. (Thank you, brief modeling career.)

Anyway. Nobody was calling to ask me to judge another *Top Chef* baking episode, which was disappointing. "Pomona Afton?" The voice was quiet, throaty, an older woman still figuring out her lower postmenopausal register, definitely not Kristen Kish's or Gail Simmons's.

"Yes?" I said.

"This is Bibi Phlume." She paused for a moment, as if she wanted to give me time to marinate in how ridiculous the name sounded. "The police have informed me of an incident that took place at *my* building."

I didn't think I was imagining how she emphasized that "my." My shoulders tensed. All thoughts of the murder fled from my mind. Well, not all thoughts, considering that the murder was the entire reason we were having this conversation at all. "Yes," I said back to Bibi. "Not a big deal. I meant to contact you about it, but I'd already emailed you about the building and hadn't heard back and didn't want to bother you, and frankly, it's such a small thing anyway."

That was a blatant lie, as directly contradicted by the urgency with which I'd hired my new armed guard (I'd requested someone who wouldn't be wearing all black leather and looking like an obvious commando. Hopefully they'd give me someone who knew how to match prints and solids so that I wouldn't feel embarrassed to be seen with him).

She called me out. "It didn't sound like such a small thing. My insurance rates are going to go up. I'm having a security system installed right this second so that nobody can get back in. Honestly, Pomona, you might want to hold off on the work anyway until after I've had more of a chance to assess my husband's estate. I apologize for the delay in emailing you back—I'm still thinking everything through. I'm not sure if we have the same goals for his portfolio."

A delicate way of saying, *Don't waste any more of your time with the place, because I'm going to sell it to the highest bidder.* Panic flared inside me. "Can I take you out to lunch?" I said. "I'd love to tell you more about the . . . incident. And we can discuss our goals as well."

She was silent for so long that the panic flared again. She was totally going to blow me off because she didn't want to give me bad news to my face. I understood. I'd done the same thing when

I didn't want to tell Jessica the reason my mom hadn't invited her to her fifty-eighth birthday party (Jessica had asked if she could bring anything to the party, which somehow my mom had interpreted as Jessica asking to bring macaroni salad, so my mom was insulted by the idea that she could be perceived as the kind of person who would throw a party that merited a bowl of macaroni salad).

But maybe Bibi's curiosity won out, or she wanted to see if I was really on the natural blue diet rumored by the tabloids (there were so few natural blue foods that the blue diet was actually a cover for an eating disorder). "All right," she said. "Meet me at Avianna tomorrow at noon."

Avianna—a buzzy new restaurant that had come out of nowhere to hit all the city's best-of lists. And all the way across town. At least it was in a location I couldn't easily take the subway to. It wasn't like I *would* take the subway, but it would mean I'd have Gabe telling me I should take the subway and giving me a judgy look when I of course would not. "It's a date."

The fly buzzing right into the spider's web. Avianna was the web, obviously. But which one of us was the fly, and which the spider?

CHAPTER Seventeen

I met Bibi the following day in a black dress, as was appropriate, I thought, for a lunch with a freshly minted widow (though paired with hot pink heels and a matching headband—it wasn't like *I* was a widow myself, and who knew who I'd run into at a hopping place like Avianna). She met me in a bright blue sheath dress, which caught me off guard. A very deliberate choice.

She also wasn't weeping as she spoke. She was smiling warmly, actually. "Pom, thanks so much for coming all the way here." Her arms closed gingerly around me in a hug that didn't actually result in any skin-to-skin contact. "So lovely to see you."

The host was kind enough to seat us at a table in the back, away from the big street-facing windows, so the only people who would be able to gawk at me would be fellow diners. I appreciated that. "So," I said sympathetically, once our waiter had come by to pour our waters and brief us on the specials. "I'm so sorry for your loss. Conrad was a good man."

Soft reggae music played from somewhere above us, barely audible over the sound of people talking quietly around us. Neither sound drowned out Bibi's snort. "He wasn't, but thank you."

I wasn't sure exactly what to say to that, which was a rarity. I smiled politely and wished the breadbasket had arrived so that I'd have something to do with my mouth other than respond.

Me being uncomfortable seemed to strike her as funny. She had a braying sort of laugh, one entirely unsuitable, I thought, for a brand-new widow. I hadn't put much thought into widowhood, but I guess I'd always pictured lots of black clothes (chic, of course; just because your husband was dead didn't mean fashion had died along with him), soft voices, not much indulgence. Though I guess if I died first, I wouldn't want Gabe to stop enjoying life. I mean, he definitely wouldn't enjoy it as much, but that was understandable, because I was a delight.

Bibi said, "I'm sorry. But the look on your face . . ."

I waited to hear what exactly the look on my face was, but just then the breadbasket arrived. The two of us busied ourselves with a caramelized onion corn bread and ramp butter (both still warm). It was so delicious that I made a mental note to look into a seasonal ramp special at the bakery (maybe in a hand pie format with some not-too-pungent cheese and some chicken). Bibi clearly agreed with me about how good it was—I couldn't help but notice that she ate the entire square. Older women in my circle, at least pre-Ozempic, tended to follow one of two paths: skinny, eats nothing; or actually eats food, carries some weight. I hoped at that age I would be secure enough with my body to confidently follow the latter. "It's very good," she said, as if reading my thoughts. "Conrad never would have come here with me—too 'ethnic' for him. One of the reasons I wanted to come now."

"Well," I said delicately. "Maybe you could have come with a friend."

She snorted again. "I don't have many friends left. One of the consequences of spending decades married to the social pariah." She picked up another chunk of corn bread. "He didn't like seeing me eat either. I'm so hungry."

Again, I wasn't sure what to say. *I'm glad you're happy he's dead?* That seemed inappropriate. *Why did you stay married to him?* So did that.

But it was as if she'd read my mind. "You're wondering why I stayed married to him, aren't you?" Her eyes went a little misty. "He was dashing back when we first started dating. Still a little nasty, but that's appealing when you're young, in a way. And then, later on, I was in too deep. He knew too much about me. If I left him, he'd have gone full scorched earth. Tell all the wrong people about who I'd slept with during our marriage, what family members I'd betrayed for Met Gala tickets, who I'd bribed for the right board seats. Oh no. That wouldn't do."

She sounded so casual about it that it was almost like she didn't realize she was admitting to having a motive. Then again, what did she care? She'd already been questioned by the police. She knew they didn't have anything concrete on her.

"He had a habit of that," she continued. "He liked collecting people's secrets." Like with Vienna. I wondered how many other secrets he'd collected. "He liked knowing things he wasn't supposed to know and holding them over people's heads."

"So," I said, just as casually. "Why did you put Vienna's earring in your dead husband's hand?"

She stared at me for a moment, shocked, then burst into that braying laugh. Phew. My instinct that she'd be more impressed by ballsiness than appalled had been correct. "What are you talking about?"

Okay. Either she was lying to me or I'd misjudged. How else could Vienna's earring have made it to Conrad, though, if Bibi hadn't brought it to him after bumping into Vienna? Timeline-wise, I wasn't sure how it would have worked, considering that, if Bibi was the killer, nobody else would've had time to bring it to him.

Unless Bibi wasn't the killer. I tabled that thought for a bit.

"So, about the building," I said, changing the subject. "I'm sure you heard it all from the police, but it really wasn't a big deal what happened." Carefully avoiding the eyes of my new bodyguard, who was seated at a table nearby enjoying his own basket of corn bread, I spilled the CliffsNotes of what had gone down, emphasizing how okay both we and the house were. "And the building itself is in great shape now after all the work we've been doing. We've stripped a lot of wallpaper, fixed a lot of the plumbing . . ."

A smile was playing on her lips. "That's nice to hear," she said. "You know, I lived in that building when I was young. My family bought it from the Melroses, who went on to something even bigger and better uptown."

William Melrose, the kid who'd doodled a bunch of superheroes. I nodded.

"It was why Conrad bought it," she said. "It was back when he was still trying to woo me. I told him how beautiful it had been and how sad I'd felt when we had to move and it had gotten broken up into multiple apartments. He had this plan to recombine the units back into one town home again, and then we'd live there. But there were always excuses about why he couldn't start the work." Her smile was now wry. "I think that knowing he wasn't going to sell it and profit from it dampened his enthusiasm for doing the work. It was a relief for him to unload it on you."

"So you want to live in it?" I asked. This was tough—it wasn't like I could try to talk her into another building I owned where she'd also lived as a child.

"You know, I've been thinking about it," she said. "I'm old now." If this were my mom, she'd pause so whoever she was speaking to could assure her that sixty was the new thirty, but Bibi just went on. "And it's only me right now, and I'm always going between New York and Palm Beach and sometimes Nantucket. I don't need a ton of space, and I do admire your mission. What if I take one of the apartments, the one on the top floor, for myself, and you can continue to use the other two for your organization?"

"That's very generous of you!" I said, and meant it, fully. The relief nearly swamped me. To keep myself from blurting out something embarrassing and emotional, I stuffed another piece of corn bread in my mouth. I did occasionally have corn bread at the bakery, but there was something almost malty in this one. Would the chef share the secret ingredient with me?

"I try," she said. "I'm happy to do it. As long as it won't be awkward with you and your parents, now that you'll be working directly with me on this."

I wrinkled my brow and let the words roll around in my head as the waiter came with our food (a Caribbean fusion take on a pastrami sandwich for her, a piri piri salad with squash and chicken for me). By the time he left, I was no closer to understanding what they'd meant. "Why would it be awkward?"

She laughed, then stopped laughing when I didn't join her. "Sorry. I thought you were joking. Dear, have they never told you why Conrad and I were never at their galas?"

She'd already said it, so I figured it was safe to say it too. "Because nobody liked Conrad?"

"Well, yes," Bibi said. "But not only that. I go by Bibi, but my full first name is Roberta." She paused to wipe a smear of Creole mayo delicately from the corner of her mouth. "Did you really not know I used to be married to your father?"

CHAPTER Eighteen

Bibi was my father's first wife?

My parents had never told me. Which checked out, I guess, because they never told me anything that might be relevant or helpful.

Or. In this case. Maybe they didn't tell me because it made my dad look a bit suspicious. I mean, he'd cheated on Bibi with my mom, then left Bibi for my mom. Bibi had married Conrad, and my parents didn't want her around, and then . . . okay, maybe it didn't make my dad look that suspicious. Which was a relief. I didn't want to have to interrogate my parents again. Suspecting your parents for murder should be a once-in-a-lifetime thing (ideally a never-in-a-lifetime thing, but for *my* parents, once was pretty good).

Still, I found myself rapidly reevaluating what my parents had said earlier about my dad's ex-wife, only attaching Bibi's face to the barbs. My mom: *She lost, and I won.* My dad: *She wasn't exactly fighting the divorce. She wanted the Nantucket house.*

Oh my God. Bibi at the gala: *Have fun with that skank.* My MOM was the "skank."

Bibi said gently, "Dear, you do realize your mouth is still hanging open."

I shut it with a snap. "I'm sorry. I'm just surprised."

That braying laugh again. God, no wonder my mother hated her. The only laugh I'd ever heard my mom make was a pointed one, usually at someone else's expense. "No, I shouldn't be surprised that you don't know. It was a long time ago."

To be fair, I hadn't known at all that my dad had been married before my mom until she let it slip last year during my murder investigation. Bibi continued, "And we were only married for three years. No kids. I think most of society immediately forgot that they'd ever attended our wedding." She raised her eyebrows. "Except for Grace, of course."

Even though my mother was maybe the worst person ever, I couldn't betray her to this woman she saw as her rival. "Oh, I don't know about that."

"I do." She snorted, taking a big bite of her sandwich and chewing thoroughly before responding again. "She spread rumors around town that she was the one who didn't invite me and Conrad to any Afton parties. That was partly true. We were invited to a few of them at first, but I stopped going because she made it all so stressful. I was wearing a Cartier sapphire brooch? She had to be wearing the Cartier panther watch. I was wearing three-inch heels? Hers had to be higher. So she stopped sending the invitations." She paused for another bite. "This sandwich is so good. You know, that's how she commissioned those trademark stilettos of hers. I was wearing the highest heels most of our favorite designers offered, but she wanted more."

Well. That sounded exactly like my mother. "Hmm," I said noncommittally.

"I grew very tired of it very quickly," she said. "A certain amount of game playing is par for the course. I mean, we've got a rarefied pocket of people who have far too much money and want to prove that they deserve it without having to work too hard, so what else are they going to do? But there are plenty of galas in the city and I didn't need to spend my time at ones where the hostess spent all of our conversations taking digs at Nantucket and anyone who wants to spend time there."

Understandable. I gave her a twist of my mouth that was somewhere between a grimace and a smile. Now I felt terrible for having seated them all together at the gala. "Well. I'll make sure to keep them away from you at any future galas or events I throw."

"Much appreciated." She shook her head. "I got so fed up sitting at that table. It's not your fault, Pom—you didn't know—but both your mother and my husband spent the night making less and less subtle digs at me. *I can't believe you can even see through eyes with pouches that big. You're going to eat all of your salmon? Don't you know that salmon is the fattiest fish? I'm so glad I have children to invite me to things like this; it must be lonely without them.* I finally couldn't take it a second longer and snapped. Told my asshole of a husband to have fun sitting with your skank of a mother. Sorry." She didn't sound that sorry. "Called my lawyer on my way to the bathroom and told him I wanted to get the divorce process moving. Conrad thought I'd been having an affair, but I was actually secretly meeting with lawyers to see if I could get him to sign something that would keep my secrets safe." She smirked. "I'd have to see him again, but not being married to Conrad meant that I wouldn't have to go places with him, which meant I'd never have to see your father—and mother—again. Which was such a relief, I almost couldn't believe it. I think I said something to your friend about it when I ran into her outside the bathroom."

"She might have mentioned something about that," I said vaguely.

"Yes. I was ready to be done with your father, and my husband as well. But not *that* done." She frowned. "I don't need his money or his estate—I have plenty of my own—but now I'm going to have to spend months or years dealing with it instead of making a clean break. What a pain."

"I'm so sorry," I said.

She waved a hand in the air. "It's fine. That's what lawyers are for. And I suppose I have the better end of the deal. You know, not being dead."

"Very true."

"But enough of that." She waved a hand in the air again, though now there was a glint of mischief in her blue, blue eyes. "You didn't come here to hear me trash my dead husband. And I didn't come here to offer you most of the building. That could've been an email."

I waited for her to tell me why we were here, then, but she seemed like she wanted me to make the connection myself. "Um, the food is really good?"

"No. I mean, yes, but no," she said, and leaned in, displacing the basket of corn bread with her elbow so that it edged menacingly close to the edge of the table. "I wanted to hear more about you. I've never had to live without my accustomed lifestyle. Except in college, where I lived in a dorm for the adventure, but everybody knew that was temporary. And you came back from your adventure with a boyfriend! How was that?"

"I've actually been in talks with a few publishers about doing a memoir about it, and then my film agent is rabid to adapt it into a series," I said. With all the excitement going on lately, I'd almost forgotten. She'd asked me if I wanted to star in it myself. I wasn't sure if I was willing to risk another Razzie.

"Huh," Bibi said. "I'd imagine that they'd have been trying to get you to write a book for ages."

"Not really," I said. My fan base was not known to be buyers of books, but everything around my grandma's murder had reached the greater cultural sphere. "Though yeah, it was something, all right. Not an experience I really want to repeat anytime soon, but I'm grateful for it."

"Well, you must be, given the boyfriend." Her eyes gleamed now with something other than mischief. "He's really quite handsome. I might consider forgoing some jewelry or vacations to dip my fingers in that for a bit. Where is he from again?"

I cleared my throat. "Here."

"No, where is he *really* from?"

"Here," I said, a little louder. I bristled at the casual way she was depicting our relationship. "And I'm not 'dipping my fingers' in anything. It's serious."

Those glittering eyes widened. "Oh, really? I thought you were just having some fun before settling down."

"Nope." The remains of my salad were limp and cold on my plate. I glanced around for the waiter, hoping I could do that subtle nod that meant bring the check, but he was nowhere to be seen.

"So you're getting married?" She reached over and casually plucked a piece of squash from my plate, popping it in her mouth. "Oh, you're done with this, aren't you?"

My stomach roiled, not at all due to the squash, which was excellent. "I don't know if marriage is that important to me," I lied breezily, wishing desperately for something to do with my mouth other than talk but not really wanting to eat the squash she'd fondled. "You can be committed without marriage."

"That's probably true," she said. "I suppose I'm not exactly the poster child for healthy marriages." She said it in a way that was so frank and matter-of-fact that I was nodding before I could help myself. "And it's probably better not to link yourself legally to someone else. Look at what I'm going through right now."

I frowned in sympathy, as if it were truly a terrible hardship to inherit an enormous portfolio of lucrative investments and enviable real estate holdings. It was tempting to make a joke that wasn't really a joke about how she could just sign it over to my nonprofit if she didn't want to deal with it all, but somehow I suspected that wouldn't go over well.

"And it's especially true when the person you're with is at such a different income level than yourself. Look at Denise Ryan's ex. He was already a tech mogul before he married her, a bartender from nowhere, and now look. That bartender from nowhere is giving away half his fortune," Bibi said. "You marry your teacher boyfriend, and then what? In twenty years he's giving away half *your* fortune."

"Denise and her ex were together since college, they just didn't marry until his company succeeded. Most of my 'fortune' is in my family trust and inheritance, which is automatically shielded from a divorce, and I assume, based on my brother's experience, the family lawyers will doubly shield it anyway," I said, annoyed at how annoyed I was. "And he wouldn't do that. He's not marrying me for my money. If anything . . ."

I trailed off before I could say it, but it was too late. Bibi had a keen eye for both food and good gossip. She leaned forward, not for a piece of my squash this time. "He doesn't want to marry you? Is that it?"

"To be fair, we've only been together about a year," I said. We'd discussed getting engaged a while ago, though. I'd really thought it was going to come soon. "It's okay if he wants to wait."

"But you didn't say he wanted to wait, did you?" she said. "You said he didn't want to get married."

I hadn't said any of that, but okay. "Again, to be fair, we haven't really talked about it."

"It sounds like you've talked about it enough," she said. "Maybe he's waiting for you to beg. Sometimes men like that."

"He wouldn't do that." *Right?*

"Trust me, as someone who's been married three times"—I was definitely going to have to google that third one. Where would she even have fit it in?—"if you've got too many differences in how you grew up, it won't last. He'll never really be able to understand our world. He'll always feel like an outsider, and, over time, it will cause resentment between the two of you. Like he moved to a different country where they speak a different language than you."

Well. All the corn bread I'd eaten balled itself into a wet, heavy lump and dropped to the bottom of my stomach. She'd hit on all my greatest fears in one short speech.

"I can see the panic in your eyes," Bibi said. "Don't worry. I can always set you up with my nephew. Chip. Do you know him? I think he went to Princeton with your brother."

Of course I knew Chip. He'd played squash, taken a beaming photo on top of Mount Kilimanjaro without the porters who'd carried all of his stuff up, and was (in)famous for vomiting out of a skydiving plane the morning of his twenty-sixth birthday. We'd hooked up a couple of times a few years ago and he'd proven himself a competent and enthusiastic lover, if not particularly inspiring. That Pom of a few years ago probably would've considered him as a good match for when all of her friends started coupling up and having kids.

This Pom couldn't stomach the thought of marrying someone who had never thanked the person who made him coffee—not because he was malicious or anything, but because he'd never think to do it, because he'd never really thought about the person making him coffee as a person. And yes, I could tell him to say thank you, and if he cared about me, he'd do it. But it would be like the time I got mad at Opal so I skipped her birthday party and jetted off to the South of France. I was still mad at Opal, just mad at Opal in the South of France. And then later she killed my grandmother.

Maybe I kind of lost the thread there. Anyway. "Thank you," I said politely to Bibi, because politeness was everything, at least when somebody was giving you a building in Chelsea for free. "I appreciate the offer, but Gabe is very important to me."

"Well. If you change your mind." She slung her bag, a classy white Chanel, off the back of her chair. "Shall we go?"

"Don't we have to pay?"

"It's on my tab," she said. "Don't worry about it. Conrad is treating." She laughed. I laughed back to be polite, even though I was slightly appalled.

"Thank you. I appreciate it."

"You're quite welcome," she said. "Though now you really can't tell your father. He'd be quite displeased."

I furrowed my brow as I plucked my own bag (a floral Chanel in a slightly more modern, boxy silhouette than hers) from my chair. "What do you mean? I thought he cheated on you. Surely he couldn't be angry that you moved on."

A new laugh from Bibi: less of a bray, more of a cackle. "Oh, my dear. Is that what he told you?"

I nodded yes, somehow feeling like I'd reverted back to a little girl, back when I'd say something adorable at the dinner table, like about how I knew how babies were made, they were handcrafted in factories in Paris and purchased by the highest bidder, and everybody would chuckle.

"Oh no, my darling," Bibi said. She glanced over her shoulder as we were maneuvering our way out of the restaurant, sidestepping people's tables and letting waiters sidestep us. "I cheated on him first. I cheated on him often. My affairs were legendary."

Her affairs couldn't have been that legendary if who she'd ended up with was Conrad Phlume, of all people. But I nodded anyway, because I wanted her to keep talking.

"He cheated on me with Grace for revenge," she continued. "And then she got pregnant, so he was stuck. He cried when I told him we'd be getting a divorce." I wasn't sure if I'd ever seen my father cry. Not even when his own father died. He'd drunk about three bottles of scotch, gone to the funeral, passed out on the couch at home, and then gone to work the next day like nothing had happened, except that he sat in his father's office instead of his own. "Oh, he was so upset when he found out I was engaged to Conrad. Called me at night while your mother was sleeping and begged me to take him back. But I had zero interest in stepchildren." She glanced back at me. "No offense."

"None taken." It wasn't me she was talking about, after all.

I would also have zero interest in raising a Nicholas. "Yeah, wow. Nobody ever told me any of this."

She snorted, opening the glass door to the restaurant and ignoring the host telling us to have a nice day. "Of course they wouldn't. Your parents are so lucky that the tabloids were all distracted by the Trump divorce of the day. Otherwise they would've been on every page."

Her shiny black car pulled up smoothly at the curb, not even having to double-park. "Anyway, Pom, this was lovely," she said as her driver stepped out to open her door. "I'll be in contact about the building. I'd love to speak with you about any work you've already done in my apartment."

I nodded. I probably should have said something appreciative again, but I seemed to have lost the ability to speak. She nodded back, then stepped inside the car and was whisked away.

My phone buzzed. God, I hoped it was my driver; I really needed to go home and stick my head under my pillow and either scream into it or try to suffocate myself. But no, of course not. It was Millicent blowing up my group chat with her and Coriander again. Pom you went to Avianna without us???

Then Coriander. Omg Pom and you didn't even sit by the front window??? How are people even supposed to know you went there?

They'd found out somehow, so there. I tucked my phone away with a sigh. I did *not* have time for them right now. Not while I was busy reevaluating everybody's potential motives. It seemed safe to say that Bibi was not a real suspect any longer—I mean, I wasn't comfortable fully counting anybody out without real evidence (I'd done that with Opal early in my investigation last time, and look how that had worked out), but she didn't seem to have much of a motive.

Not as much of a motive as some other people in the mix. Like, maybe a man who'd been abandoned by the woman he loved for a man he despised, and was still smarting about it years later, but whose feelings had been held mostly at bay by scotch and by the distance imposed by his wife. Only to have that distance evaporated by his oblivious daughter, leading to an explosive confrontation with that man he despised, which ended in a push from a high place and a fall onto a sharp object.

Where had my parents been lately, anyway? Suspiciously absent, that's where. I was used to them popping up out of nowhere like they'd done the morning of the gala. But they'd been hiding away, like they were afraid of being perceived by their brilliant investigator of a daughter.

Don't bleed on the couch, Richard. My mom had said that over the phone the day after the gala. She said my dad had had a nosebleed. Or . . . maybe his knuckles had split open from punching Conrad Phlume. I couldn't believe I hadn't thought more about it. When was the last time I'd seen my dad with a nosebleed?

Gabe looked up as I walked through our door, still stewing. "How was your lunch?"

I flopped down dramatically on our couch, sprawling with one arm over the side, groaning out the sound of a dying moose. "I think my parents might have killed someone."

"Again?"

The moose was definitely dead now. "Again."

CHAPTER Nineteen

The one positive about having parents who consistently underestimated you in every way was that it wasn't all that hard to manipulate them. For example, if they thought you were too stupid to solve an actual murder (even though you'd already done it once before, but who's counting?), they wouldn't assume an innocent dinner invitation was actually an interrogation.

Or so I triumphantly told Gabe the next afternoon, only to have his face slacken with dismay. "Did you forget my mom was supposed to come over for dinner tonight?"

Yes. Yes, I had forgotten. But, judging from that look on his face, that was the wrong answer. So I said, confidently, because you can get away with saying anything as long as you say it confidently (mental note: chapter title for my memoir): "Of course not. I was thinking that it would be a great night for the parents to meet. You've been saying that we should get them together."

He blinked at me, probably hating that I was correct. "Right. I have been."

I continued, growing in confidence as I went. "It's best to do it like this, I think. Just rip the Band-Aid off." My mom wouldn't be too mean or lie too much in front of a witness. She'd want to make sure she looked good in case Andrea was selling secrets to the tabloids. "It'll be great."

"Right," Gabe said dubiously. "Okay. Well, I guess it's too late to uninvite anyone." Thanks for the vote of confidence, beloved boyfriend. "And also to change the menu, right? I mean, nothing I make is going to impress your parents, and your mom doesn't eat anything anyway, so it's okay if I still make my roast chicken, potatoes, and salad?" I nodded, because everything he said was true. Also, his roast chicken over potatoes was delicious. "And then maybe you can pick up bread and some cakes from the bakery for dessert? My mom loves the pink lemonade tarts."

A bubble of pride burst inside me. I'd spent weeks tinkering with those tarts, making them pink without using any artificial coloring (the secret was a little bit of rhubarb, but not too much, or it would make the tarts too tart, which, ironically, you did not want). "Sure," I said brightly. Gabe stared at me for another moment.

"You're going to interrogate them, aren't you?"

I patted him fondly on one stubbly cheek. "Not 'them.' Just my dad."

Another pause, another stare. "I suppose there's no way to talk you out of this, is there?"

"Hey," I said. "How long do we want to let a murderer run free?"

He had no answer to that, but I could see it in his eyes. *You're so right, Pom. Let loose the hounds of justice and let them bay until said justice is found, even if it wakes us up too early and is extremely annoying. I am your faithful sidekick, ready to serve. Your instincts are, as always, entirely brilliant.* "Thank you," I said generously.

He blinked. "For what?"

Honestly, I was glad we weren't pushing out this whole thing. I already felt like I was going to throw up at the idea that—again, freaking *again*—I had to interrogate my parents for murder, and I knew it wouldn't fade until—again, hopefully freaking again—they were cleared. So at least I only had a couple of hours of my stomach swimming and me trying to tame it into submission with some yoga before our dinner party began.

Andrea was the first to arrive, a bottle of wine in her hand. "This is for you," she said, handing it to me, then leaning in to kiss both of my cheeks. "You don't have to open it tonight."

"No, of course we will," I said, even though it was a heavy, fruity red, totally wrong for chicken, and I didn't recognize the label, which didn't bode well for eliciting anything but puckers from my parents. "It looks delicious. Thank you."

"Of course." She leaned back, smiling wide. It was amazing how she hadn't aged at all since her years as my nanny (fingers crossed Gabe had inherited those age-defying genes). Her black hair was threaded with silver, but flowed thick and lustrous to her shoulders; yes, she was curvy and soft in a way that would make my mom recoil and call her doctor, but Andrea was winning the wrinkle game even though she was up against my mom's cheat code of surgery. "I have to be honest, I'm a little nervous about seeing your parents again."

As I would be, too, if I were her, but I chose not to say that. "Don't be nervous! You used to see them every day, and it was fine."

She didn't fiddle with her hair or toy with the edges of a sleeve, but she did press her lips together, which was her calm, unflappable version of fidgeting. "Not in this context."

Not in a context of equals, she meant. When she used to see them every day, she was their employee. She hadn't been young or pretty or rich enough for my dad to even remember her name, and my mom was one of those people who liked to pretend she didn't have a nanny for her kids when asked by women's magazines or newspaper columnists about how she "did it all."

"It'll be fine," I said cheerfully, not entirely sure I meant it. "Come in."

She went to the bathroom, and Gabe swooped in behind me to whisper in my ear. Advisable, since his mother had the hearing of a bat, something I'd learned when I was ten and decided I wanted to have a lemonade stand like all the kids did in the books I read, except obviously I only wanted to sell the best product possible, which meant using the sweet, juicy lemons I'd tried on the Amalfi Coast, which meant coordinating via whisper between an overnight shipping company in Italy and my dad's stolen credit card. (Like, I was only trying to do right by my customers???)

Anyway, he said, "Are you sure this is a good idea? We could call your parents and tell them we've been exposed to the flu or something."

"My mom loves getting sick, because it means she has an excuse to lie in bed and not exercise for her usual two hours a day and to order my dad to bring her things," I said. "No. Our parents have to be in the same room together sometime. Let's get it over with now." I was talking about myself as much as them. "You don't want the first time they meet as equals to be at our wedding, right? That would be awkward." I glanced over my shoulder to see if panic or excitement or any emotion that could give me a hint about how he was feeling, really, seriously, please, flashed over his face. Nothing. As usual, the man was impassive as a rock.

We were interrupted by a knock at the door. My mom didn't wait for me to respond, just pushed the door in. How had she gotten past the doorman and my security guy? I really needed to get my locks changed.

"Pom," she said, leaning in for a bony cheek bump, leaning back with a waft of her subtle perfume, which Reginald Poivre formulated especially for her and somehow left you with the impression that you'd walked by an undercover film star (not movie star. There's a difference). "So lovely to be here. I noticed a loose tile in your lobby's mosaic. You might want to inform the doorman. You do have a doorman, don't you?"

"Of course I have a doorman," I said. "You probably swept right by him. His name is Byron. You have a friend named Byron, don't you?"

She was as stone-faced as Gabe. "I don't recall."

She did, of course, recall. Who could forget the months of rumors splashed across every tabloid about her and Byron, her all-too-personal trainer? But she still hadn't figured out how to respond by the time my dad cleared his throat behind her, prompting her to move on. Hopefully she wouldn't take it out on Andrea.

"Oh, how nice to see you, Angela," I heard from the other room.

Great.

I bared my teeth at my dad. "Thanks for coming."

"I'm sorry," he said, and we both knew he was apologizing on behalf of my mom. He liked to do things like that: apologize without even trying to do anything about whatever he was apologizing for.

Most of me knew that this was just him, and he was who he was, and at this point in his life he wasn't going to change. There was a little part of me that still believed, though, a small, bright part I didn't want to douse yet. "You know, you could say something."

"I know," he said. "I'm sorry."

My eyes immediately dropped to his hand, which was covered in a wrist brace. "What happened?"

He shook his arm out, frowning. "The carpal tunnel flaring up again."

"I see," I said. Convenient. "How about your nose?"

He looked at me blankly. "My what?"

"Your nosebleeds," I said. "Mom said you've been getting them lately, remember? 'Don't get blood on the couch.'" I let the words hang in the air for a moment before the blankness in his eyes crystallized into recognition. "You should probably get that looked at."

"Right, right, the nosebleeds," he said. "Yes, yes, I should."

I let him hug me, certain that he was lying. But he couldn't be a killer, right? I'd find out over Gabe's delicious roast chicken and schmaltzy potatoes and magical salad dressing (the secret was pickled shallots, which apparently wasn't a secret at all but a standard recipe, which sounds fake, but okay).

We served the food pretty much immediately so that we only had to suffer so much small talk about the weather and . . . that was it, basically, since that was about all my parents and Andrea had in common. I needed my parents to relax a bit and feel like they were superior before springing any murder talk on them. At least at the table they could talk about the food, and I wanted to get something in front of them before my mom could ask about—

"And where is Gabe's father?" my mom asked.

Double great. Gabe had wondered beforehand if I might request to my parents that they not say anything about the subject, but I'd shut that down immediately, because telling my mom not to mention something would mean she'd concoct the absolute most painful way to mention it at the most inopportune moment.

Andrea's face pinched. I cringed inside. Even knowing that this was the best way to handle it, considering that we'd be able to wrap it up and move on without my mom bringing it up over and over again, I couldn't help but feel like an absolute garbage person. "He lives in Texas," she said. I prayed she wouldn't say anything else and give my parents any more ammunition.

Gabe's face was like stone. His father wasn't in his life much. He'd left him, Andrea, and Caleb, Gabe's brother, when Gabe was three. He was an above-average father in the realm of sending birthday cards mostly on time and issuing invitations to visit him and his new family in Texas anytime, except for whatever time Gabe suggested, because somehow he was always busy then. I'd never actually met him, only heard his voice briefly on the phone the day after Gabe's birthday.

"Try some of the salad," I said hastily, motioning to the huge pile of it on my mom's plate, where it crowded out the paper-thin slice of chicken she'd taken to be polite. "Gabe makes this really good dressing."

My mom gingerly placed a leaf into her mouth and chewed like it was trying to bite her back. "Mmm," she said unconvincingly. "Very oily."

I wasn't sure if that was a backhanded compliment or if she was genuinely trying to be nice. I chose to believe the latter. "It's much better than the salad at my gala, though of course the memory is tainted," I said, as casually as possible. "I can't believe we haven't talked about it yet. You were sitting next to Conrad Phlume that night. How are you feeling?"

"Oh, it's devastating, of course, even though he was such a nasty person," my mom said with not a little bit of glee. "It's a tragedy whenever someone loses their life. Especially when it was someone who was sitting at your table, which means the police come to question you more than once even though you tell them you have an extremely important hot yoga class to go to."

"That's the true tragedy," I said somberly. My mom nodded as if I were finally the daughter she'd wished for her whole life. Hopefully Andrea knew I wasn't actually this shallow and callous. "Dad, how about you? How are you feeling?"

He glanced up from his lap, where he probably had his phone open so that he could follow the Japanese stock market or get angry at the news. "Me? Oh, I'm fine. I'm always fine."

"How did you guys know Conrad again?" I asked. "You didn't invite him to your galas for years before everybody else stopped doing it. *So* ahead of the curve."

"I usually am," preened my mother. But I didn't want to hear her prattle off some lie about how they'd met Conrad and his wife years ago at some gala or other where my mother was valiantly trying to save a herd of small children from falling into a fiery cauldron over which Bibi was cackling like a witch.

"Dad?" I pressed him. He looked up. Was I seeing things, or was there a faint sheen of sweat on his face? He licked his upper lip.

"What?"

"How do you know Conrad and his wife?"

He gave an awkward little stutter of a laugh. "Them? Oh, uh, I . . ." I stared him down, refusing to avert my eyes. He sweated more. Licked his upper lip again. Ugh, gross. "I, uh, it was a . . ."

My mom sighed. "Oh, stop it, Richard," she snapped. "She clearly knows." She turned to me. "How did you find out? Did you talk to that woman about us?"

"Not *about* you," I said. "I spoke to Bibi about the murder. We had what was actually a very pleasant lunch, and yes, she shared that she'd previously been married to my father."

Mom huffed. "'Married' is a generous word for it. Left behind and—"

"Enough," I said, refusing to look away from my dad. He was literally squirming in his seat. You'd think that, as an experienced businessman who did a ton of negotiations, he'd be used to uncomfortable conversations. "Why did you guys never tell me?"

"There was no reason to," my dad said miserably enough where I almost felt sorry for him. "We never saw them. Roberta and I had never had kids, so the break was clean. It was before you were born. What would have been the point?"

Fair enough. I didn't know if I'd want to talk to my future children about the people I'd dated in the past (sure, my ex-fiancé would inherit that ancestral castle, which might be worth mentioning, but there were so many ghosts in it! Also, his mother got to live there until she died and would haunt the place too). "Okay. I understand."

But meanwhile, as Gabe and Andrea glanced back and forth between me and my dad as if we were players in a tennis match, my mom was narrowing her eyes. "You're investigating again, aren't you?"

There was no point in lying. I might be really good at it, but my mom was even better at sniffing me out. So I just kept my eyes on my dad as he slowly, uncomfortably withered in his chair. "Dad, can I see your hand?"

He held up his left hand, the one not covered by the wrist brace. I sighed. Come on, man. "The other hand, obviously."

"Oh, this is so cute," Mom sneered. "You think you're Miss Marple, don't you? Darling, you stumbled onto the answer to the last one, and now you're getting in over your—"

I talked over her, eyes still trained on my dad. *"Your other hand."*

Mom, clearly seeing that her attempt to shrink me wasn't working, turned to my dad. "Richard, you don't have to—"

"Dad, let me see—"

He stopped us both by raising his right arm and undoing the straps that held on the brace. It was kind of anticlimactic—undoing it with his left hand only was clearly a struggle, but nobody wanted to break the spell and jump in to help him. Eventually it fell with a soft thud onto his chicken. I sucked in a breath as he rotated it for us all to see.

There was no carpal tunnel there. Not unless carpal tunnel created fading bruising down the back of your hand, and scabs where the knuckles had clearly split (it didn't, did it?). "It's much better than it was the night of the gala," he said, still holding it in the air as if it were a trophy. "I don't know how I got out of there without the police stopping me. There was blood running down my arm into the sleeve of my tuxedo. It was totally ruined. I'm going to have to go to the tailor and get measured for a new one, which I'm not happy about."

I held that breath I'd sucked in. "Was it you?" I asked. "Did you kill him?"

He gazed back at me, his eyes vacant, his jaw set under his trim beard. Which was graying, I was somehow surprised to see. Had it always been that gray? "I'm not going to lie and say I'd never thought about it," he said. "But it had been years since I'd come face-to-face with him. Seeing him there, it was like it was thirty years ago again. All those same emotions washed over me like a tidal wave. Of fire."

My dad never had been one for metaphors, but I shot my mom a warning look before she could point that out. She sat back in her chair and scowled, stuffing another lettuce leaf in her mouth and grimacing as she chewed. Andrea and Gabe both sat totally still, rapt, as if the slightest movement might stop my dad from confessing. "I realized I'd never actually spoken to him about what happened. Or Roberta, aside from a bit there at the end." The begging, I assumed. "So when I saw him heading up to the second floor for a cigar or something, I thought I would follow and talk to him. Just talk. It had been a lot of years, after all. Maybe he would apologize to me."

Not to get off topic, but this might have been the longest string of words my dad had spoken to me in . . . well, ever. We weren't much of a talking family, and my dad and I had never had many interests in common. I had no idea what all the business numbers meant or what a golf handicap was. He had no idea what the difference was between a cowl, butterfly, or petal sleeve, or why I would want to dedicate my time and resources to helping the less fortunate.

Dad went on, his eyebrows drawing together. Had he always had so many wrinkles in his forehead? "We went up the stairs and around the corner to a nook in the hallway with pillars in the way of the staircase. He stopped at the railing and looked down at the party below, but he turned around when he heard my footsteps. He looked surprised to see me. 'Oh, it's you?' he said.

"How dare he. 'Oh, it's you?' As if he was surprised to see me there. It was the same thing he'd said at our table. This was my daughter's first gala. Of course I'd be there."

The genuine bafflement in his voice almost made me feel a little bad about purposely not inviting him. Almost.

He went on. "I didn't beat around the bush. None of us have time for that, not at our age. I asked him, 'Why?' And can you believe it?" He shook his head. "He had the nerve to squint at me and ask, 'What are you talking about?'"

I raised an eyebrow, then lowered it as I realized I probably looked way too much like my mother. "Are you saying he didn't remember stealing your wife?" I winced a little saying it—no human being could be stolen; Bibi had played an equal part in the dissolution of their marriage—but I knew that wasn't how my dad saw it, and I really wanted him to be primed for an honest answer.

"It seemed that way," Dad said darkly. "Or else he wanted me to think so, because he's a smug asshole. Either way, I punched him."

"You punched him?" I cried. Not in surprise: that much had been obvious by the state of his hand. It was just hard to imagine my mild-mannered father, who could barely carry on an uncomfortable conversation, physically assaulting someone.

"Hard. In the face," said Dad. "In the eye, to be precise. He shouted and reeled back toward the railing."

"And that's when he fell off," I breathed. "You didn't mean it, but that's how it happened."

"Are you joking, Pomona?" said my mom. She turned to my dad. "She's joking, isn't she, Richard?"

He was staring at me. "It's a pretty awful joke, if so," he said. "No, Pom. I didn't kill him, I only punched him. It hurt my hand. I had to go ice it. Also, he tried to punch me back, and I wasn't there to get into a fight. I wouldn't do anything to ruin my daughter's very first gala."

That was rich, coming from the person who'd started the fight. I didn't bring that up. Not out loud, at least.

"I can tell what you're thinking," Dad said. "And thank you. Yes, I am a good father." I bit my tongue. "And I have an alibi. I went to one of the bars along the side to get a napkin and ice for my hand. I was there chatting with the bartender at the time Conrad fell. I told him I'd gotten so angry at the injustice being done to those kids you're helping that I couldn't help but punch a pillar."

"Wow. Okay," I said. That explained why he hadn't appeared in any of the photos taken around the time of the murder. "Thanks for letting me know. I appreciate it."

He straightened his shoulders, lifting his chin as if preparing for me to place a medal around his neck. "You're welcome."

My mom muttered something, shaking her head, then glanced at me as if waiting for me to ask her to repeat herself. I didn't, because anything she muttered under her breath wasn't something I particularly wanted to hear.

But she repeated herself anyway. "I cannot believe that our daughter once again thought we were murderers. The shame of it. And in front of the help." She cast a withering gaze at Andrea, who looked more amused than anything.

"Andrea is not the help," I said wearily.

"You know what I mean," said my mother.

"I do," I said. "And it was incredibly rude." I stopped short of saying she should apologize, because she would twist it into some awful passive-aggressive dig at Andrea that would hurt worse than what she'd already said. Andrea still just looked amused, honestly. She knew my mother.

Mom shook her head. "Honestly. I have such ungrateful children." She muttered something else, but this time I actually wanted to hear it.

"Children? Are you talking about both me and Nicholas?"

"Traitors, both of you," she said. "He tries to overthrow his own father on the board, and you keep thinking we've murdered someone. Such terrible children."

"Nicholas *what*?" I said, shocked. Though not that shocked, honestly. Staging a coup wasn't all that out of character for my brother.

"It's that Jessica's influence," she said. "I know it. My darling boy would never do something like that on his own."

My dad was wrapping his arm back up in his brace, but looked up to say, "Let's not talk about this here, dear. Pom's not involved in the business. Andrea, your oldest son is a detective with the NYPD, isn't he? Very impressive."

I had to give it to my dad when he'd earned it: It was a masterful change of subject that made this dinner party slightly less horrible. After Andrea bragged about her sons for a while, my dad actually bragged about me, how my bakery was profitable and not losing money like the businesses of his friends' daughters (respectively: a publishing company focused on poetry about poetry; a boutique that sold only clothes knitted from faux goat wool; a pet yoga business, as in yoga *for* pets, no snakes allowed) and how proud he was of me for sticking it out in the real world, and not only sticking it out but thriving and solving a murder while doing it. It would've been nice if he could've looked at me while saying any of it or had indeed ever said any of it to me before, but it made me all teary-eyed anyway.

Same with my mom—as my dad went on, her face got more and more pinched and sour. When she clearly couldn't take another second of someone else being praised instead of her, she interjected, "Richard, we'd best head out soon. Don't forget you have that call with Jack about the purchase of that bed-and-breakfast."

Right, Jack Wohl. He'd been at the gala, too, also unpictured in the alibi photos. I didn't know him well, only that my parents and the Afton company as a whole were pretty heavily invested in his hedge fund. "How's Jack doing?" I said casually.

"Oh, fine," Mom said. "All business talk, as always. Though I did hear a rumor . . ."

"It's not a rumor," said Dad. "Fred saw them out together."

"Fred could be lying for attention," said Mom.

My mom was the only one in this circle who lied for attention, but okay. "What's this rumor?"

"It's not a rumor," Dad repeated, a little annoyed, as if I hadn't heard him the first time. "Fred saw Jack Wohl out with Denise Ryan."

That was not an exciting rumor. "So? She might have been asking him to donate to her nonprofit. Or investing in something herself and needed his help."

My mom snorted. "That was *not* a dress you wear to a business meeting."

"How do you know?" I said. "You weren't even there."

Mom sighed. "Well. It was great seeing you, Angela."

"It was great seeing you too," said Andrea, with the grace not to call my mom Gail or Gloria. I didn't bother lying to them and saying it had been great to see them as well, just gave them limp goodbye hugs as they left. When the door closed behind them, a weight lifted off my shoulders, like after taking off my wings the year I'd walked in the Victoria's Secret fashion show (those wings were surprisingly heavy, and I felt considerably more floaty and angelic once they were off. There was probably a metaphor there).

Andrea looked just as relieved to see them go. She stayed for a few minutes to chitchat, probably to make sure she wouldn't run into them on the sidewalk, then made her escape. "Well," said Gabe. "At least it wasn't one of your parents. Probably."

It was a relief, I supposed, to know that neither of my parents had murdered anyone this time. But, honestly, last time my mom had given me a clue that had pointed me to the next place to go. The next thread to pull. This time?

Ruling out my dad put me at a dead end. I didn't know who else to look at, or what else to look for.

CHAPTER Twenty

I needed more time to noodle upon my next suspect. There were still a number of people who weren't in an alibi photo, but I couldn't just go around spraying off interrogations willy-nilly. People would start to talk. No, I needed to be laser focused. I needed another motive. Conrad's habit of hoarding people's secrets must have come back to bite him, but those secrets had died with him. Which was a motive in itself. All I needed to know was *whose* secret had pushed him over the edge.

Literally.

So after I'd moaned and groaned and moped around the apartment a bit, I told Gabe, "Let's take a weekend for us. Let's go somewhere and have fun and not think about murder or dark secrets or anything horrible." I had to solve this murder to save my nonprofit and therefore the kids who needed it—needed me—but that could wait a weekend. Self-care was important too.

He stood up a little straighter, eyes gleaming. "Where?"

I took a moment to think. I didn't really want to go anywhere the social scene would find me. Most of the people I'd wanted to befriend, like Kitty and Libby and John, were still shunning me, and I couldn't be seen with the ones who didn't, because then the former would never take me back. And Gabe had seemed a little intimidated and stressed by our trip to Kevin

Miller's private island, so probably I didn't want to make a grand gesture like that again (there was also the small point of me being grounded from the jet). I was about to suggest going up to the house in the Berkshires, but stopped right before the words crossed my lips. My parents wouldn't be there, but it was still an Afton family home. Same for going to the Afton Philadelphia or Afton Portland.

I took a deep breath, already regretting what I was about to say. "How about that national park you've been wanting to go to? The one in Virginia? We can drive there."

"Shenandoah?"

"Yeah." I was already mad at myself. "We can get your tent and camping gear out of the storage cage in the basement and . . . use it. Go camping or whatever. It will be . . . fun."

Gabe's entire face lit up, which made it worth it. Almost. Kind of. "It's going to be so much fun. Sleeping in the great outdoors in all kinds of weather. Going to the bathroom outside. Cooking cans of beans over the campfire. Wearing the same clothes the entire time no matter how muddy and sweaty they get."

I did my absolute best to arrange my face so that it didn't look as if I were about to cry. "Yes. All of that."

A wry smile twitched at his lips. "Pom, you don't have to do this. I knew going into this relationship that you probably were not going to be my camping partner."

But maybe that was what was missing from our relationship. He accompanied me for all this stuff that was second nature and beloved to me, like galas and sunning on private islands, but I didn't do the things with him that he loved. Like—God—sleeping in a flimsy canvas cover that didn't totally keep out the mosquitos, all while marinating in the same sweaty clothes from your active day. "I can be, though," I said earnestly. "I want to be."

I really, really did not. But I would, if that's what I had to do. I squared my shoulders, lifting my chin, readying myself for the misery ahead.

Gabe sighed. "Look, I know what you're trying to do. And I appreciate it. But I would rather just go hike Shenandoah with Caleb when he has some time off than go with you, knowing you hate every second of it."

"I wouldn't hate every second of it," I said. "I'd enjoy being there with you."

He leaned in and gave me a gentle kiss on the lips. The tension in my shoulders melted, a little of the stress in my stomach easing away. "Why don't we do something that we'd both enjoy? Like the Queens Night Market. I've been meaning to go back for ages, but we were a little distracted last summer."

I knew what I'd just said, but I still couldn't keep myself from grimacing. A national park was one thing. But Queens? I'd had quite enough of Queens last year.

But this wasn't about me. I mean, it *was* about me—most things were—but it was also about Gabe. I said, "I'd go anywhere with you."

• • •

Even back to Queens. We stepped out of our car into a cool but sticky evening, the smells of grilling meat and candied nuts drifting through the air around us. Hand in hand, we walked through a packed park, kids playing volleyball on one side of us and more kids riding bikes on the other, stands selling ices and churros and cold drinks lining the sides of this central pathway. Ahead of us sprawled an enormous grass field lined with tents and already bustling with people.

"I can't believe you've lived in the city most of your life and you've still never been here," Gabe said, craning his neck over the line of people ahead of us waiting to go through the security gate. "It's one of my favorite places in the city. Only open during the spring and summer."

"You'd rather come here than go on another Jackson Heights food tour?" I asked. Aside from the whole catching-a-murderer thing, that was the only other time I'd come out to Queens with him. It had been fun, honestly. The food had been amazing. I perked up.

"The thing is that when we went to Jackson Heights, we only got to try, like, four restaurants," Gabe said. "Here, everything you order is only a few bites, so you can try food from a whole bunch of different places, and everything is also less than six dollars. And there are cuisines from all over the world, ones you never see in restaurants, even here in New York."

"Great," I said enthusiastically. "I'm excited."

The market grounds smelled like we'd stepped inside a kitchen where they were boiling broth and baking pastries and roasting meat over an open fire. I wiped sweat off my forehead, not even minding that the fumes would stick to me because they smelled so good. I did grimace, but only because I'd sighted the bathroom facilities, and they were all Porta Potties. The one time I'd been to a concert and those were the only facilities available, I'd instantly had the family assistant call and make sure I could go backstage. Somehow I suspected similar accommodations would not be possible here.

But I could just purposely not have anything to drink tonight, and hopefully avoid having to use them. I was already eyeballing the Native American fry bread stand. I pointed. Gabe craned his neck with childlike enthusiasm, popping up and down on his toes. Thumping pop music from a DJ played in the background. "There first?"

In quick succession, we ate fry bread topped with maple syrup and strawberries, then Afghan dumplings, Korean corn dogs, and a Sichuan treat called ice jelly that was sweet and chewy and icy and fruity and like nothing else I'd ever had before. "I kind of want one in the other flavor, but I don't really want to wait in that line again," I said, eyeing the Sichuanese stand. It was a shame I hadn't known ahead of time about the line situation. I could have hired a few people to handle that for us. I opened my mouth, ready to voice the thought to Gabe, because maybe there were a few people out in the park who'd want to earn a few extra dollars by standing around, then closed it, because that was not the spirit of the outing. Then opened it again. "We really have to try that Transylvanian ice cream cake thing. It could be fun to do something like that at the bakery."

"It would," agreed Gabe. Then frowned a little, looking over my shoulder. "Hey, Pom, isn't that—"

"Oh my God, Pom? What are *you* doing here?" Lips hit both my cheeks as hands wrested me roughly to one side. That impressive tonal combination of genuine, sweet surprise and fake dismay could only belong to one person.

I widened my eyes, not even bothering trying to match it. I'd spent years concocting my own mix of what I hoped would come off as pleasure to the less attuned listener, but also annoyance to those who knew what to look for. "Persimmon! What a surprise! Out here in Queens?"

She was beautifully dewy in a jumpsuit from The Avenue's last-season collection patterned with climbing ivy, which made me feel a little conscious of the way the meat sweats were already soaking through my ecru sundress. She said, smoothly, "Kevin wanted to try it, and I was all for it. Queens is the new frontier."

"Is it so new?" I said. "I've been out here quite a few times already. But it's so nice to see you here."

Translation: I was here *before* it was cool. Which was technically true. Kind of. I mean, Gabe had dragged me here. He'd grown up here. Did that mean Gabe was more in the know than me?

Before I could wrestle with that discomfiting question, Kevin Miller caught up to his girlfriend, panting with the effort, probably because he was old. "Pom, Gabe, so nice to see you." He smiled at us with a mouthful of gleaming white teeth. Veneers, definitely. "Isn't this place grand?"

He probably had a chapter in one of his stupid books about how waiting in lines as a poor child gave him the grit and strength of character to rise above the streets to the skyscraper where he could look down on everybody else, blah, blah, blah. "So grand," I said. "I love Queens."

"Have you tried the yak yet?" Kevin asked. To be 100 percent honest, I wasn't sure what a yak was. But before either of us could answer, he clapped Gabe on the back. "Come on. I've been dying to try it. Let's go get in line."

Sure enough, as the four of us were walking through the crowd toward the, I guess, yak stand, Kevin rhapsodized about how the Queens Night Market reminded him of the street fairs of his youth, when booths selling funnel cake and fried Oreos and hot dogs would shut down an entire block for the day. "It's not the same now," he said wistfully. "It's stressful always getting recognized in public."

Not a single person here had recognized him so far, but I didn't bring that up. "I'm sure," I said. Somebody nearby snapped what they thought was a surreptitious photo of me, despite my sunglasses and floppy hat. Nobody could take a secret photo of me. I had a radar for them.

The line for the yak was, surprisingly, at least as long as the other lines. We joined the end. I looked wistfully at a group passing by holding spools of cotton candy shaped like Pikachu. "So, Pom," Persimmon said. "I heard about your little run-in at the Phlumes' old town house the other day. Everybody's talking about it. How frightening. I'm so glad you're okay."

"Thanks," I said. How kind of her. "Me too."

"Personally," she purred, eyes glinting. Yup, there it came. "I'm so glad I'm not the kind of person who always needs to be involved in such things."

"What things, Persimmon?" I asked wearily.

Gabe jumped in. Honestly, I was proud of him for recognizing this time that she and I were battling it out. Such growth. "Which dumplings should we try? There's yak, yak cheese, chicken . . ."

"Why not all three?" Kevin asked. "That's my philosophy." He frowned down at his phone, then smiled wide. "Oh, excellent."

"What is it, darling?" Persimmon abandoned our battle to cuddle up by his side. He didn't put his arm around her, too busy scrolling. "Oh, did the deal come through?"

"Yes, Jack just texted. We got it."

"Lovely," she said. She beamed a toothy smile at me and Gabe. "You two will have to come visit once we've gotten it set up."

"Visit where?"

"I recently purchased this charming little bed-and-breakfast upstate," said Kevin. Not quite a private island, but probably easier to get to from the city.

Wait. I furrowed my brow. Bed-and-breakfast. Jack. Jack Wohl? My parents had mentioned him yesterday regarding purchasing a bed-and-breakfast for the family business. It could easily be two different Jacks and two different bed-and-breakfasts, but that was an awfully big coincidence if so.

Kevin was really into hotels lately—he'd approached me about the Chelsea town house too. Was he trying to break into the industry?

My attention was drawn away by another couple of girls who thought they were being sneaky, posing for a selfie while their lens pointed at me. I rolled my eyes under my sunglasses, skin itching. Maybe I shouldn't have come out in public today. Maybe I should've just stayed up high in my apartment, with Squeaky on my lap, where I was safe.

The girls tittered, the sound like the soft camel leather of a Soubry bag ripping down the middle. My hands clenched into fists. It was so hard not to give them the finger, but then that would go viral, and what would people think? Everybody would call me trashy again. One slipup, that was all it took.

"Truly, Pom, you're so brave," Persimmon cooed like a pigeon. "So strong. If people were saying about me what they are saying about you, I'm not sure I'd be strong enough to show my face in public."

I'd had it. "See, if I were you, I'd definitely feel comfortable going out in public," I snapped. "Considering nobody knows who you are, and the people who do know you're a giant bitch."

Persimmon reared back like I'd slapped her. I might as well have—she wasn't used to a direct attack like that. She sucked in a great gasp of air, hopefully getting a good lungful of the super-spicy steam coming from the Sudanese place nearby. "What?"

The only way to salvage this situation and not turn it into a huge thing would be to laugh as if I were joking. She'd know I wasn't, but she'd be able to pretend. Both Kevin and Gabe were watching us with scrunched-up faces, waiting for me to giggle.

I just couldn't do it. I did keep my face even instead of scowling, though, for the sake of anyone sneaking pictures of me. A photo of me looking angry could be twisted into so many headlines. "I said that you're kind of a giant bitch," I said. "You're mean to me whenever we speak, and I don't know why, because I've never been mean to you." I paused and considered. "Well, except when you've been mean to me first."

"Pom," Kevin and Gabe both said at once, then looked at each other uncomfortably. Persimmon, meanwhile, gasped. Her eyes shimmered glossily, little wet drops clinging like tiny diamonds to her lashes. Damn it—she was the kind of person who grew more beautiful when she cried. "Would you excuse me, please? I need . . . the restroom . . ."

And she fled. The three of us watched her go. Before Kevin could defend his girlfriend's honor and Gabe responded to defend *my* honor and they got into a fistfight that would only start rumors that I was pregnant and I didn't know whose baby it was, I followed. "Excuse me," I called over my shoulder. I sped off, partially to outrun the horror that was going near a Porta Potty. God, the lengths I was going to for other people these days.

Persimmon had bullied her way to the front of the restroom

line, probably because it was hard to refuse a woman who cried like that girl in the fairy tale who wept jewels, so she was just going into a stall as I caught up. Again, before I could think too hard about what I was doing, I shouldered my way in behind her and shut the latch with a clunk.

Thank God for the tiniest of mercies: She'd chosen the accessible stall despite not needing any accommodations, so it was sizably larger than the other choices. Didn't smell any better, though, and there was a puddle of something indeterminate on the ground in front of the (thankfully closed) toilet lid.

"Pom," Persimmon gasped, her face shock-white, like she'd just now realized it was me who'd followed her in and not a murderer. "What are you . . ."

"We need to talk," I said.

She gasped again, then wrinkled her entire face. "Okay. But you couldn't wait until I got out?"

"I didn't want you to be able to make an excuse and run off," I said, already regretting it. The side of my arm that had brushed the plastic of the door was tingling, like I'd contracted some kind of flesh-eating bacteria.

She swayed a bit. Maybe the bacteria had gone straight for her brain. "If I swear on my one-of-a-kind peacock Birkin that I won't run off, can we go talk outside?"

Savvy of her to sneak in a reference not only to her one-of-a-kind Birkin (that I obviously didn't have) but also to the peacocks I hadn't been able to obtain for my gala. It almost made me reconsider what I wanted to say, but I held firm to my convictions as we burst out of the dank stall into the delicious-smelling air of the market, then moved to the side of the crowd, beside a stall that seemed to be selling some kind of twisty cake on a stick. I added a new conviction to the holdings that I would pick up one of those after this conversation was over and plan something for the bakery that echoed its fun shape, which would attract a lot of attention on social media.

"Look, I'm sorry for saying something mean," I said. "Of course people know who you are." Way more people knew who I was, and most of the people who knew her were huge fans of her rock-star father and not her, but I was being nice here. "I was already in a bad mood, and I blew up. I shouldn't have called you a giant bitch. Twice."

Somebody walked by holding not only the cake on a stick, but a twisty fried potato on a stick. I looked longingly after them as Persimmon responded. "I'm sorry too. I *was* being kind of bitchy."

Well. That was a step. I didn't think she'd be inviting me into her cool elite friend group with open arms anytime soon, but at least we could hopefully stop this nasty game playing. "I think we have more in common than not," I said. "Both of our boyfriends come from humble backgrounds." God, I hoped this wouldn't get back to Gabe; he would hate it. "And if you hate me, fine. Hate me. I'm okay with that." I was bluffing; I wanted everyone in the entire world to love me. "But I don't hate you. I think you're pretty cool, actually, and I wanted to be your friend until you started being all mean to me."

Her lips twitched again, this time a little bit like she was about to scream. "You're so different."

"What?"

"I guess we haven't seen a ton of each other since I stopped partying," she said. Which was true, not that I hadn't tried. "The Pom I remember was fun and mean and it was almost a sport for her, or I guess you, to twist your words into the absolute perfect little dagger disguised as a kiss. All you wanted to do was party. Nobody took you seriously. Now all of a sudden you're here, like, all mature and everything, and nobody knows how to take you."

I assumed that "nobody" was her.

"It's like Denise," Persimmon continued. "She spent all those years being the smiling face by the side of her husband, and now all of a sudden she's this big charity person? You might be able to buy the public's opinion, but you can't buy yourself into a new friend group." She muttered something I couldn't quite catch. "You can't just talk the talk, you have to walk the walk, for long enough for people to know you won't get tired and flop on the ground before you get there and tell someone to bring you an ice-cold water."

She stopped long enough where I figured it was safe to respond. "I don't think Denise is giving away her fortune to find a new friend group; I think she wants to do good. Like me." I made myself shrug, because this next part wasn't so honest. "And if you never think I'm a serious person, then fine. Don't. But I am, and I will be, and I hope everyone will see that."

She gazed at me for a moment. "I think they're starting to," she said finally. This time, I hoped that "they" was her. "And I should probably apologize too. I know I haven't been the nicest person. It's just . . ." She exhaled deeply. "It took *so* long for people like Libby and Kitty to even speak to me. I still always feel like I'm on thin ice whenever I'm around them. Vienna only won them over once she'd separated from you. I was kind of worried that if you and I were seen as being too chummy, then . . . well . . ."

Then she'd be on the outs too. I nodded grimly, totally understanding, even as I didn't like it. She was new money too. Newer money than me. My grandparents had made ours; hers had come from her parents, and through performing, not respectable means like investments or real estate. So she was on even thinner ice than me or Vienna.

Speaking of Vienna. "That's a bridge too far," I said, and she looked confused before I clarified. "Vienna is so good. She's such a good person. Maybe I deserve the distance, but she doesn't."

Her face didn't change. "Vienna . . ."

"Vienna's my best friend," I said. "And I want to be part of Libby and Kitty's crowd, I want to be taken seriously, I want people to stop making up rumors about the most salacious thing they can imagine me doing." The current winner of the title: a sex act with one of the dinosaur skeletons at the Museum of Natural History. "But none of it's worth it if I have to be mean to my friend. That's how I'm trying to live."

She blinked, as if she'd truly never considered it before. "Huh. Vienna's always been really kind to me too. And I've . . ." More blinking in fast succession. "I should be better to her. I'm going to try to be better to her."

"I'm glad," I said sincerely. Then nodded at the cake stand. "I'm going to lose my mind if I don't get one of those cakes on a stick. You want to share? We can bring one back to our guys to make up for ditching them." Hopefully they'd found something to talk about. Probably how delicious and/or terrible yak was.

"Sure."

We got in line, and neither of us even complained as it inched forward, even though it was in direct sunlight and I could practically feel the skin cancer bubbling up on my shoulders (I'd done so much tanning as a teenager that I knew it was only a matter of time). "So, you and Kevin," I said. "You make a cute couple."

She wrinkled her nose, but her light tone didn't reflect whatever feeling was scrunched up there. "You think so? People definitely judge us for the age difference, but it wasn't like we met on an app where his age range was set only to girls in their twenties. We met at a benefit for young musicians where he was funding a scholarship, and I don't think he even realized that I was twenty years younger than him." Her lips quirked. "He's trying out wearing a wig today. Apparently he's self-conscious about balding, which, hello, really drives the age difference home."

I was in a tricky position here—either I could nod along and risk her realizing she'd said she looked old and that I was agreeing with her, or I could disagree, tell her how young and fresh she looked, and then her boyfriend would come off as a creep. Fortunately, she spoke again, before I had to make a decision. "I thought it would be tougher than it was," she said. "Considering where he came from. Honestly, I was a little excited about being with somebody who might shake things up a little. But even Libby and Kitty like him. I guess he's been in society so long that he knows all the unspoken rules." We moved up in line. She gave me a sidelong glance, which was impressive, considering the delicious smells wafting toward us from the booth. "Not like your man."

I sighed. "So you've noticed?" We both snorted. Little snorts, not big ones like Bibi's. "It's definitely a change. But I think it's a bigger one for him. During my fall from grace, I was totally shocked by how most people live out there. I had no idea what I was doing. Did you know that most people in this city don't have laundry machines in their apartment?"

"Hmm." Her brow wrinkled as if she was thinking hard. "I'm not sure if I have laundry machines. My clean laundry just . . . appears."

We stepped up to the front of the line and ordered a brown sugar cake. I realized belatedly, as they handed it to us, that there was no real, neat way to use a utensil to eat this cake or to divide it between us. We'd have to gnaw at the cake, biting over each other's teeth marks like savages. "Thank you," I called as we stepped away. Persimmon hadn't thanked the vendor. As much as she'd like to think she was so different from my old friends . . .

"Anyway, I think it's been hard for him to try and fit into our world," I continued as we stepped aside. I wouldn't go into too many details—I didn't know Persimmon well enough to really spill; who knew what she might spread around or try to use against me later—but it wasn't like Gabe's struggles were some well-kept secret. "I've been meaning to ask Kevin if he has any advice. Maybe I should buy Gabe his book."

"Ugh, don't bother." Persimmon leaned in conspiratorially. Her hair brushed my cheek. Honestly, it smelled better than the cake. I had to try whatever she was using. "He didn't even write it."

"Well, obviously. No one writes their own books." Writing a business book, like writing a political book, was basically a money-laundering scheme. My grandparents had a book all about their rise to success as the founders of Afton Hotels. They'd given a bunch of interviews to some ghostwriter, who'd actually written the book, and then the hotel bulk-bought, like, a million copies to give away at business retreats and stuff and wrote it all off on their taxes.

Maybe I could break the cycle. A little thrill ran through me at the thought. Everybody wanted my memoir, and I'd assumed I'd have to find an excellent ghostwriter with the skill of capturing my voice—a difficult, if not impossible, task. But maybe I wouldn't do that. Maybe I'd tell my own story. Writing a book couldn't be *that* hard.

I shook the thought away. Not the time. "The fact that he didn't write it doesn't mean there isn't anything good in there. I assume the ghostwriter spent lots of time with him to try and make it as accurate as possible."

Persimmon rolled her eyes. "Are you kidding? I read the thing back when we first started dating to try and get to know him better without, you know, talking to him. The whole thing's full of empty inspirational platitudes. 'The only one who can pull yourself up is you.' 'The best defense is a good offense.' 'If I could do it, anyone can do it.' Blah, blah, blah."

Unfortunate. Maybe he wasn't as charitable as he wanted people to think and didn't really want people to be able to imitate his ascent. Just pay to hear all about it.

Before I could respond and ask her what she thought about my own potential book deal, my phone buzzed. Then buzzed again. It was possible it might have been buzzing all throughout our altercation and I had been too busy showing how serious I was to notice.

The first thing I saw as I pulled it out was a bunch of text notifications, topmost from Gabe. Could the man please have some patience while I was off mending a cataclysmic rift in society? The first one he sent me told me that yak tasted like gamy beef. The second, I guess from a new line he was waiting in, asked if I'd rather have pork bao or shrimp bao; the third asked if I wanted some watermelon boba tea because the girls next to him in line told him it was "dreamy."

But then it took a turn. Pom, why are reporters calling me?

Oh. That's why.

It's not true, is it?

No. I know it's not true. Of course it's not true.

I'm not supposed to talk to them, right? I don't want to talk to them.

Somebody just cornered me behind the pierogi tent. Help!

I grimaced. One exclamation point from Gabe was the exact equivalent of seven exclamation points (and probably an emoji or two) from a regular person.

I ignored most of the other texts, which were from family and friends with an assortment of variations on *Is it true???* I did take a second to dip into the one from Vienna, which gave me the name of a "fixer" who could "take care" of "this" for me before "it" got any bigger.

???????

I clicked over to Google, which I probably should've done in the first place, and to my usual Google Alert for my name. It popped up right away. The headline:

> Trouble in Pomona Afton's Paradise? Not only is the socialite and Razzie Award–winning actress's charity venture crumbling, but there are rumblings about her relationship too.

Crap.

CHAPTER Twenty-One

I was a little embarrassed to admit it, which was why I'd never say it out loud, but my first thought, after *Crap*, was petty annoyance. Why did they keep having to bring up my Razzie Award? It had been five years, and I'd been doing a nice thing by helping out the indie director I was seeing—he needed my star power to make his movie a success. I'd agreed before realizing my role would be a gender-bent Hardy Boy (the blond one, even though I was a natural brunette) who also, inexplicably, was unveiled in the third act as an alien, upon which the other brother had to kill her (my death scene had been the featured clip). The movie had flopped. The director had dumped me and gone on to produce the latest big-budget fantasy adaptation from HBO.

My second thought was panic. I read through the article, which had already been cross-posted and shared pretty much everywhere you could cross-post or share something, and felt that cold pool of dread in my stomach opening. The article painted me as the same party girl I'd always been, frittering my life away on silly things, someone who was easily dissuaded from any life path or choice.

Pom's never been able to stick with something for very long, an anonymous "friend" told the journalist.

> We all think she was hoping her entry into the charitable scene would make a major splash, and it did, but in all the wrong ways. She's already looking for a way out. Maybe getting into DJing.

"Is it true?" Persimmon asked. I jumped, nearly spearing myself on the end of the cake skewer. I'd totally forgotten she was there.

"Of course not," I said adamantly. "I've changed. I'm not giving up."

But the article wasn't only about my professional life, and that's what really made me bristle. I was used to unfounded speculation about me (if I'd been pregnant as many times as the tabloids said, I'd have my own synchronized swimming team by now. We'd sweep the Olympic nominations and I'd beam proudly on the sidelines as all the gold medals shone and, okay, this was getting away from me). But Gabe? He wasn't used to this.

> The shine on her relationship is wearing off now too, said the same or perhaps a different anonymous "friend."

> She's used to guys who can fly her to Bali for a weekend or buy her the newest Cartier watch before it even comes out, not a teacher living on a teacher's salary.

Oh God. Full-body cringe. "I don't even *wear* watches." The venom in my voice caught me off guard. Persimmon actually took a step back. "What's the point of a watch? If I want something that looks nice on my wrist, I'll wear a bracelet. If I want to know the time, I'll check my phone. Nobody needs the time permanently attached to their wrist."

But that wasn't the important thing here. Even I knew that. "I've got to call Gabe," I said, stepping away. "I've got to . . ."

I've got to set things straight. Not even with the public. My fans knew perfectly well how I felt about watches. And I'd have time to address things with my donors and the people I cared about.

But Gabe. He came first.

The call went to voicemail. I called again. Went to voicemail again. Before I could call a third time, my phone buzzed with a text. From Gabe. Got overwhelmed so I'm already on the subway home. See you there.

I bit my tongue, then realized it was a text and crossed my fingers so that I couldn't respond and ask him why, if he was so worried about being in a public place where people would accost him, he would go on the subway of all places instead of a nice private black car.

"I need to go," I said, stepping away, and then I was accosted. I didn't full-body cringe this time; I'd already slid into my old damage-control mode, the poker face and languid posture and bored tone to all the *no comments* that would come out of my mouth. It was good I was wearing sunglasses, though, to hide my eyes. There was no keeping them from worrying. Not when I had so much more to worry about than I did in the past.

"No comment," I said automatically, then realized it wasn't a kid with a phone held up taking video or a reporter with a phone to their lips as a microphone (the news world had really lost a lot of its flair when big flash cameras and tape recorders all merged with phones). It was Kevin Miller. "Oh, hi. Sorry, I have to—"

"Try the Moldovan waffle rolls?" His smile was so white it almost glowed. "It's like a waffle corn dog and a cheesecake had a sordid affair."

The way he said "sordid affair" made me feel a little like I'd gotten Moldovan waffle roll sticky on my hands, no matter how delicious it sounded. I wiped them unconsciously against my sides. "I've actually been to Moldova. With an ex. Yes, he was in the Russian mob." I wasn't sure why I was babbling. "Anyway, it was so nice to see you, but I have to—"

"Actually, I wanted to talk to you more. It's fortuitous to run into you here before you have to leave." A flash of those white teeth again. "Lucky. It's lucky to have run into you here."

Irritation bubbled in me, almost hard to read over the worry already boiling away in there. Did he think I didn't know what "fortuitous" meant? I'd gotten a fifteen hundred on the SAT. Granted, I hadn't been the one to take it, but he didn't know that. "I'm sorry. I wish I had time, but I don't. I need to go. Right now."

He didn't move, so I pushed past him. Honestly, it felt great to get a little of that aggression out. "No problem," he called after me. "We'll talk later."

I pushed my way through the rest of the crowd, but not as hard as I'd pushed Kevin, since it would've been way too easy for someone to snap a photo and publish it with, *Crazed Pomona Afton Shoves People Away in Panic After Exposé!* Back in my black car, I let myself breathe. The smell of soft, polished leather and the hum of calming string music—somehow the driver always knew exactly what I needed; I'd have to make sure he got a big holiday tip—relaxed me enough where I could think actual thoughts and not panicked sentence fragments.

This would be fine. All I had to do was show Gabe a few of the most egregiously, demonstrably false pieces published about me in the past few years to illustrate how often the press lied. *Pomona Afton Skips Grandfather's Funeral to Party at Exclusive Speakeasy* (there were literally pictures of me at the funeral; my face had been hidden enough by fashionable black netting that people didn't realize it until later). *Pomona Afton Takes Wasteful Private Jet Flight of Ten Miles to Skip Traffic* (people didn't seem to realize that refueling and repositioning flights were things). *Duchess Pomona Afton? Crown Jewel Spotted on American Socialite's Ring Finger* (technically not true, but only because my brief engagement had been to an earl). Then Gabe would realize how much fun the public had making things up about me and understand that they saw me as, like, a character on a soap opera or something. Not as a real person with a real life who could be affected for real by the storylines they whipped up.

So I was breathing a little easier when the car pulled up to our building. I almost didn't look at my phone when it started buzzing.

Almost. As I waved to the doorman, keeping my head down in case any neighbors were staring, I glanced down at it, because what if it was Gabe?

It wasn't. It was my mother. And as much as I desperately wanted to leave her on read, I knew she'd only keep calling until I blocked her, upon which she'd start calling from whoever else's phone she could find, and I couldn't block the entirety of her staff. "What is it?" I said curtly into the phone.

Her sigh gusted into my ear. "Pom, is that any way to greet your beloved parents who you've already accused of murder twice in this lifetime?"

Way to hit the guilt buttons. I stepped into the elevator and hit the button for my floor—two below penthouse level, which my mother never ceased to remind me—as I said, "Are you calling about the article? Because I'm not breaking up with Gabe."

"I'm calling because apparently you were photographed with Kevin Miller," my mother said huffily. "And yes, also because of the article, but we can discuss that later. What were you doing out with him?"

The elevator dinged for my floor. I went into my apartment, where I was promptly greeted by Squeaky and not Gabe. "I wasn't out with him. I ran into him while I was out," I said, poking my head into every room, even my bedroom-size closet. No Gabe. He must still be on the subway. "There's a difference."

Due diligence done, I plopped myself down on our couch, Squeaky hopping up into my lap and sprawling out over my legs. I could talk to my parents until Gabe showed back up. Honestly, it was fine. Talking to them would distract me from how anxious I was over Gabe's reaction. "Not in the eyes of anyone who sees," said my mom. She paused after she said it, like I was supposed to be taking that moment to appreciate how profound she was. I used it to scratch that spot behind Squeaky's ears that made him purr like a vintage Maserati. "You do realize what he's done, right?"

My superior investigative skills made me think it had something to do with that bed-and-breakfast. "Is it because you lost out on the new hotel?"

"Bed-and-breakfast," my dad chimed in, because of course he was there, too, apparently not holding too much of a grudge against me for suspecting he was a killer. "There's a difference."

"It's not only that he bought the bed-and-breakfast out from under our noses," my mom said. "It's who he did it with. Did you know he's been colluding with Nicholas?"

Why would my brother, the heir apparent to Afton Hotels, be teaming up with a rival? "That doesn't make any sense."

"You would know any of this if you ever bothered to come to board meetings or showed any interest in the family business at all," said my mother. I rolled my eyes. "Nicholas is trying to demonstrate to the board that he'd be a superior head of the business to your father. Apparently he's beginning to sway people. Getting one over on us by purchasing this bed-and-breakfast out from under us isn't going to help our case."

A daring move, for Nicholas. If he failed, he might be tossed out himself. Though I doubted my father would have the guts to do that to his only son. Who else would the family company go to? *Me?* I snorted. "And he got Kevin on his side?"

"I'm sure your brother promised him some stake in the company if he succeeds," said Mom. "I know this is that girlfriend's influence. Nicholas would never think to do such a thing on his own."

"Jessica's not his girlfriend, she's his fiancée." I could practically hear my mother's shudder through the phone. "And I don't think it has anything to do with her." Should I say something about how my dad was bad at his job? Probably not after so recently accusing him of murder. That might be too much for one week. "What if you gave Nicholas more responsibility in the company? A better title? That might make him happy enough to chill out on the coup for a bit."

"Hmm," my dad said. My mom moved on, probably because she'd rather choke on a martini olive than tell me I'd had a good idea.

"Anyway, Pom, let's talk about you and your options as I see them. I think we say it was mutual. Much respect on both sides, will stay friends, blah, blah, blah, all that."

"What are you talking about?"

"Your breakup with the nanny's son," Mom said. "I don't think you want any more drama in the press. Will he move out of your apartment without fuss, or are you going to need to evict him? Because that wouldn't be ideal."

"Would you stop calling him that?" I said. "And I won't need to evict him, because, as I told you, the article is not true. I love Gabe. He loves me. We are not breaking up. The press is always telling lies about me. It'll blow over in a week or two like it always does. I don't even know why you're focusing so much on one stupid article."

"This one won't blow over as quickly as they used to," my mom said. "That was true when all you did was party and the most controversial thing you did was take an occasional drug or sing along to a song and say a certain word aloud that you weren't supposed to say."

The word was "fucking." Why did she have to make it sound like I'd said some awful slur?

She continued brightly, "Now you're trying to do something big and real. The press hates that. People are going to want to tear you down for trying to change how they see you. It won't stop. Trust me, it happened to me."

I doubted that very much, mostly because my mother had

never done anything good for anyone in her entire life. But I bit anyway. "What do you mean?"

"When I was in college, I decided I wanted to save the world. We needed to fix the ozone layer, I believe. And I met a boy in the environmental club. We held a lot of fundraisers and I raised a lot of money. Together, we were unstoppable. For a few months." That tracked. "But cracks started opening in our relationship soon after. He would get up in arms that I'd used the family plane to visit my grandparents or hop over to the family lodge for some skiing rather than flying commercial, or that I wouldn't stop using the only hair spray that could tease my hair into the fashion of the day, as if I were reaching up there and ripping a hole into the ozone layer myself. We were just too different. It never would have worked."

I took a deep breath. "That's not even close to the same thing."

"Isn't it, though?"

"No," I said firmly. It would be the same thing if I were raising money for kids in need but personally anti giving scholarships. Or something. The situations were totally, completely different.

Right?

Crap. Now I was all in my own head. "Look, I know that Gabe and I are different people and that we come from extremely different backgrounds. I know that we were raised very differently and that we still look at things differently. I know that maybe we won't always see eye to eye."

I was about to continue with something grand like, *And it doesn't matter, because our love will conquer all*, but my mom interrupted with, "I'm so glad you see it my way. I've heard through the grapevine that Nicholas's old college friend Chip is interested in you now that you've moved past your drunk-at-sunrise phase."

Bibi had seemed interested in setting me and Chip up too. What was it with this guy? It almost made me intrigued enough to look him up. I mean, if both my mother *and* Bibi, diametrical opposites, thought he'd be a good fit, then I was just curious—oh my God, no. What was I thinking? I loved *Gabe*. I wanted to stay with *Gabe*. I wanted things to work out with *Gabe*. Eventually *Gabe* and I would run into Chip and his wife (slim, brunette, wide-set eyes like mine because he could never truly get over me) at a gala and make polite conversation and Chip would hit on me in a way he thought was slick but was actually really obvious and I'd turn him down because, HELLO, I LOVED GABE.

"Some differences you can't get past. That's why our relationship would never work," I said through clenched teeth, talking about Chip, because he had some nerve judging me for my drunk-at-sunrise phase when he'd gone through a phase himself where he wouldn't stop hanging his underwear off various official flagpoles (the 9/11 Memorial one had been in especially poor taste), but before I could say that, Squeaky jumped off my lap, purring hard as he trotted somewhere behind me. The only reason he'd jump off my lap would be to greet his other favorite person, which meant . . .

"Gabe?" I said, turning around and lowering my phone. My mom continued our conversation in a tiny voice with the couch cushions. I hadn't even heard him come in.

When had he come in? How much had he heard?

Enough where his eyes were glossy. No tears striped his cheeks, but I'd never so much as seen him look like he was going to cry. "Gabe," I said again, standing. Taking a step toward him. "It's not what it—"

I stopped, my stomach lurching, as he took a step back. Away from me. "I heard enough," he said, his voice a croak. He didn't even stoop down to pet Squeaky or scoop him up into his arms. "Pom. I was going to propose. On Kevin's island. The original plan was to propose after the gala, but the murder killed that plan." Neither of us laughed at that terrible pun. His face was ashy. I felt kind of like I was going to throw up, but I was frozen in place, so I'd choke. "I thought it would be the perfect plan B: find a beautiful, isolated stretch of pristine beach, ask someone at the party to take photos from a distance, ask you to marry me, just the two of us. But then I heard what you were saying to Persimmon . . ."

My stomach lurched again. I'd been trying to one-up Persimmon as she bragged about her future proposal from Kevin. Of course Gabe would have dropped his plan after hearing that crap.

"And now this . . ." He shook his head. Took another step back. Had I heard a creak before, when I started talking about how different Gabe and I were?

Probably. Because that would've been the absolute worst spot for him to start listening. "Gabe, it's not what it sounds like," I said.

But he was still shaking his head, still moving back, ignoring Squeaky, who was headbutting his leg to get pets in an increasingly frustrated manner. "Even so," he said. "It's too much. It's too much right now. I need some time away. You stay here. I'm going to . . ." He turned, showing me his back. "I'm going to go stay with Caleb for a bit. I need some time to think."

He took that last step toward the door, then paused. Knelt down to scratch Squeaky behind the ears and give him a kiss on his head. "Be good, Meatball," he said, and then, like a magician, he was gone.

If it were just what he'd overheard me say on the phone, I'd run after him and plead my case. But that, combined with the whole proposal thing . . .

Honestly? The idea of an isolated beach proposal didn't make me jump with joy. Did I really want the over-the-top proposal I'd described to Persimmon? No. It sounded like a lot of work, and what if the giant ring got lost in the coral, and also I didn't really want to show up at a party soaking wet while everybody else was nice and dry. But I really wanted something in between the two, and what if that meant I was shallow after all? That there was too much of Old Pom in me? That I wasn't the woman Gabe thought I was, the woman he deserved?

Was I really any different than I was before? Maybe I'd tried and tried and tried to climb out of the Old Pom pit, only to realize that the walls were too high and too slippery and that I was stuck here in my old self.

My phone buzzed. I glanced at it, hoping that it was Gabe saying he'd made a mistake but that he'd forgotten his keys so I'd need to let him up, but resigned to the fact that it was my mother who'd heard from a neighbor about what Gabe just said and wanted to gloat.

It wasn't either one of them. It was my long-dormant—at least on my side—group chat with Millicent and Coriander. They, at least, didn't assume that the article was true.

Ugh Pom what the internet is saying about you 😫

Pom come out with us and show them how much you don't care

Let's flip them all the bird!!!

What was the point of resisting?

CHAPTER Twenty-Two

Getting ready for my night out felt like slipping into a dress from last season I'd found at the back of my closet that was somehow still in style. When I looked at myself in the mirror, it felt as if I was seeing a friend from the past, Old Pom in her black bodycon dress with mussed hair and big, ironic pearls dripping from her ears and her throat.

I met my friends outside one of our old haunts downtown. They rushed over to me on the sidewalk for cheek kisses and hugs where we barely touched, partially because Coriander's metallic silver dress had little spikes around the collar. "Oh my God, Pom, it's so good to finally see you," Millicent gushed, clad in a sparkly pink jumpsuit that looked as if she'd plucked it from a human-size Barbie Dreamhouse. Had her voice always been this nasal to the point where it grated against my nerves?

"Yeah, you've really been out of the loop," Coriander said. Had she always twirled her blond hair with her fingers in this way that made me want to chop her fingers off one by one with gardening shears? "We have to fill you in."

I leaned in, smiling mechanically, as they led me inside. The entryway was small and dark, the stairs going down narrow and claustrophobic. "I can't wait. Tell me everything." I couldn't stop glancing around me, keeping an eye out for anyone who might be seeing me, judging me. Old habit from the past year.

Our usual routine was bar before club, so that we could get all of the talking out of the way before music drowned everything out. This particular bar was speakeasy style, located in a basement and littered with gas lamps, Tiffany stained glass, and shelf upon shelf of herbal-looking tonic and clear liquids in elegant perfume bottles behind the stately mahogany bar. It was crowded already; I nodded to a few people I recognized and a few people I was pretty sure I didn't but who would get a thrill from The Pomona Afton nodding at them like she did.

For the next hour, over drinks that tasted like medicine or licorice or sometimes both, Millicent and Coriander filled me in on the last few months of happenings in their sphere. My old sphere, the one I had spurned for the new one that had spurned me. Old friends who had gotten together. Who had broken up. Who had gotten together then broken up then gotten together again but would probably break up soon. Who had gotten threatened with eviction proceedings from their parents after throwing one too many loud parties, who had been arrested for dealing or driving under the influence but got off without jail time. Who had been thinking about starting a fashion line (Millicent) and who had sworn off drinking wine for the near future because of the tannins (Coriander).

"What exactly are tannins?" I asked Coriander. Her face wrinkled up, eyes wide with fright. Before she had to admit she had no idea what they were or why she was avoiding them, I changed the subject. "Do you know Chip? Apparently everyone thinks we should be together for some reason."

"Chip? Princeton Chip?" Millicent asked. "Oh no. I've slept with him and he's so mid."

"So mid," Coriander echoed. Was she supporting her friend or did that mean she'd also slept with him and found him mid?

Probably better not to ask. "Anyway," I said. Moving on.

"What's the big news, now that we've gotten through all the petty drama?"

They regarded me with four big blank eyes. Coriander took a sip of her drink, a parsley soda with gin and tonic. "What do you mean?"

"That *was* all the big news," Millicent clarified, in case I hadn't gotten it from Coriander's question.

Right. It hit me at once all over again how small and insignificant everything in my old world had been. A big accomplishment for me back then had been when I'd plotted with a whole group to wear bright red to Catherine Sounder's Hamptons pink party. Which—I smiled at the memory—had been a lot of fun, actually.

Maybe it would be nice to kind of turn my brain off for a night and not think about the weight of the world or anything too big or important. Though, of course, anyone who saw me out tonight would assume I wanted to turn it off permanently again.

To avoid thinking about it too much, I took a big gulp of my extremely fennel-y drink, then another. It seared its way down my throat, lit a fire in my stomach. Made me relax enough to take the little orange pill Coriander fetched for me from her pearl compact without asking what it was.

Once the effects started to hit, we cleared out for somewhere louder and sloppier, a new club that had opened in the past year that looked and sounded exactly like every other club I'd been to: flashing multicolored lights; a cloaked DJ spinning beats; a thumping bass; round tables cordoned off in the back that we were ushered to immediately.

Champagne rained down my throat. I felt every inch of its glittering journey, the pooling of it, now warm, in my gullet. The effects of Coriander's pill: I'd kind of hoped it was one that would chill me out, but it was doing the opposite; it heightened every sensation, made every light sharper, stretched each second out into a gooey strand of taffy.

This was the place to be tonight. Everybody who was everybody, at least in my old sphere, was here. Random people I hadn't seen in ages stopped by to say hi, telling me how good I looked, asking me how I was, commenting on the music or the lighting or the champagne before I had a chance to answer.

Everywhere I looked I saw Gabe.

No, that wasn't fair. Because sometimes also in my peripheral vision there was a swoosh of black hair and I thought it was Vienna, or a lithe, willowy gesture that made me think of Persimmon. The shine of light on pearl that made me think *Libby*, or the angle of a waist that shouted *Kitty*. People who would never be caught stepping foot in here, who would look down on me for my presence on this dance floor.

But mostly it was Gabe. Gabe's hand brushing along my shoulder, Gabe's lips quirking up in a quick glimpse of a smile as he indulged a speech from me about how Squeaky totally preferred chicken with thyme to chicken with rosemary that I knew was ridiculous but that I felt comfortable making anyway because I knew he wouldn't think *I* was ridiculous for it. Gabe's eyebrows rising, impressed, as I told him about the newest initiative I was doing to help people and use everything I'd been given to make the world better.

I took another gulp of champagne. A group of girls my age materialized before us, big smiles on their faces, phones in their hands, all gesturing toward me. I didn't need to be able to hear them to know what they were asking for: a picture.

Millicent flicked her hand at them like they were flies. They raised their phones and took pictures anyway, giggling as they ran off. Great. Now everybody would see those pictures and think all of the rumors were true. *Pomona Afton, seen partying without her poverty-stricken boyfriend. Pomona Afton, out frittering away her money instead of helping some other poverty-stricken kid go to school. Pomona Afton, her head empty, as always.*

I tossed back the rest of the champagne and threw myself from the booth, nearly falling over as I turned to extend a hand toward Millicent and Coriander. Great. Hopefully somebody got a photo of that too. Ideally with my underwear showing. "Let's dance!"

We stumbled onto the dance floor. The music swept me up, thumping so loud I felt it through my whole body like a heartbeat, vibrating through my muscles and relaxing them better than the best massage (okay, not the *best* massage, but that one had been deep underground in a Turkish cave and helped along by earthquakes, an experience I was not looking to repeat anytime soon). I shouted along the lyrics to some pop song from a few years ago remixed into something edgy and new, throwing my arms up in the air and shaking my body until sweat dampened the back of my neck. Scream-singing made me feel free, cleared my mind, forced me to be in the moment. Let me forget everything about the article, the photos, Gabe.

God, I'd *missed* this. This was the first moment without that nagging thought of *what will* they *think?* hovering in the back of my mind. That was why I'd always loved clubbing, and why I loved it now.

I'd changed so much. Why was that same thought still there?

A very damp man was dancing up to me, his smell sharp enough to cut through the general funk of sweaty bodies packed into a small space. I grimaced and danced away. Where was I? It was hard to remember over the thump-thump-thump of the bass, the chorus of people yelling lyrics around me so that we all felt like one glorious organism.

Oh yeah. That was exactly where I'd been.

Millicent and Coriander danced up to me. Each grabbed one of my hands and swung it, and even with all I'd been feeling toward them lately—the annoyance, the frustration, the itch to get away—it was so nice to be here with them in this place, in this time, in this era. "I love you guys!" I yelled. They didn't yell it back, which, rude. Though maybe it was that they hadn't heard me. "I missed this!"

I had no idea how long we danced for, because the songs never really ended, only morphed into new songs. There was a metaphor in there somewhere, but I couldn't think too hard about it. I just danced and danced and danced until my lips were dry and my throat was sore. Once I could no longer ignore the demands of my body, I shook my way off to the side and flopped, exhausted, back onto the cushioned bench surrounding our table.

I'd had enough alcohol for one night, so I poured myself a glass of water. Then poured myself another glass when I realized I'd accidentally poured myself the spicy water. No, that wasn't right. Carbonated. *That* was right. The effects of the drug were finally wearing off, leaving my mind a little jumbled.

But not too jumbled to remember what I'd said and thought on the dance floor. How much I'd missed this. I hadn't let myself go clubbing at all over the past year, worried about what people might think. If they'd assume my new leaf was equally as tawdry as the old leaf. But now, here I was, still worried about what people would think. Why? What was the *point*? I'd been so worried about what my sphere would think, then what my new sphere would think, then what Gabe would think . . .

. . . that I'd forgotten to ask *myself* what I thought. Why couldn't I be a person who was determined to do good in the world who *also* liked to go dance and party sometimes? Because I enjoyed all of those things. I should be able to *do* all of those things. Why couldn't I be a person who liked doing important, serious things and also sometimes going clubbing without being judged?

Maybe because I couldn't do *anything* without being judged. Even when I'd done everything right, Kitty and Libby and them had still snubbed me. And if that was the case, what if I just . . . stopped caring about what they thought?

I sank back into the cushion, gobsmacked. I could just stop

caring. I could do the best I could and, if that got me smack talk from my new sphere or my old sphere or the public, so what? What did it matter? I'd know I was doing my best. I'd know I was doing what mattered.

I almost felt like I was going to cry.

"It's soooo hot in here," Millicent said, sliding into the seat beside me. Coriander slumped into the bench on my other side, sandwiching me between them.

Maybe they didn't quite fit into my new world. Maybe they weren't the kind of friends who would help me change the world for the better, or enrich my mind. But they were really good and fun at clubbing, and we had a long history together. Maybe that could be enough.

I leaned in and gave Coriander an impromptu hug. "I'm glad I came out with you tonight."

She responded by bursting into tears. I would've been alarmed, except that Coriander was excellent at bursting into tears. She did it when somebody shoulder-checked her on the sidewalk because she was staring down at her phone, taking up the whole walkway, or when it looked like somebody might beat her in tennis—basically, whenever she wanted to make someone feel bad. How long would it work? I wondered. Everybody felt bad for a sobbing teenage girl. Nobody pitied a sobbing middle-aged woman.

Anyway, I sat for a moment, waiting for her to get the worst of it out. Once she was sniffling and dabbing at her flawless mascara with a tissue plucked from her black leather The Avenue clutch, I said, a little wary, "Why do you want me to feel bad for you right now?"

Coriander sniffled again, dabbing at her cheek. Upon closer reflection, it was hardly wet. Okay, now I was more than a little wary. She'd definitely done something bad and didn't want me to be angry. "Cor?"

Millicent's hand alighted on my bare arm like a butterfly. "We only did it because we love you."

"You did it?" My mouth dropped open. "You killed Conrad Phlume?" Images flashed through my head: Coriander, furious about my tricking her into wearing ugly glasses; Conrad taking a swipe at Millicent's boob or something; the two of them losing it and shoving him off the landing.

"What?" Coriander squawked at the same time Millicent cried, "Oh my God, no!"

So much for that. I thought I'd be disappointed once again at not finding the culprits, but instead I found myself relieved. Having one friend go down for murder was more than enough for one lifetime, thank you very much. "Then what are you talking about?"

Coriander's lower lip pushed out. I really hoped the tears weren't about to restart. "The mean posts about you. And also the mean article about you. We were the 'anonymous sources.'"

CHAPTER Twenty-Three

My jaw literally dropped at Coriander's confession that she and Millicent had been behind the mean posts and mean article, but not because I was shocked. They'd done meaner things in the past, honestly; this was nothing. It was that I kind of wanted my teeth out to bite them.

Maybe the effects of the drug hadn't entirely worn off. I shut my mouth firmly so that there wouldn't be articles the next day about how Pomona Afton had left unsanitary teeth marks in her friend's arm and should be put down for the public's safety. "What? Why? How could you?"

"We missed you so much," Millicent said, her voice wobbling now too. Impressively so, considering I could hear it over the music. "After Opal went to jail, you, like, dropped off the face of the planet. You wouldn't answer our texts or calls even though *we* didn't even kill anyone."

"Yeah," Coriander said, as if I were the one who'd betrayed them, as if not murdering someone's relative was the highest bar of friendship. "So after the gala, we were kind of drunk."

"A lot drunk," said Millicent.

"Okay, a lot drunk," said Coriander. "The pink drink named after you that you served was really good, actually."

"Thank you," I replied, oddly pleased. At least I'd done one thing right that night.

"We were jealous of all your new important friends and your boyfriend you were spending all your time with. We thought that maybe, if they didn't like you anymore, you would come back to us."

I probably should've been angrier than I was, but, having had one friend murder a blood relative already, other friends saying mean things about me on social media wasn't really that bad. Also, they loved me! They'd been bullying me out of love! I mean, probably part of it was because they enjoyed the attention they got from hanging out with The Pomona Afton, but at least part of it was that they actually liked me. Hopefully.

Still, I couldn't let this go unpunished, or they'd keep leaking secrets about me. I fixed my face into the sternest expression I possibly could, carefully facing away from the dance floor so that nobody would be able to snap a pic of me looking angry. Who knew how they'd spin that? "Wow. I can't believe you would do that to me." I shook my head slowly, taking a long sip of water to let them marinate in their shame and fear a little longer. "And you're supposed to be my friends." A little lie to drive the guilt in even deeper. "My *best* friends."

They gibbered and cried some more as I sipped my water, crossing and uncrossing my legs. Honestly, this was kind of okay. The more upset they thought I was, the more they'd do to make it up to me in the future. Coriander would get me into the good graces of her cousin, a designer who created the absolute best high-end kitchen implements—maybe I could finally get off the waitlist for that personalized baby-pink mixer. Millicent had a phobia of show tunes, but I bet she'd go see something on Broadway with me now, maybe the jukebox musical I knew Vienna wouldn't be caught dead at.

Marginally more cheerful, I stood, still frowning very hard.

"I'm going to go home now and cry myself to sleep. Don't even try to follow, or I'll never speak to you again."

"Pom!" they both shrieked tearfully behind me as I walked off in a mostly straight line, relieved that the effects of the drug seemed largely to have worn off. I made sure to keep a smile fixed to my face as I pressed buttons on my phone to call my driver.

And then I actually did go home and sniffle a little into my pillow, Squeaky curled into the back of my knees. But, of course, it had nothing to do with Millicent and Coriander. It was that empty side of the bed, the one that ached with Gabe's absence, the one you might think Squeaky would spread out into but, nope, he'd rather stick as close to me as possible and stab me with his claws whenever I moved.

• • •

I was still sad the next morning when I woke up, the backs of my legs speckled with claw marks. I did not want to be alone. So I called Vienna. *Please pick up.*

She did. *I love you, Vienna.* "Hi!" I said. "I'm going through a little bit of a crisis. What are you up to?"

"Hi!" she said back, not thrown even a bit. We'd been through so many crises together. "I was actually about to text you, because, weirdly, Persimmon just texted me to go out to brunch. Apparently it was something you said? Are you two hanging out without me now?" She was joking, but also not joking.

"Of course not," I said. "We ran into each other last night. We're cool now. Where are you going?"

"I'll send you the address."

My car pulled up in front of Vienna's favorite brunch spot, which was near the Whitney Museum, alllllll the way west in the Meatpacking District, presumably because it was where she'd go before visiting the museum. It was high-ceilinged, softly lit, strewn with small, uncomfortable-looking tables and glowing things I wasn't sure were lamps or art pieces, the opposite of the small, cozy breakfast spot Gabe liked to go to north of our apartment. An acoustic guitar player strummed in one corner beside a singer who sounded a little bit like Enya and, wait, might actually have been Enya. On the one wall that wasn't hung with colorful abstract art, huge arched windows looked out over the Hudson River, the sun dazzling over the gray water.

I found Vienna sitting with Kitty, Libby, John, a few others, and Persimmon in the corner, beneath a massive painting of a bunch of pink dots over red smudges. Vienna was sitting on the literal edge of her seat, her thighs probably burning with the effort. The smile she gave me was a little nervous, a little shy. "Pom." She stood to greet me, leaning in for a brief hug. Though it was early, she had on a full face of makeup above a boxy silk tee and gray pencil slacks.

"Vee," I said, conscious that I, in my flowy white maxi skirt and cropped pink leather jacket, was about a hundred decibels louder in appearance than anyone else at this table.

But c'est la vie. The rest of the circle echoed her greeting; Persimmon, rewearing that cute ivy jumpsuit from yesterday, was the only one who stood up for a hug. "Good to see you, Pom," she said, her voice so genuine that Vienna and the rest of the circle raised their eyebrows. "How are you feeling?"

I glanced around the circle. A few eyes flicked up from my loud ensemble, lips pinching with disapproval. You know what? Screw them. Being honest with Persimmon had gone great for both me and Vienna. Being honest with myself had gone great too. Might as well keep doing it. "I'm feeling fantastic, actually," I said, pulling a chair over with a terrible screech on the subway-tiled floor. Half the group winced. I ignored it and plopped down, crossing my legs so that my skirt billowed out and brushed the legs of the people next to me. "I'm exhausted because I was out clubbing all last night. I know, *classy*." The other half of the group winced, probably because I'd just echoed their sarcastic thought. "But it turns out I really love clubbing and I've missed it a lot over the past year. You can want to do good in the world and appreciate art and have a blast at the club too."

From all the side-eye I was getting, I was pretty sure they didn't agree. But so what? What was the worst they could do? Maybe boycott my galas and parties and deprive me of a crucial source of funding. Ostracize me socially and spread terrible rumors about me, I supposed. Also make it too awkward for Vienna to continue being my friend.

Okay, thinking about all that had been a mistake. I took a shaky breath and fixed a bright smile on my face. No going back now. "Anyway, honesty feels great. Anyone else want to share anything?"

My eyes found Vienna, who was studiously avoiding mine. She was clearly not ready to share the secret Conrad had blackmailed her over. It wasn't my place to share it for her, but it would definitely come out eventually. These things always did. I hoped she'd be able to share it on her own terms before someone else did it for her.

"I suppose I can share," said Kitty. "Last night I took home a signed first edition of *Jane Eyre* from the New York Public Library benefit and silent auction. One of my absolute favorite books."

I nodded along enthusiastically, deciding not to mention that when *Jane Eyre* had been assigned in school, I'd barely made it through the SparkNotes. Even from those I didn't love the sound of it—we're supposed to be rooting for a "romantic hero" who locked his mad wife in an attic and then lied to his creepily younger lover and, oh, right, employee, about it? No way. "How fun."

It hadn't been quite what I'd meant by sharing, but Libby took her lead. "Also last night, I cohosted a party meant to raise awareness of alternative contraception methods," she said. I nodded, kind of interested this time. My IUD was great, but it was coming time for replacement and the insertion had been a bitch. If there was something out there to use that didn't make me feel as if I were being sliced in half for a weekend but that I also didn't have to worry about forgetting to take at the same time every day, I was all for it.

"Cool."

The rest of the semicircle chimed in with their altruistic and/or scholarly pursuits of the week, some more pompous-sounding than others. I nodded along, fighting the urge to feel silly and small. I couldn't host a benefit or raise awareness for a genocide *every* night. Surely it was okay to just have fun sometimes.

"Well, I, for one, just went out for a late dinner with my parents," said Vienna. I knew her saying this was a kindness for me; knowing Vienna and her parents, it had probably been a dinner to raise money to save rare birds in Taiwan or music education in the Bronx. "And then it was so nice to hear from Persimmon this morning. I feel like it's been so long since I've been here."

The rest of the circle nodded along, nobody mentioning the fact that she hadn't been here in so long because they'd all been shunning her. Nobody ever would either. The social rules said we'd glide right over it as if it had never happened. Eventually everybody would forget. Everybody except Vienna.

It made me feel protective of her. I turned back to Persimmon, not wanting to focus on how they'd treated my best friend. "How did you like the night market?"

Her smile seemed a little mechanical. "Oh. It was nice. It turns out that yak isn't too bad." She toyed with her hair, avoiding my eyes. She hadn't even gotten to try the yak, had she? "And then Kevin and I went back into the city to see a show."

She named a beautiful show on Broadway about mothers and daughters that I'd cried at. Mostly because my own mother would never sing songs about how she'd do anything to protect me, even kill someone (she would totally kill someone, just not to protect me). When I'd gone backstage to meet the actors afterward, it had taken some serious self-control not to ask the woman playing the mother if she wanted to adopt me.

"You guys are so cute together," Kitty cooed, taking a sip of her tomato juice. Persimmon smiled back, just a moment too late.

"Yeah. Sure." Was that sarcasm? Had something gone wrong between when I ran into them last night and now?

Maybe I was thinking that because it was a distraction from the fact that, even though I'd had a major personal epiphany, my boyfriend wasn't there to know it and might not even care. Maybe it was because it was nice to think that somebody else was a bigger mess than me. Maybe it was because I was the best friend anyone could ever have. Probably that one. But whatever it was, the curiosity grew again. "Hey, Persimmon," I said, standing. "Could you come with me to the bathroom? I need help with my . . . buttons."

Nobody in the circle looked surprised, which was kind of insulting. Really, did they think that somebody as experienced in avoiding upskirt photos as I was would wear something I couldn't get off by myself? (Unless I was at the Met Gala, of course. The rules were different for the Met Gala.) Vienna gave me an odd look. Probably she'd noticed I wasn't wearing any buttons. I tried to give her a significant look back, all like, *I have a good reason for this*, and just had to hope she'd get it and wasn't insulted I was snubbing her.

Persimmon, to her credit, was game, maybe because this friendship we'd created was so small and new and fragile. She stood. "Sure."

Our trip to these restrooms was way better than our trip to the Porta Potties. They were located down a long hallway lined with more art, less grand than the huge canvases in the main space yet somehow more moving (I made a mental note to ask the manager about a small painting of a girl perched on a rock gazing out over the ocean—it would work perfectly in my guest room).

Both single-occupancy rooms were vacant. I took a quick peek inside the farther one to make sure it was the accessible one and therefore larger before ushering Persimmon inside.

Up close, there were dark smudges under her eyes held in bags the size of dumplings. "You look exhausted," I said, surprised.

"Thanks," she said dryly. "Where are your buttons?"

I waved a hand in the air. "Oh, that was just a lie to get you alone," I told her. She glanced, eyes wide, at the lock on the door. "Don't worry. I'm not going to murder you. They'd catch me in, like, a second."

"But you would murder me otherwise?"

"No, of course not." Sometimes I forgot that most other people didn't constantly have murder on the mind. Maybe I *should* open up that detective agency. "Anyway. I wanted to make sure you were okay. You seemed off out there. Did something happen after you left the night market?"

Her eyes widened, as if she were more surprised by me being a good friend than she was about me potentially murdering her, which, honestly, rude. "Wow. Actually. Yes. Yeah, it did."

"Do you want to talk about it?" I said generously.

She was quiet for a moment, both of us looking around the bathroom. They'd wallpapered it with pages from art books, so that all around us lounged naked women and also horses, a strange combination from the decorator. "Your boyfriend isn't here."

If I wanted her to be honest with me, I probably had to be honest, too, as distasteful as that was. "That article wasn't exactly kind to the two of us. He's taking a little space."

"I see. I'm sorry." She was quiet for another moment, which gave me some time to be sad about that space Gabe was taking. Then again, if he'd been with me last night, I probably wouldn't have gone clubbing with Millicent and Coriander, and I probably wouldn't have had my life-changing epiphany, and maybe that epiphany would be key to making sure the two of us wouldn't want to take space from each other in the future, so it could be that the article had saved us all.

Millicent and Coriander: casually mean saviors of humanity.

Persimmon went on. "Kevin's being really shady lately. He's definitely hiding something, and I think it might be an affair. Last night he got a call right in front of me and I couldn't avoid thinking about it any longer."

My instinct was to go in for a hug, and she didn't stiffen when I leaned in, so I let it happen. "I'm sorry," I said into her hair. It smelled like tangerines. Or maybe persimmons. What did persimmons smell like anyway? "He'd be insane to be having an affair when he's got you."

"I know, right?" She pulled back, eyes flashing. "Men are supposed to cheat on their old wives with young women, not cheat on their young girlfriends."

"Right," I said firmly, then realized what she'd actually said. "Wait, what?"

"It's just the way of the world," she said, which was depressing but also, I supposed, expected, considering what she'd seen from her father. Last I'd heard, he was on his third wife. Or fourth? The wife couldn't be that much older than Persimmon, if she was indeed older at all. "I thought that, by being the younger woman with the older man, I'd be . . . safe." She sank down onto the toilet seat, which was, thankfully, closed. "Now I don't know what to do."

There was nowhere else for me to sit down, so I hovered uncomfortably above her. "What happened with the call?"

Somebody knocked on the door. We both ignored it. "He's been taking frequent phone calls in the other room. He changed the password on his phone. And he's been coming home with marks on him he can't explain. But yesterday I saw the name on his phone before he snatched it away and went outside with it. Why would he be hiding a call with a Jessica if it wasn't because of an affair?" She wrinkled her nose. "The name 'Jessica' just sounds whorish, honestly."

Jessica. I laughed, which made Persimmon's eyes widen, as if she thought I was mocking her. "I think I know what's going on," I said. "Jessica is my brother's fiancée. I learned from my parents earlier that my brother and Kevin have been colluding to try and take over the Afton family business. My brother's probably been using her phone so that his calls don't show up on the family phone bill."

"Oh my God. Are you serious?" Persimmon rubbed her head. The person at the door knocked again, more insistently this time. Persimmon glanced at the door, then back at me. "Oh. You know, that actually makes a lot of sense."

"What do you mean?"

"When I asked about it, he told me that he'd made a bargain with the caller," she said. "That he was helping out the caller so that the caller would help him with something. He wouldn't tell me details, which is why I figured he was lying." She let out a breezy laugh. "You know, I suspected Denise Ryan. They had a very cozy lunch the other day. But she's way too old, right? He would never cheat on me with someone who's *so* much older. Oh my God, I feel way better now."

I wished I could say the same. The pieces were slowly slotting together on multiple fronts, slipping and sliding in a way that made me queasy.

"Nobody is quite who they claim to be," I said slowly.

Before I could say anything else, the knocking on the door turned into a thunderstorm. "Please!" someone called desperately from the hallway.

"We should probably let them in," said Persimmon, and opened the door before I could ask her for one more moment in the quiet. Somebody shoved past us in a blur. Together, we headed back to the dining room, where half the circle was standing, bags thrown over shoulders or fastened over waists, brushing goodbye kisses over cheeks. I was too deep in thought to be insulted that everybody was leaving so soon after I'd arrived. After all, so what? I was sick of trying to pretend to be somebody I wasn't. That only worked for so long, could only make you so happy.

As I was beginning to understand.

I swooped in on Vienna for a quick hug. "I'm really glad I came," I said, grabbing my own bag. My stomach lurched with the movement.

"I'm glad you came too," Vienna said. She squinted at me, cocked her head. "Did you just figure something out?"

I gave her an enigmatic smile in response. The answer was, of course, yes. I'd cracked it again, or, at least, I was pretty sure I had. I had a few calls to make. To Nicholas. To Jessica. To Jack Wohl. To whomever those calls would lead to.

Into the car. "To the bakery," I directed. If I was going to have to rock the foundation of my entire world, I wanted to do it from the safety of my favorite place.

CHAPTER Twenty-Four

I was incredibly productive over the next several hours. I made a bunch of phone calls and even a field trip to find Nicholas when he ignored my phone calls. I made a literal chart and timeline of how I thought things must have gone, and backed it all up with what I'd heard on the phone (or, in Nicholas's case, in the pool of the Afton, where he was swimming laps and only ignoring me by virtue of not having his phone). I took out some nervous energy on customers who were yelling at my employees for no reason and, in bursts of wild inspiration, planned the bakery's specials menu for the next month. Ellie wasn't totally sure how we would accomplish everything-bagel-and-cream-cheese Danishes, but I told her I'd figure it out. I'd have a lot more downtime soon.

By the time I came up for air, it was dark outside, and my heart was racing, probably because everything I'd eaten today had come from the bakery and contained a metric ton of sugar. "What time is it?" I asked nobody, then decided it didn't matter. I'd accomplished a lot today. But there was one more thing I needed to do, and it was the most important thing of all.

It took another hour to figure out how exactly I was going to do it. Part of me wanted to do that grand gesture of a stereotypical movie scene where, to beg for forgiveness, you got a boom box and played it outside someone's window at night to get their attention. But the rest of me figured that going to Queens was a big enough gesture, and also that playing a loud boom box on a quiet residential street this late at night would get me drawn and quartered. Also, I had no idea where I'd get a boom box. I wasn't sure I'd ever actually seen one in real life.

"I'm so sorry to wake you up," I told Gabe's brother Caleb at the door. He'd come armed with a baseball bat, which said something about Queens (mostly that they didn't have doormen to hold the bats for them).

"What makes you think you woke me?" he groused, rubbing his eyes. Black hair stuck out every which way, including in tufts from the collar of his faded white NYPD shirt.

"Anyway," I said, clearing my throat. "I need to talk to Gabe. It's very important."

"You could've just called him," Caleb grumbled. I had called him. He hadn't picked up. Probably because he was sleeping. Hopefully not because he was so mad at me that he couldn't handle the thought of hearing my voice.

Thankfully, Caleb turned his back toward the hall inside, gesturing for me to come into their small row house. Which meant that Gabe presumably wasn't *that* mad at me that he'd told Caleb not to let me through the doors, no matter what. "Upstairs, second door on the right."

The first step was creaky, so I stuck to the outside edges of the others as I crept my way upstairs (old habit from when I used to sneak out of the Hamptons house as a teenager to meet my twenty-five-year-old boyfriend, which, come on, teenage Pom, did you not pick up on the creeper vibes from the fact that he always had a bubble-gum vape hanging out of his mouth?) and counted the doors carefully, hoping as I eased the second one on the right open that I wasn't actually intruding on one of Caleb's two young children. I stood there as my eyes adjusted, aware that I probably looked like a monster silhouetted in the dim light of the hallway.

Fortunately, I knew immediately the shape of Gabe's lump

under the blanket on the twin bed; Gabe must have displaced one of his nephews to his brother's room. I stepped inside, closing the door behind me and plunging us back into darkness. "Gabe?" I whispered.

He let out a little snore in response. My heart twisted. At first those little snores had woken me up. Now it was hard to sleep without them. "Gabe?" I said, slightly louder. I didn't want to touch him—it felt like crossing some kind of boundary. Well, more of a boundary than creeping into his room in the middle of the night.

He grunted and stirred, flopping over and putting his pillow over his head. I took a step closer. "Hey. Gabe. Wake up."

That got him. He pulled the pillow off, pushing himself up to an awkward sit that turned into a real sit on the edge of the bed as he saw me. "Pom? Are you real?" he said, blinking hard, rubbing at his eyes like he wasn't seeing the room right. "What are you doing here?"

"I am real. Realer than I've ever been," I said dramatically, plopping down on the edge of the bed. He hadn't invited me to sit down, but my feet were killing me after all the pacing I'd done in the back of the bakery while thinking things through. "I had an epiphany. I've been trying so hard to be this perfect person who Vienna's cool friends and the public all approve of. I've been trying so hard to be perfectly charitable and grown-up and mature and in that process I've made myself maybe not miserable, but a little sad. Because it turns out that I do still love some things from my life before. Like going out clubbing. I can do good for the world and enjoy art and go clubbing and go to fashion shows all at once."

I paused to consider what that would actually look like. "Well, not literally. Unless?" A hybrid art show–fashion show held at a club for charity? It wasn't the worst idea I'd ever had (that was the line of designer puke bags for private jets I'd tried to start). "Okay, I'll table that for later. The point is, even though

I've changed a lot since last year, it turns out I haven't changed into an entirely different person. There are still parts of the old me I want to hang on to."

Gabe was still blinking hard. Maybe I should've given him more time to wake up before really diving in. Oh well. Too late now. I forged onward. "When I was talking to Persimmon about proposals on Kevin's island, I was exaggerating a bit for effect. Because she was showing off and I wanted to show off in return. But it wasn't totally a lie. An intimate proposal all alone sounds beautiful. For someone else." He was blinking less now, sitting up straighter. "Not that your idea was bad. But I . . . I love the idea of being asked in a big way that makes me feel important and special and where there are a lot of eyes on me. I just do. I'm sorry that it came out the way it did and not in a conversation between the two of us, the way it should have."

I swallowed hard. He was still just staring at me, mouth a little open. "Also, I'm sorry you overheard me on the phone with my parents," I said. "I know people say this all the time and it turns out to be a lie, but it really, *really* wasn't what it sounded like. They were saying I should break up with you and I was telling them no, that I loved you, to stop saying those things about you, that I had nothing in common with this rich jerk they wanted me to date instead. It all just came out in the worst possible way. I promise. They know I love you, which is why they were working so hard to convince me that we shouldn't be together." Now he was frowning; why did I bring up how much my mom hated him? "Don't forget they also work really hard all the time to convince me that I shouldn't be myself. They suck. We should see them less.

"But," I continued. "Ultimately it's not the engagement that matters. It's the marriage, right? So if a small, private engagement is what you want, then that's what I want, because I want more than anything to be married to you. So." I squared my shoulders, lifted my chin, tried to look as regal as I could sitting in a bedroom in Queens. "You can ask me right now, and I'll say yes."

Gabe just blinked hard at me for a few seconds that felt like minutes. Eventually he sighed, running a hand down his stubbled face. "Pom." My name came out in an exhale. "I'm not going to ask you to marry me."

It felt like I was a sheet of paper and my teacher had crumpled me up before my calligraphy lesson was even done. "Oh. Okay." My voice was tiny. "Okay. I'll go. I'm sorry. I just thought—"

"Because I want more than anything to be married to you, too, and a private engagement in a bedroom in Queens where you don't even have your nails painted the right color for the photos afterward is definitely not what you want," he continued. I stopped halfway through a stand, my thighs quivering with the strain. "We're going to wait until I can give you what you want. And what you deserve."

This was why I'd done so many rounds of Pilates: so I could hover here in place, half crouched, afraid to either sit or to stand, like doing either might break the spell. He went on, "Pom, I hate clubbing. I don't really understand fine art, the kind that's in the galleries we tour. But they're both things you care about, and I care about the wonderful swirling whole of you, so they're important to me too." I wasn't sure describing clubbing as something I cared about was the best way to do it, but I certainly wasn't going to interrupt someone who was saying nice things about me. "You don't stop being the brave, brilliant, hilarious, beautiful, fascinating woman I love just because you like to go dance for a night and blow off steam. Are you worried it makes you silly or superficial? Because I shouldn't have to tell you this, but it doesn't."

He took a deep breath, raking his hand through his hair, which somehow stood up even more on end. "Do I ever want to go clubbing *with* you? No, unless for some reason I really have to. But you don't want to ever go to hockey games with me, do you? Or camping?"

"No." I shuddered, which released enough of the tension

where I plopped back down on the bed. It seemed safe to say at this point I wouldn't have to run off. "God, no."

"Exactly." He shifted closer to me so that he could take my hand, thread my fingers through his, rest it in my lap. "I can do those things with Caleb, or a friend. Not every person has to be there for everything. Hell, I don't think one single person *can* be there for everything. That goes for friendships too. You can have Vienna and Persimmon and the rest of them for your galas and art gallery tours and fancy bars and, I don't know, operas or whatever, and you can be friends with Millicent and Coriander for clubbing, and whoever else for whatever else." He leaned in, resting his forehead against mine. It was incredible how the mere act of touching his skin, breathing in that faint coffee and soap smell, was enough to instantly soothe any nerves that might have been bristling. "And I want to be there for everything. Except clubbing."

I closed my eyes, reveling in the warmth of him against me. "You never have to come clubbing with me."

"I love you so much right now." His lips found mine in a soft, gentle kiss, one with promises of what we'd do later, when we weren't in his brother's small, creaky house.

"I love you so much too." Was this what being a mature adult was like? Arguing with someone and miscommunicating and then just . . . making up without spreading nasty rumors about each other or lighting anybody's left-behind clothing on fire? Because if so, it was so much less stressful than what I was used to. I'd nearly burned down multiple apartment buildings disposing of friends' exes' treasured vintage polo shirts or cashmere lounge pants. Arson wasn't my thing these days. Unless it was solving a crime that included—oh! Right! My eyes popped open.

"Also," I said, pulling back a bit, but not too far. "By the way, I think I know who the killer is. I still have to confirm one more thing, but, yeah."

"You could've led with that," he said, and it touched my heart that he didn't look surprised, as if he'd expected me to figure it out. It felt great to have someone think I was smart. Something I was still getting used to.

"No. I wanted to get us squared away first," I said. "But now that we've figured out our relationship, we can figure out how to get a confession."

Gabe inclined his head toward the door. "How about we just go to my brother, tell him our theory, and let the police take it from there?"

I snorted. "Yeah, because they've done such a great job at investigating so far that *Pomona Afton* figured it out before them." I shook my head. "No way. If I have to do all the work, I want all the glory."

To his credit, he didn't try to dissuade me. He only sighed. "Is it going to be dangerous?"

Now we were in it. I could feel my eyes sparkling. "Only a little."

CHAPTER Twenty-Five

It began with a party. It would end with a party too.

One week later, after I'd gone through some dusty old records and made some phone calls, I was exactly where I'd been the morning of my first gala, clothing myself like I was putting on armor. (If armor doubled as an absolutely darling marigold gown.) As I finished, I placed the makeup brush on the surface of my vanity with a monumental thud that made me think of resting a sword. "How do I look?"

"Incredible," Vienna and Gabe said at the same time, which was impressive, actually. I must just look *that* good. I took a deep breath, focusing on that and not the nerves swimming in my stomach like the basket of live eels a very exclusive sushi restaurant in a Tokyo basement had actually proposed I eat.

"Do you feel ready?"

"No," the two said, also at the same time, which was equally impressive but more unnerving.

Oh well. Too late now. The space was already reserved and decorated, the last-minute invitations responded to. Granted, it was a space in the New York Afton, a place I would be perfectly happy to ghost, considering who still lived there and the memories that lived along with them. But society was rabid to get there and discuss everything that happened at the last gala, along with, hopefully, making those big donations they were supposed to make at that last gala. *It's for the kids*, I told myself. *And your reputation.* Also, a little bit for personal glory, but I didn't need to remind myself of that.

Vienna, Gabe, and I arrived early to greet guests, them flanking me like bodyguards (and the armed security I'd hired trailing behind me, also like a bodyguard). Time tilted as I stepped through the front doors of the Afton, my heels clicking on the marble tile, the faces at the front desk turning to smile at me even though one of them was in the middle of very sympathetically frowning at a grown man having a tantrum over having been assigned a room with an unlucky number. "Good evening, Ms. Afton!" they chorused.

I smiled back at them automatically. It didn't used to be automatic like this; Old Pom would've probably just given them a sour look and swept past, all like, *How dare you interact with me when I don't want to be interacted with?* But Old Pom had never worked at a coffee shop where customers felt free to treat her like a machine that occasionally wept with frustration when it couldn't figure what all its buttons did. "Good evening."

Down the grand hallway and into the even grander ballroom, which had already been booked for the night but which my mom had immediately freed up when I told her I wanted it (sorry, wedding of Michelle Horowitz and Ryan Tango. I hope clearing your registry and gifting you a honeymoon fund healthy enough to take you around the world a few times makes up for it). It looked just as it did when the hotel was built in the 1920s: marble floors with inlays; white and golden arches lining the walls; dazzling chandeliers; a ceiling covered in paintings of the sky that would probably be at home in Versailles.

I'd gone with relatively simple arrangements for decor: white cloths for the round tables; a low stage for the band; a table set up in the corner stacked with brochures my former assistant had spent hours upon hours compiling with experiences of students in the system who'd benefited already from my foundation and which guests would likely toss on their way out the door. "It looks nice," Vienna said.

"Thank you." Deep breath in. Deep breath out. "What if it doesn't work?"

"It'll work," Vienna said. Gabe was a bit more pragmatic.

"Don't forget the backup."

All of our eyes strayed to the armed man behind us, who regarded us seriously in turn. Gabe said, "That's not what I meant."

"I know."

Over the next half hour, I ran around fixing little details, which was great for distracting me from the nerves. Then people started to arrive, and the nerves came flooding right back.

The artists came first, probably to maximize the amount of free champagne and hors d'oeuvres they'd be able to consume. "Vienna, a pleasure," said Isaiah first, a little bashfully. "It's good to see you. You know I'm so sorry I couldn't—"

"Save it," Vienna said curtly. "You had to do what was best for you."

And it had been best for him—his gallery show in Brooklyn had sold out; his next show would be in Manhattan, where the art world would see if his work could hold up on a bigger stage. "I'm still sorry," he said. "I hope you'll come to my next show. As the guest of honor."

Everybody had such short memories. "We'll see," Vienna said.

Isaiah turned to me. "Pomona, thank you so much for inviting me."

"Of course."

He turned seamlessly to Gabe. "I'm hoping you'll find something more suitable for you at my next show."

Gabe cleared his throat. "Um. Sure."

"You actually inspired me," Isaiah said, hand making drawings in the air. It was hard to see what shapes he was trying to make; the big, chunky rings on every finger were quite distracting.

"I'm thinking, for you, a painting. Multicolored, neon, glowing lights advertising the opening of a store. In the window, an assortment of dildos in every color. In the middle, one real penis."

Gabe choked. "Oh."

Isaiah winked. "Don't worry. When you see it, I'm sure it'll speak to you." Before Gabe could speak anything to that, Isaiah swanned away toward the waiter carrying the tray of mini lobster rolls. He was carrying a big bag, I noted. He'd be feasting on lobster for days.

Despite all the nerves trying to come up my throat, I couldn't resist the grin that snaked its way onto my face once the artist was fully out of earshot. "What do you think, Gabe? Does it speak to you? Should we hang it in the place of pride in our living room?"

"Oh, it speaks to me, all right," Gabe grumbled. "It says, *Gabe, art is fake and nobody has any idea what they're doing.*"

Cora and her husband entered next. "Pom!" she said, stepping hesitantly, then less hesitantly as she saw what was, hopefully, a welcoming expression on my face. "I wasn't expecting an invite now that you know who I really am."

"You are not your family," I said, leaning in automatically for a cheek kiss as her husband gave Gabe what I assumed from the wince on his face was a bone-crushing handshake. "I know that better than anyone." I hesitated for a moment, then said, hating myself a little bit as it came out, "Have you been to see her recently?"

I couldn't bear to say her name, but obviously we all knew who I was talking about. Cora responded softly, "She's doing okay. Somehow she has a feather mattress in her cell, and she raised a stink in the cafeteria because supposedly she's allergic to soy, which is in pretty much everything, and I'm not sure how the dots were connected but now she has a private chef sending her meals."

Despite the circumstances, in that she'd made a blood relative of mine very bloody and that she'd also tried to kill me, I was glad to hear Opal was doing okay. Well, about as okay as you could do in prison. "Another few years and she'll have become, like, a mob boss," I said. Cora laughed weakly, her smile now forced. I nodded and moved her along before either of us had to acknowledge the weirdness of the situation.

A bunch of others came in next. Millicent and Coriander, Coriander wearing those ugly decoy glasses again as if they would win her extra points with me, the two of them literally tripping over each other to say how beautifully the room was decorated and how noble my cause was. "Thank you," I cooed, air-kissing them both. "And what exactly is that cause?"

"Uhh . . ."

"Uhhhhh . . ."

I swooped in to rescue them after a moment. Okay, after a few moments. (Sue me, I enjoyed watching them squirm.) (No, don't actually sue me, please—I was going to have to be in court enough to testify after tonight.) "I'm glad you both came," I said, very kindly, more kindly than they deserved. "We'll go out again soon. I hear there's that new underground club in the Village that plays nothing but amped-up classical music?"

"Thank you, thank you," Millicent gushed, blinking tears out of her eyes. Coriander probably was, too, only you could barely see her eyes past those big, ugly frames. "You won't regret it."

"I hope not," I said. "I've always liked Beethoven."

Next up came Nicholas and Jessica, who looked very chic tonight in an Emblème handkerchief dress that looked a little like a fun, sexy Persian rug. "Pom!" Jessica said brightly, swooping in for air kisses like a pro. "I'm obsessed with the new cardamom currant buns! They're so good!"

I beamed. "Thank you! Ellie and Sage were pushing me toward cardamom lime, but I'm glad I stuck to my guns."

"Me too." She gave my hands another squeeze and moved deftly to the side to greet Gabe. Which, rather unpleasantly, left Nicholas before me.

"Big brother!" I said, trying to match her chirpiness, but it elicited nothing but a dour stare. *Deep breath.*

"You made me miss an important business meeting when you hijacked the jet."

I rolled my eyes. "You make it sound like I put a gun to Captain Ted's head. Anyway, how's the business?"

His face didn't change. He clearly had no idea our parents had told me what he'd been up to, which was a fair assumption, considering my parents very rarely told me anything of importance. "Not excellent, as you would know if you ever came to a board meeting," he huffed.

"Why would I come to a board meeting when I'm not on the board?"

"You are on the board."

My eyes widened. "I am? Really?"

He let out a long-suffering sigh. "You're an Afton. All Aftons have a place on the board."

"Huh." Good to know. Maybe if I'd gone to board meetings, I'd have learned about his attempted coup sooner. With one final roll of his eyes, he and Jessica moved farther into the ballroom.

To be replaced by my parents. Great. "Oh, darling," Mom said, placing her hands on my shoulders and pushing me back slightly so she could look me over, top to bottom. "Who told you yellow was your color, and did you tell them immediately that they needed to go to the doctor for an eye exam?"

I gritted my teeth. Going low-contact would begin soon, I told myself. I just had to get through tonight. "Hello to you, too, Mom. You look beautiful." I hated to admit that she actually did. Black was her color, which suited her personality just fine. "Hi, Dad."

"Hi, Pom."

Providence granted me a wonderful gift when Bibi swept in just then in a whirlwind of scarlet silk, too quickly for my parents to get out of the way. "Richard," she said, all teeth. "Grace."

My mother bared her teeth in response. "Roberta." A beat. My mom stood there for a moment in silence, emphasizing it, as if to say, *This is where I'd greet your husband, except that he's dead.*

Bibi gestured behind her. "Come," she said, and God, I hoped she hadn't brought a dog I'd have to have security come remove, but no—trailing behind her was perhaps the most handsome man I'd ever seen. He seemed to be in his late thirties or early forties, significantly younger than her but not so young as to be creepy, with cheekbones and a jawline that had clearly been sculpted by a god. "Pom, I hope you don't mind me bringing a guest. This is Frédéric."

"Charmed," Frédéric said in a light French accent.

Though I was in an extremely happy and healthy relationship, I still flushed as those plush lips graced the back of my hand. "Charmed, indeed."

Bibi linked her elbow through Frédéric's and the two of them glided into the ballroom, leaving my dad staring after her slack-jawed and my mom's forehead vein pulsing with barely repressed rage.

You know, good for Bibi.

Denise Ryan came next, no handsome man following her in, dressed in the same black bodycon dress she'd worn to the first gala, as if she was hoping for a repeat of the night. "Thanks so much for the invitation, Pom. I know we still need to sit down and hash the donation out. Believe me, we'll do that soon."

"Oh, sure," I said. She launched into a speech about how she was no longer flying via private jet because of the environmental impact—*not* that she was judging me, not at all, rest assured—and because the money could do so much better elsewhere, but it was almost impossible getting anything done on a commercial flight, and she spent so much of her time on commercial flights these days, flying back and forth between Seattle and the East Coast, where her kids were in college, and—

I interrupted her with a warm but firm pat on the shoulder. "We both know that's not true."

She paled. "What?"

I leaned in, lowering my voice so that nobody around us would be able to hear. "How long do you think you're going to be able to keep this up?"

She cleared her throat. "I'm afraid I have no idea what you're talking about."

"So the prenup you signed when you and your husband got married *didn't* prevent you from receiving half the wealth of his company?" I asked. All the muscles in her jaw clenched. "From what I hear, you received a sizable payout, but nowhere near what you've been alleging. How long till it runs out?"

One of those clenched muscles twitched. "I'm fighting it in court and have been talking it through with my friends who really know my financials." Friends like Jack Wohl and Kevin Miller. "It wasn't my fault that a reporter asked me what I wanted to do with my half of the money without knowing the facts. What was I supposed to say? Tell her that I'd been screwed over?"

"Everybody's going to find out soon that you lied."

She drew back, frowning hard. "He wouldn't have been able to build that company without me! Whatever that stupid paper says, I deserve half of it."

"I'm sure you do," I said. I was dead serious. "But anyway, I invited you to be nice. You can stop pretending you're going to donate, though. It's a waste of both our time. Why don't you go in and find your seat?"

With one more annoyed look, she hustled in, followed by Jack Wohl, who greeted me with a surprisingly limp handshake, and a fluttering crowd of second-tier socialites, who it was painful for me to greet while most of my new crowd were no-shows. But I needed to fill out the space, and their money was as good as anyone else's, I supposed, even if there was less of it.

Once they'd cleared the entrance, Kevin and Persimmon

waltzed in, her clinging to his arm as if she might fall over without it. (Which might have been true, considering how high and narrow her ivory silk heels were. A bold choice for New York, where even a few moments on the sidewalk between car and door could turn anything white the color of smog.) "Pom," Kevin said, smiling broadly, holding out his hand for a shake. As opposed to Jack Wohl's, his was perfect, strong and firm without being crushing. "When are you coming back to the island? Or to our new bed-and-breakfast?" *The one your brother and I bought together with the plan to turn it into an Afton*, he didn't say.

I smiled enigmatically. "We'll have to see."

He didn't follow up on that, fortunately. Persimmon leaned in for our customary cheek kisses. Up this close, I could tell the skin around her eyes was a little swollen, though any redness had been deftly hidden by her makeup. "Are you okay?" I whispered.

"I will be," she whispered back, I guess deciding that tonight's theme was being enigmatic. She pulled back and moved inside, tottering gracefully to her table. She extended her arm for Kevin to help her sit, but it took him a few seconds to notice, because of his tablemates: Denise, my parents, Cora, and her husband (the artists were in the back of the room. I didn't want them in the inevitable photos).

I greeted a few more stragglers, and then the doors slammed shut, the lights going dark. No, they didn't—the doors closed gently and hardly made a noise, guided by the expert workers of the hotel, and the lights still shone golden from their chandeliers. A slam and darkness just suited a dramatic reveal.

Showtime.

CHAPTER Twenty-Six

Again, I was being dramatic. It wasn't quite showtime yet. Trying to expose a murderer to a bunch of hangry guests was a recipe for disaster—I wanted people sitting on the edge of their seats to see what would happen next, not to peek toward the kitchen doors in hopes the salads were coming out. So instead I sat there on the edge of *my* seat, on pins and needles, mixing metaphors because I was *that* nervous. At least I had Gabe and Vienna on either side of me. Vienna even managed to pick at her salad despite her nerves, though I'm not sure much more than a couple of pieces of lettuce actually made it into her stomach.

I was glad I didn't have any lettuce in mine as I stood and made my way to the podium, because it probably would've come right back up in neon green. "Greetings, everybody," I said, surveying the crowd. They twinkled with diamonds, shimmered with well-done plastic surgery. Was this my future? To sit among them year after year, eating a few bites of overcooked chicken as I tried to give my money to worthy causes?

No. There would be more. *I* would be more. I was already more, really. How many of these socialites could say they'd solved not one, but two murders?

Okay. I was getting *slightly* ahead of myself. I wouldn't know if I'd solved this second one for real until this was over. To be entirely honest, I wasn't completely sure I'd still be alive when this was over. I was about to take some pretty major risks, because you know what they say: big risk, big reward.

And I was never one to settle for something small.

I flashed the crowd my most dazzling smile. "I appreciate you all coming out tonight after what happened last time. I promise you there won't be a repeat." I paused and considered. "Well, I promise that I'll do my best to make sure there won't be a repeat. There's only so much I can do. Anyway!" I pressed on before they could think too hard about what I'd said. "I wanted to start the evening with a moment of silence for Mr. Conrad Phlume. He was more than a murder victim, and he shouldn't only be remembered that way."

Unfortunately, it was hard to come up with nicer ideas about how he should be remembered, since nobody had liked him. I couldn't even point out his grieving widow, because her attention was focused so keenly under her table that I knew her date's foot was definitely somewhere it was not supposed to be. So I continued, "Nobody deserves to be murdered, and his death leaves a hole torn in the world that nobody will ever be able to sew up. Let us sit and remember him."

Maybe that's what the guests did—I didn't know. Bibi was focused on her date's inappropriate foot, and my mom was staring daggers at her, and Persimmon was chewing off her nails, and Gabe was sitting so rigid in his seat that if somebody tapped him on the head he might split down the middle. I took the moment to case the rest of the room, check out the exits, make sure they all lined up with what I remembered from my childhood games of hide-and-seek with Farrah and Jordan (who, last I'd seen in the group chat, were off partying in Bali for a friend's birthday).

The moment ended. I continued, injecting as much brightness into my voice as I could. "His name will forever be attached to the building he donated to me." Demonstrably false—names on buildings had ways of being replaced once the original name had fallen out of collective memory or someone else donated more money—but the crowd murmured appreciatively anyway, probably because they liked the idea of their own named buildings staying like that forever. "And the entire city will be able to see it and enjoy it, because, with his widow's blessing"—Bibi nodded at me, her eyes twinkling from her game of footsie, face dewy—"she's officially signed the deed over to me so that I can donate the Conrad Phlume Memorial Library to the city."

A murmur went up around the room. Denise Ryan raised her eyebrows, Kevin Miller muttered what looked like a curse under his breath, my parents leaned their heads into one another's, and Cora smiled at me. I went on, "While going through the papers in the building's basement, we discovered some fascinating records. We made them available to the city archivist, who deemed the building a historically significant site and expressed their wish to make the building a combination library and museum. They'll be going through all the records with a fine-tooth comb and digging up information on all the people who lived there to create a time capsule of twentieth-century Chelsea society."

All that was absolute garbage, but from the way people were nodding and murmuring, they didn't know that. "Thank you, thank you. It's not 100 percent official yet—I still have to sign the paperwork tomorrow morning at the courthouse. Hopefully nothing happens to me before then, because I don't think my parents—my heirs—would be able to resist selling it for a bunch of money." That got a laugh from the people who didn't like my parents, which was a lot of people, and a sour look from my mom. My dad seemed to be focused on his phone again. Probably for the best. "I'm grateful that Conrad Phlume's legacy will be able to be enjoyed not only by the students I'm helping with my nonprofits, but by everybody in the city he loved. Thank you, and I hope you have a wonderful night."

I sailed back to my seat on the sounds of applause, sliding

into it with a modest smile before my plate of mostly untouched chicken. "What do you think?" Gabe asked, leaning in so that nobody but me and Vienna could hear. "Do you think it worked?"

I shrugged, trying not to let my deep inhale shake too much. "We'll see soon enough."

The rest of the night passed as galas tended to: lots of schmoozing, lots of mediocre champagne (sparkling apple juice for me; I had to stay on top of things), lots of persuading people to give a minuscule portion of their fortune to people whose entire life that minuscule portion would change. I kept busy, circling the room, pausing at a few points to discuss my after-party plans. "Oh, I don't know," I said with a pointed yawn each time. "I'm exhausted from planning this party on such short notice. I'm not really in the mood to go out. All I want to do is go home and go to sleep." A glance toward the door, as if I could perceive the weather from this windowless room. "It's such a beautiful night too." Thank goodness it wasn't raining. "I might just walk home."

My parents sidled up to me toward the end of the evening, right when I was between schmoozes and the thought that I was about to put my life in great danger was nipping at my very fashionable heels. "Are you sure about donating that building?" my mom said. "You could sell it and have enough to fund your little organization for the rest of your life."

I inclined my head modestly. "I'm absolutely, 100 percent sure. No person and no amount of money could change my mind."

"She's sure, Grace," Dad said before Mom could try and argue with me more. "It's her life. Her decision."

"A poor decision," my mom huffed. "But whatever. I suppose you're an adult now. You're allowed to make all the poor decisions you'd like."

I glanced around. The room was clearing out, people off to their next party or to bed. "Speaking of poor decisions." Gabe and Vienna were still here, obviously, chatting by one wall, keeping an eye on me. "The doorman who keeps letting you up to my apartment has been reprimanded. One more warning and he'll lose his job."

Mom's mouth dropped open. "Pomona, I—"

"And I've changed the locks in case you manage to sneak by him anyway." I kept my tone low but pleasant, so that hopefully anyone not actively nearby and listening in would think we were having a nice conversation. "You're my parents. I want to have a relationship with you. Ideally a good one. But, God, you make it hard."

"Pom—" my dad protested weakly, but I wasn't done.

"Gabe is the love of my life, whether you like it or not. You need to accept it if you want a relationship with me. Do you understand? Stop saying mean things about him and trying to convince me that he's not the right one for me, or we will be seeing very, very little of each other."

"Pom—" they said at once. This time I *was* done, but I didn't want to hear whatever they were going to say.

"Do you understand?" I asked again. "All you need to say is yes or no."

My mom's face was mutinous, eyes roiling like lightning might come bursting out, but I was done caring. "Whatever. Fine."

I would take that as a yes. "Good. Great." We stood there staring at each other for a moment longer, but I didn't really want to wait for that lightning to hit me. "Okay. See you soon. *I'll* call *you*. Because if you call me, maybe I won't pick up."

I excused myself, breath racing and heart pounding like I'd just won a marathon. Nicholas and Jessica accosted me before I could make it to Gabe and Vienna on the other side of the room. "Pom, did you just—"

"Yes, I did, and yes, I recommend it," I told my brother. He knit his brows together in consternation. "I feel great now." I felt kind of sick and shaky, actually—I was definitely never going to run a real marathon—but that wasn't entirely due to the confrontation with my parents; it was because of what lay ahead. "Imagine having boundaries."

"Sounds amazing," Jessica said wistfully. Poor Jessica. Well, if Nicholas's coup succeeded, the bright side was that my parents probably wouldn't want anything to do with her and him for a while.

"Sorry," I told her, but Jessica stopped me with a hand on my arm. Jessica, this was *not* the night. She smiled kindly at me, as if she could hear my tone and wanted me to know she forgave me for being so sharp at her in my head.

"Pom, I wanted to ask you something I've been meaning to ask for quite a bit. And this seems like the perfect night to do it, while we're both dressed up like this." Jessica tucked a lock of hair behind her ear. I ground my teeth with frustration. "Will you be my bridesmaid?"

Gabe's eyes were bugging out toward me. Again, Jessica, this was not the time. I was honored and touched and everything, but I had a murder investigation to wrap up. "Unofficially, of course," I told her. "But I'll give you my formal response when you've presented me with your official request." Her bug eyes echoed Gabe's. I sighed. "You haven't prepared bridesmaid boxes? I hope I'm the first one you asked. We'll deal with it tomorrow, okay? Call me."

"Okay," Jessica said faintly as I pushed through her and my brother like a pair of doors. Gabe and Vienna waited, two of the last people in the room other than my family members (my mom was now publicly and noisily crying on the other side of the room, but I could see the absence of actual tears from here).

"Okay, Pom," Vienna said, leaning in for cheek kisses that smelled like roses. I inhaled deep, reminding myself that roses were pretty but they also had thorns. "I'm going to head out. Are you ready?"

I stretched my arms over my head; even though there weren't many people there to see it, I had to do it for myself, to be in the right mindset. "Yup. Ready to go."

"Okay." Vienna's lips actually grazed my cheek. "Good luck."

The breath I drew in was deep and shaky. "Thanks."

Just like that, she was off. The next breath I drew in was a little less shaky. Gabe gestured me forward; together, we left the ballroom, walked down the glittering hallway into the lobby. I smiled automatically at the people behind the front desk. "Should we walk home?"

Gabe waited until we were walking through the big double doors out onto the street to respond. "Pom. It was pretty rude what you said back there to your parents."

I blinked. We stopped on the sidewalk in front of the Afton. Somebody towing luggage had to go around us. "Excuse me?"

He cleared his throat. "It was pretty rude what you said back there to your parents. About it being hard to have a relationship with them."

I placed a hand on my hip, making luggage dodge my elbow. "Excuse me? I thought you'd be happy to hear it, considering the whole argument was about, like, defending you."

"Well, I'm not." He shook his head emphatically. Somebody down the street honked as if in agreement. "Don't bring me into the middle of the relationship between you and your parents. I don't want to be blamed for making things hard."

"I wasn't blaming you," I said. "I was just saying that—"

"It's the same thing," he said. I frowned at him, crossing my arms. "Even if you're not blaming me, your parents will. Keep me out of it."

I tossed my hair. It didn't hit anything, but I straightened myself as if it had. "I'll do what I want."

"Fine. Do whatever you want. As usual." He clenched his jaw. "I need some time to cool off. I'm going to take the subway."

"That's the worst way to cool off!" I called after him as he started walking away. His steps stuttered, as if he wanted to stop, but he balled his fists at his sides and kept going.

So be it. Nerves jangled in my stomach. I didn't really want to be alone right now, but I would walk home as planned. Alone.

Conveniently, I'd brought along cute glittery sneakers to switch out with my heels. I slung the heels over my shoulder as I walked north, as the tall buildings and bright lights of the hotels and stores on the south end of Central Park turned into the grand, stately prewar buildings of the Upper East Side. Doormen lurked inside, but few of them hung out beneath their awnings this late at night.

So when the gun barrel poked into my lower back and the rough voice said into my ear, "Come with me," there was nobody there to notice.

CHAPTER Twenty-Seven

For somebody in the process of being abducted, I felt remarkably calm. I had armed security, who was following at a safe distance; if things went too far, he'd step in. "Are you going to hurt me?" I asked over my shoulder. The assailant was wearing one of those sheer black stocking things pulled over his—because it was definitely a him—head. The nerves that had been dancing in my stomach zipped and zapped with electricity. The mask was a decent sign, right? It meant he was worried that I'd eventually identify him, once I was away from here and presumably alive? "I have a lot of money, you know. I can pay you."

"I don't want your money," said the assailant, voice muffled. I didn't recognize it, but that wasn't surprising, considering the muffling. "By the way, I've taken care of your security guard. You didn't think I'd be that stupid not to see him following, did you?"

I stopped, rigid in my tracks. The assailant bumped into my back, the gun digging in hard. He'd "taken care of" my security guy? What did that even mean? "Did you hurt him?"

"Don't worry about that," the assailant said, voice low and menacing. Not helpful: I was worried! Very worried!

I was suddenly much less remarkably calm. "Are you sure I can't tempt you with my money?"

Apparently not. He said, "Walk left. I won't hurt you as long as you cooperate."

To my left was an opening in the stone wall that surrounded Central Park. Beyond it loomed the park itself, dark and ominous and spooky without its usual daytime or early evening crowds of people. The occasional standing streetlamp made pools of light along the paved paths, but otherwise there was nothing there. Nobody to rescue me.

Still, what choice did I have? I held my head high as I marched into the park, guided by the man with the gun. It felt like an out-of-body experience; I could almost see myself from above, still in my dress and my sleek gala hair, walking stiffly down the path and into the gloom. He steered me past a playground, where one of the swings creaked back and forth as if a ghost were kicking its legs, and into the dense thicket of the Ramble. Trees knotted together overhead, blocking any light from the moon. The trickling of a stream sounded somewhere in the distance.

My entire body was stiff with tension. The assailant released me, and I lurched forward, but I couldn't see enough around me to find a safe place to land my feet. I spun to face him. It turned out that the mask he was wearing was sheer, one meant to shield him from cameras but not necessarily from human eyes. I could see him right through it. The steely blue eyes. The straight nose. The determined cut of his square jaw. That thing I'd thought earlier about it being a good thing he didn't think I'd be able to identify him if I walked free lurched back unpleasantly into the front of my mind.

"Good evening, Kevin," I said, trying not to sound weak and scared. Kevin Miller stared silently back at me, his lips pressed together. Hilariously—if anything could be hilarious right now—he was still wearing his gala tuxedo, though he'd also changed into sneakers. Black, of course. "What did you do to my security guy?"

Kevin pulled the black sleeve off his face with the hand not holding the gun, then sighed with what sounded like relief. It had to be hard to breathe through that thing. "I didn't hurt him. He's just been . . . detained."

I cringed a little at that. Assuming we all made it out of here, I'd have to give him an enormous tip. "Well. Thanks for not hurting him, I guess." Hopefully that boded well for me too?

"I'm not going to hurt you either," Kevin said, flicking some beads of sweat from his brow. For all he was saying, the gun didn't waver. "I mean it, Pom. I don't want to hurt you. And I promise I won't, as long as we can come to an . . . understanding."

Something hooted overhead. An owl? I didn't know owls even lived in Central Park. "What kind of understanding?"

He shifted back on his feet. With the lack of light, it was hard to see anything of his eyes but a glint. I couldn't tell if he was panicking, or cocky, or calm. "The building. Pom, you're going to come out tomorrow and tell everybody that you're very sorry, but you have to backtrack on your plan to donate the building and its archive because you've already signed the deed over to me. For a fair price, of course. Above market, even."

I furrowed my brow, though I wasn't sure if he could see it, and made sure to infect my voice with as much of Old Pom as I could still manage. Sometimes it was useful to have the entire world think you were stupid. Probably it was half the reason I was still alive. "I don't understand."

"I want that building. No, I *need* that building." He sounded patient, like all of my teachers had the first time they tried to explain something to me. "And I don't want there to be any more violence in that process."

"*You* killed Conrad," I said grimly. I was already here at gunpoint. He knew I'd put it together eventually, even if I didn't know now. Assuming he let me go.

He was silent for a moment, probably thinking about whether he should admit to it or not. But remember: He thought I was stupid. Yes, I'd solved one murder, but everybody thought I'd blundered my way into the solution. He sighed, air leaking out of a punctured tire. "Just sign the building over to me."

"Why did you do it?" I persisted. "Did he hit you, and you hit him back?" I knew that Kevin hadn't hit Conrad; my dad had. But Kevin didn't know I knew that. Kevin didn't know I knew anything. "In that case, it's self-defense. Right? You wouldn't go to jail for that."

He was silent again, another long moment. Something scurried in the brush around us. He said, finally, "I didn't hit him. He didn't hit me. It was . . ." Pause. Nothing scurried this time. The entire world hung silent, suspended, as if it, too, were holding its breath. "He fell."

"But he didn't just fall, right?" I scrunched up my brows even more. "I remember the police said he had to have been pushed, or he wouldn't have hit the sculpture with enough force for it to pierce his body the way it did."

"I didn't mean to push him!" The words burst out. I actually took a step back from the force. "He just . . . He wouldn't shut up. It was only supposed to be a little shove to make him stop talking." *You didn't mean to push him, or it was only supposed to be a little shove?* It probably wouldn't be helpful to clarify that right now. "I didn't realize . . ." A hard swallow. "I didn't realize he was so close to the railing, or that the railing was so low." A pause. "If anything, this is the venue's fault. What kind of safety rating is that? It's unconscionable."

"He wouldn't stop talking." I brought him back to earlier in the conversation, before we started talking about historical buildings and grandfathered-in accessibility ratings. "About what?" I let the words hang there. When it didn't sound like he was eager to go on, I tossed him a crumb. "It was because he put two and two together from his last look around the building, didn't he? You'd seemed desperate to take it off his hands. He must have wondered why."

"I don't know what you're talking about." But he didn't sound angry anymore. He sounded . . . tired.

Because he did know what I was talking about. And he knew that I knew what we were talking about.

And he'd already killed one person to cover it up.

"I think you do." We both knew it. I might as well stop being coy. "William."

He sucked in a sharp breath. "How did you figure it out?"

"There's only so long you can pretend to be someone you're not," I said somberly. "That's something I learned firsthand." I paused to let my profound wisdom sink in. "Also, the way you were trying to use my brother. I thought it was weird that my brother cared so much about what I did with that house, but then, after I learned the two of you were collaborating, I talked to him more. You told him you'd help him take over Afton Hotels if he got me to sell you the building. That's why you were so interested in whether Gabe wanted to be part of the business, weren't you? So that you could use him instead, since he's closer to me. You were *so* interested in that building.

"It made me take another look at the records. Isaiah, the artist, said that you'd wanted his painting of all those superheroes. And I remembered that William, the kid who'd lived in the brownstone, had doodled superheroes that wound up in the records. And under the wallpaper. And all over that house. Your parents must have been annoyed they had to wallpaper over your big, looping signature. I did a little more research, and found out the truth."

His mouth opened, as if ready to accuse me of lying, then closed again when he realized I'd told him I had receipts.

"That's how you got into the house the day you went after me and Vienna and then out of the basement, isn't it?" I gestured at his head. He still had on that wig Persimmon told me he was wearing to disguise balding, though in reality it was probably to cover up the big bruise or bump I'd given him when I smashed him with the filing cabinet. "You still had the keys from the old days, when you lived there."

He hissed. Literally hissed, like a cat. He probably wasn't used to people telling him he had to do things he didn't want to do. Not then, not ever.

I sighed. "It's over, William. You should just admit to it while you have some dignity left."

He was silent for a while. Just as I was thinking maybe I could jump at him and surprise him, he said, very quietly, "Nobody's called me that in many years." He sighed. "And I wasn't coming after you and Vienna. I didn't even know you were there. I was . . . talking to the records."

Right. *Where are you hiding? When I find you, I'm going to rip you to pieces.* It was a little silly, but it made more sense.

He went on, "I knew there was more in the house that could point to me, but getting those would at least buy me time where I could hopefully get back in and find it. As a child I hid a time capsule beneath one of the loose floorboards, but I couldn't remember exactly where. I'd written all under the walls. I needed that building."

Grim satisfaction. I said, "William's not your legal name anymore, right? When did you change it?"

"When I went to college," he said. "I introduced myself to my roommate and told him I'd grown up in New York. He said, 'Wow, that's so badass. Ever get in a knife fight on the subway?' I'd never taken the subway, of course, but the awe in his voice, Pom . . . He thought I was a fighter. A survivor. A badass. Nobody had ever spoken to William Melrose, the weak, nerdy kid born with a silver spoon in his mouth, like that. So I went along with it. Told him I went by my middle name, Kevin, which was actually the name of our family chef. And just like that, I became someone else."

"You embellished it over the years," I said. "Until Kevin was a whole different person. Your entire brand's been built on this idea that you're Kevin Miller, a guy who worked his way up from nothing. It all falls apart if they find out you're actually William Melrose."

"That's what I told Conrad." His tone was almost pleading, but the gun didn't move. His arm had to be aching by now. "After that speech of his, I knew he'd discovered the truth." That speech when both Vienna and I had thought he'd been talking to her. "I'd almost forgotten about the place, didn't even realize what was there until what he said. I cornered him afterward to beg him to let me buy that building and destroy all the records. Nothing against your organization, Pom—I would've donated an equivalent building or amount of money in its place. I couldn't let the secret get out.

"But Conrad laughed at me," Kevin continued, his voice growing choked. "He told me I'd been lying to people for far too long, and he couldn't wait to see the movie based on my life. Which I wouldn't get to see, because I'd be in prison for fraud." He cleared his throat. "I didn't mean to kill him. Just shove him and make him shut up. But he was injured already from some other altercation"—the one with my dad—"and he staggered back."

I let the words hang there in the air for a moment, much like Conrad Phlume hadn't hung there for a moment after toppling over the railing. "Wow," I said. "So. Even if I sell you the building, you know I know your secret. One you've already killed to protect."

"I meant what I said about not wanting to hurt you," he said earnestly. "You're my girlfriend's friend. We should go on a double date sometime."

An absurd laugh couldn't help but bubble up my throat. "They do say the best way to make couple friends is to hold them at gunpoint. They can't say no."

"I like you, Pom," Kevin said, smiling in what almost seemed to be a genuine way. "Let's be friends."

"'Let's be friends,'" I repeated. "Hmm. Would you like to tell me how Vienna's earring wound up in Conrad's hand?"

That smile vanished in what might as well have been a puff of smoke. "I . . ."

"You thought it was mine, didn't you?" I said. "That's why, after you noticed it on the ground and picked it up, you gave it to Conrad before you pushed him off the ledge. Which would seem to suggest you didn't just shove him a little to stop him from talking. You pushed him. Hard. Intending to kill him, and to frame me."

Something dark glinted in his eyes. "I would stop right there, Pom. I don't want to have to hurt you."

"You're not going to hurt me no matter what," I said. "Because there aren't any bullets in that gun."

He scoffed. "You're wrong. I loaded it myself this morning."

"I'm right," I said. I so did enjoy saying those words, and my God, hopefully they were correct. "Persimmon unloaded it herself this afternoon. She sent me a video. Would you like to see?"

"You're wrong," he said, but he sounded less sure of himself this time. "She wouldn't do that."

"Oh, but she would," I said. "She helped me put it all together, by the way. Although she thought you were having an affair. With Denise Ryan, at first. You weren't, were you? You were just trying to help her cover up her own secret."

"You can't think—"

"I think we've got enough." I raised my voice. "It's time."

The whole area lit up like a Christmas tree. All of a sudden, I was surrounded by a crowd of people: Gabe, Vienna, Persimmon, my security guy, a bunch of cops. I very nearly collapsed with relief. I'd been pretty sure this would all work out, but not 100 percent sure. "I'm not stupid," I said, staring at Kevin. He was blinking hard, his eyes still adjusting to the light, but I hoped he could see the triumph on my face. "And I win."

Kevin didn't have anything to say back to that. He appeared

to be in shock, blinking hard and fast as the police cuffed him and read him his rights, as if he'd never thought he would *actually* see the consequences for what he'd done.

I supposed that was one thing about being William Melrose that remained.

Gabe emerged from the crowd of people and immediately enveloped me in his arms, bringing me in so tight it was almost hard to breathe. "I wish you'd let me come with you."

"You know it had to be me alone," I said, my voice muffled by his chest. "That's why we had to fake that fight. Otherwise he'd never believe I was out walking alone."

"I know." His own voice was a growl. "But I didn't like it. Never again."

I looked over toward the security guy. "And he's okay?"

"Yes," Gabe said. "Kevin pushed him into the trunk of a locked car. We let him out right away."

Vienna let out a tinkling, almost musical laugh, reminding me she was there. "Of course you'll never have to do this again, Gabe. What are the odds that you'll ever have to solve another murder?"

Gabe and I exchanged a dark glance. That was almost exactly what we'd said the last time. It had to be true this time, though.

Right?

Persimmon had been silent, turning her back to us as she watched the police lead Kevin away. I disentangled myself from Gabe and, with a quick look and raised eyebrow, left him to talk with his brother the cop while Vienna and I descended on our friend. "Thank you again for helping us earlier," I said. "This whole thing was stressful enough, but it would've been a lot more stressful if there had been bullets in that gun."

"You're welcome," she said quietly, her shoulders drooping forward as if she were a wilted flower. "I'm glad you're okay. But I'm sorry this all happened."

Honestly, I was surprised she wasn't angrier. She was my friend, but not a close enough friend where I could trust her not to run immediately to her boyfriend with the details of our investigation if I'd shared them with her.

So I'd lied. I'd told her I was going to help her make absolutely sure Kevin wasn't having an affair and wouldn't have an affair even if someone stunning (e.g., me) came on to him, and that she had to remove the bullets in his gun in case he got really, really angry at me. I'd made her send me a video of it just in case she rolled her eyes at the thought he might shoot someone over an affair and told me she'd done it when she really hadn't.

I told her, "I'm glad I'm okay, too, and also sorry that it all happened. I'm especially sorry that I had to lie to you. This must come as a major shock."

She sighed. "At least he wasn't cheating on me, right?"

She'd be okay.

The group of us joined back up as we began heading out of the park, Kevin already gone. Gabe slipped his hand into mine. "This moment, actually," he said. "It's a triumphant one. A memorable one. But . . ." He knelt forward, slipping his hand out of mine and turning himself around to face me. On one knee. "Do you know what would make it more memorable?"

My jaw dropped open. Oh God. No. Not here. Not now. "Gabe—"

"Making sure your shoelace is tied so that you don't trip and fall flat on your face." Gabe ducked his head, but I could still see the smirk on his lips as he knotted my laces. He knew *exactly* what he was doing.

I shoved him gently on one shoulder once he'd stood. "Funny guy."

"I try."

I inhaled deeply as we neared Fifth Avenue, tilting my head back and regarding the sky. It was partially washed out from the city's light pollution, but you could still see a nice scattering of stars. Central Park was one of my favorite places. It was also free to spend time in. "I do love Central Park, though. You know. For future reference."

Gabe flashed me a lopsided smile. "I'll keep the future in mind."

And off we went into the night, leaving the past behind.

EPILOGUE

Two weeks later

It was an early summer Sunday, the weather warm enough where I didn't need a coat but cool enough where I wouldn't immediately be drowning in sweat upon stepping outside. I'd gone to the spa with Vienna the day before and had a fresh, pearly pink coat of polish on my nails. Gabe had hinted that I should wear something cute on our usual walk in the park.

In other words: It was happening, people.

Nerves danced in my stomach as we laced up our shoes (I went with my glittery sneakers, in case the photographer wanted a full-body shot). "You ready? You got everything?" I asked.

Gabe gave me a bemused smile from the floor, where he was lacing up his own sneakers. Running shoes. Okay. We could always photoshop them out. "I think so?"

To be absolutely fair in the telling: I'd decided it was happening three times already. Once when it had just finished pouring and a misty rainbow stretched high overhead; twice when Gabe suggested we take a walk by Belvedere Castle, which we never did.

But today. My hopes rose as I saw he wasn't wearing the smelly running shorts he sometimes did but real jeans with deep pockets, where he could easily be storing a ring box. Even one big enough to house the four-carat diamond ring I'd told him was an heirloom from my grandma but was actually sourced by *moi* in top secret from the family jeweler (Gabe might have too much pride to admit it, but he knew perfectly well that Pomona Afton couldn't walk around in the small ring he'd be able to buy me himself). "Ready?"

I tossed my hair, hoping it looked as bouncy on the outside as it did in my head. "So ready."

My excitement climbed as he steered us toward Belvedere Castle again. Third time was the charm, right? Together, we climbed up the steep stone steps to the very top of the building, where only a couple of people hung out on the platform. Gabe walked me to the edge, where Central Park sprawled around us green and golden and bright: the Shakespeare Garden, where my friends and I would study in high school to feel smarter; the ancient Egyptian obelisk stabbing the sky beside the great glass walls of the Met; Turtle Pond and its adorable shelled inhabitants I'd named in middle school. Turtles lived a long time, didn't they? Hopefully Shelldon and Mishell were still around.

And, of course, on the other side stretched the Ramble, its dense and thorny tangles hiding where I'd made Kevin confess. I didn't face that way, though. I chose to look the other way, at the good things.

"Pom," Gabe said. I squinted at the pair of people regarding the landscape several feet away from us. They were the perfect distance away for a photo. One held a fancy digital camera by his side, the other a phone. And their angle? Ideal in lighting terms for where we were standing.

"Yes?" I turned to Gabe to find him down on one knee.

Oh.

Okay.

This was actually happening.

My face split into such a wide smile, the *oh my God oh my God oh my God* on repeat in my head drowning out the first part of his speech. Which was fine; the videographer was absolutely catching it right now and I'd be able to watch it later.

I knew all the important parts, anyway.

"Pomona Abigail Afton," Gabe said. "At first, I never thought we'd even like each other. Then we became friends, and I was sure you'd never think of me the way I thought of you. But then you did. And it's been the greatest joy and privilege of my life, to be able to share it with you." He paused. Tears were sparkling in my eyes, hopefully in a way that said *old-school movie star*. "I want to share the rest of it with you too. Pom, will you marry me?"

I clapped a perfectly manicured hand to my mouth. "Yes. Yes. A hundred times, yes."

He stood and slid the ring onto my finger. I turned it this way and that, dazzled by the way the sun shone through it. And then, of course, he kissed me. The photographer snapped away, capturing every angle.

When we broke apart, I was out of breath, elated, filled with joy like a balloon close to popping. It took me a moment to realize that we were surrounded by the sound of . . . people clapping?

"Look," Gabe said, gesturing down below. I peered over the railing (careful not to get too close to the edge). It was amazing how I could fit even more joy inside me, because below us cheered so many of the people who mattered. Andrea and Caleb and his family, including my soon-to-be nephews. Nicholas and Jessica, who—shoot, was wearing Grandma's actual heirloom diamond ring. Hopefully that wouldn't come up in conversation.

And there were our friends. Many of them, from all facets of our life. Gabe's high school and college and grad school buddies. Vienna and Persimmon and others from that strata of society. Millicent and Coriander and more of my party friends. My heart swelled, seeing them all here together. It felt like it had been made whole.

I squeezed Gabe's hand. "Our wedding is going to be epic."

"Absolutely," Gabe said. "Wait, how epic?"

My head tilted, already full of ideas. I was definitely getting those designer peacocks this time, come hell or high water. And a private resort on the water. Not on a private island, because I wanted at least a couple of paparazzi to be able to sneak in. But I also kind of wanted to be on top of a really tall building. Was it possible to do both at once? Was it too much to—

A scream. I jerked back to the present just in time to see the photographer lurch back from the edge, as if he'd been about to fall. "Oh my God," I said. "Are you okay?"

He flashed a dirty look over his shoulder at the videographer, who was stubbornly not looking back at him. "Your angle isn't more important than my life, asshole."

I furrowed my brow. I was an expert at photo angles by this point in my life. And that spot where the videographer had almost bumped him off? It wasn't even close to the ideal angle to capture this—

No. Purposely, I turned away. Even if I was the greatest investigator of murder this city had ever known, this was not the time to focus on it. So I nestled into Gabe's side, beaming down at the cheering crowd of loved ones below, and prepared to celebrate us.

ACKNOWLEDGMENTS

Pomona Afton may think that writing a book can't possibly be that hard, but I can assure you that it is. Thank you so much to the most excellent team at Emily Bestler Books and Atria for guiding Pomona from unedited Word document to sparkling finished book, especially Lara Jones, Libby McGuire, Emily Bestler, Dana Trocker, Megan Rudloff, Zakiya Jamal, James Iacobelli, Paige Lytle, and Shelby Pumphrey. Sanny Chiu, thanks for hitting this cover out of the park. Thank you so very much to my agent, Merrilee Heifetz, and the rest of the team at Writers House, especially Rebecca Eskildsen, for all that you do. Ali Lefkowitz and the team at Anonymous Content, thanks for taking Pom to Hollywood.

Friends and family, I love and appreciate you.

This was the first book I wrote since having a baby, and, unsurprisingly, it was way harder than it used to be. But I did it and I'm really proud of myself! Jeremy, thank you not just for being the love of my life but for being the best possible partner and enabling me to write this book while caring for a baby. Miriam, you were the one who made writing this book way harder, but you're the best and I wouldn't have it any other way.

www.ingramcontent.com/pod-product-compliance
Lightning Source LLC
Chambersburg PA
CBHW011934190326
41492CB00003B/37

* 9 7 8 1 6 6 8 0 7 5 6 8 5 *